CHAPTERS

Chapter 1: The Cold Shore - Page 4

Chapter 2: The Frail Prince - Page 11

Chapter 3: The Welsh Winter - Page 22

Chapter 4: The Widow's Weeds - Page 32

Chapter 5: The Gilded Cage - Page 41

Chapter 6: The Ambassador - Page 51

Chapter 7: The Sun Rises - Page 66

Chapter 8: Our Coronation - Page 77

Chapter 9: A Son For England - Page 89

Chapter 10: The Empty Cradle - Page 101

Chapter 11: Queen Regent - Page 109

Chapter 12: My Jewel, Maria - Page 117

Chapter 13: The Shadow in the Gallery - Page 128

Chapter 14: The King's Scruple - Page 136

Chapter 15: The Poisoned Text - Page 144

Chapter 16: The Cardinal's Plea - Page 153

Chapter 17: A Court of Whispers - Page 161

Chapter 18: My Daughter's Right - Page 170

Chapter 19: The Emperor's Ear - Page 178

Chapter 20: The Insult - Page 186

Chapter 21: The Summons - Page 193

Chapter 22: The Eve of Judgment - Page 200

Chapter 23: The Court at Blackfriars - Page 208

Chapter 24: The Queen's Appeal - Page 218

Chapter 25: "I Call God to Witness" - Page 228

Chapter 26: The Defiant Exit - Page 237

Chapter 27: The Last Glimpse - Page 246

Chapter 28: My Shabby Palaces - Page 254

Chapter 29: The Break with Rome - Page 262

Chapter 30: "Princess Dowager" - Page 270

Chapter 31: The Cruelest Cut - Page 281

Chapter 32: The Love of the People - Page 293

Chapter 33: The Walls of Kimbolton - Page 301

Chapter 34: A Sickness of the Heart - Page 309

Chapter 35: The Last Letter - Page 317

Chapter 36: The Final Sacrament - Page 324

Chapter 37: The Unconquered Queen - Page 332

Chapter 1
The Cold Shore

My fingers, stiff with a cold I have never known, trace the familiar, comforting face of the Virgin on a small, jewel-encrusted icon. She is my anchor in this churning grey sea, a piece of Spain, a piece of Heaven in a world that feels like purgatory. For weeks, this ship has been my prison. We left Coruña with such hope, my ladies and I, only for the Bay of Biscay to rise up like a beast from the deep. I truly believed I would die, that my destiny would be swallowed by the black water. To survive such a tempest can only be a sign of God's favor. He has tested me, and I have endured.

Now, we lie at anchor in a place they call Plymouth. They call this persistent, weeping mist rain. In Granada, even the storms have warmth. This is a liquid cold that seeps not only into my bones, but into my soul. My duenna, Doña Elvira Manuel, watches me from across the cabin, her face a stern mask of Castilian propriety. Her gaze is a constant reminder: a princess of Spain does not shiver. A princess of Spain does not show weakness.

The ship creaks beneath me, a groaning complaint against the English harbor's embrace. Through the salt-stained window, I can see nothing but grey—grey water meeting grey sky in a horizon that might not exist at all. The English vessels that surround us are dark shapes in the mist, their standards hanging limp in the wet air. Is this what my new kingdom offers? This colorless welcome?

A sudden lurch of the ship sends a small chest sliding across the cabin floor. There is a sharp crack, and a scent, impossibly rich and warm, fills the damp air. Jasmine and orange blossom. A vial of my Spanish perfume has shattered. My servant, Catalina de Motril, her dark eyes wide with alarm, moves to clean the mess, but I raise a hand to stop her. I close my eyes and breathe it in, a fleeting, poignant memory of the sun-baked courtyards of the Alhambra, the home I left in May, so many months ago.

The scent brings visions: my mother's hands arranging orange blossoms in my hair for the farewell feast, the jasmine vines that climbed the walls of my chambers, their white stars opening to the warm night air. I can almost feel the marble beneath my feet, still holding the day's heat long after sunset. But the vision shatters as quickly as the vial. The cold returns, made more bitter by the brief respite.

I must not dwell on it. I am not Catalina anymore. I am the Princess of Wales. My mother, Queen Isabella, a ruler in her own right, taught me that a royal woman's heart is a fortress, her duty its only gatekeeper. She taught me law and theology, history and philosophy, so that I would be a worthy partner to a king, not merely a vessel for his heirs. She, who rode in armor at the head of her own army, would not abide a daughter who wept over a broken bottle of perfume.

"Your Highness," Doña Elvira's voice cuts through my reverie, sharp as Toledo steel. "The English delegation approaches."

I straighten my spine, feeling the weight of the damp velvet against my shoulders. My ladies flutter around me like dark birds, adjusting my veil, smoothing the heavy brocade of my skirts. The fabric is all wrong for this climate—too heavy, yet not warm enough. Everything Spanish seems to wilt in this perpetual dampness.

The delegation that boards our ship is a study in contrasts. The English lords wear their finest, but I can see the wear at the edges, the careful mending. Their Latin, when they attempt it, is accented strangely, making the sacred language sound foreign even to itself. They bow low, these pale men with their pale eyes, and I see them taking my measure just as I take theirs.

The Bishop of Bath speaks for them, his Latin more polished than the others. He welcomes me to England in the name of King Henry VII. His words are correct, formal, but there is something calculating in his gaze. These are not subjects greeting their future queen with joy. These are men assessing a foreign bride, weighing my worth in dowry gold and political alliance.

The summons comes soon after. It is time. My ladies dress me in heavy velvet, the Spanish fashion strange and dark against the pale English faces that peer at us from the docks. The gown is crimson, the color of authority, of Spanish power. Let them see whom they receive—not some frightened girl, but the daughter of the Catholic Kings who conquered Granada, who sent Columbus to claim a new world.

As I step onto the gangplank, the wind whips my veil across my face. The wood is slick with moisture, treacherous beneath my feet. Below me, the soil of England waits. It looks dark and sodden, nothing like the golden earth of my home. For a moment, vertigo seizes me. This narrow plank between ship and shore is the bridge between everything I was and everything I must become.

My foot touches English soil for the first time, and I feel the weight of it, the permanence. There is no returning. The ships that brought me will sail back to Spain, but I will remain. This wet earth will be my earth. These grey skies will be my skies. This is not a visit or a sojourn. This is my life now.

My first act on this foreign shore is to seek a church, to kneel on the cold stone and give thanks to God for my safe passage. The English lords seem surprised by my insistence, but they lead me through the muddy streets of Plymouth to a small stone church. It is a humble building that smells of sea salt and old stone, so unlike the incense-heavy cathedrals of Castile. The altar is plain, almost austere. There are no golden retablos, no carved saints watching from their niches. But God is here, the same God who watched over me in the storm.

I kneel on the hard stone, feeling the cold seep through my skirts. The Latin prayers come easily to my lips, though they echo strangely in this bare space. *Gratias tibi ago, Domine.* I give thanks for my deliverance from the storm, for the destiny that awaits me, for the strength to face it. But beneath the formal prayers, my heart speaks its own desperate language: *Give me the courage of my mother.*

Give me the wisdom to navigate this strange land. Give me the strength to be the queen You have called me to be.

I pray for my husband, Prince Arthur, the boy I have been betrothed to since I was three, the boy I know only through formal Latin letters. In those letters, he seemed learned and courteous, but letters can lie. What manner of man will he be? Will he be strong enough to stand beside a daughter of Spain? Will he understand that I bring him not just a dowry, but the blood of ancient royalty, the legacy of Castile and Aragon?

I pray that I may be a worthy queen for this land, a land to which I, too, have a claim through the blood of my great-grandmother, Katherine of Lancaster. That connection feels thin as spider's silk in this moment, but it is there—a thread of legitimacy stretching back through the generations. I am not entirely foreign here. Some part of me has always belonged to England.

When I rise from my prayers, my knees ache from the cold stone, but my spirit feels steadier. I emerge from the church to find that the grey day is already fading into a greyer dusk. The English lords wait with barely concealed impatience, eager to begin the long journey inland. They have prepared a litter for me, hung with cloth-of-gold that already shows spots of mildew from the damp air.

I stand for a moment on the church steps, looking out at this town that has given me my first taste of England. The buildings huddle together against the weather, their timber frames dark with moisture. The people who have gathered to glimpse their future queen—for that is what I am to them now—stare with curious, wary eyes. I am a foreign curiosity, a Spanish exotic, as out of place as a palm tree in this northern port.

But I will not be always thus. I think of my mother's words before I left: "You go not as a beggar, but as a conqueror of hearts. You carry the blood of warriors and saints. England will be blessed to have you." At the time, secure in the sun of Spain, I believed her completely. Now, surrounded by these pale, watchful faces, I must choose to believe her still.

I pull my Spanish veil tighter, a shield against the curious stares and the biting air. The heavy fabric is embroidered with pomegranates, the symbol of Granada, of my parents' great victory over the Moors. Each seed represents fertility, abundance, the promise of dynasty. How many seeds will I plant in this English soil? How many will take root in this inhospitable climate?

The litter bearers step forward, ready to carry me to whatever lodging has been prepared. But I hesitate, turning back to look at the harbor where my ship lies at anchor. Tomorrow or the next day, we will begin the journey inland to meet my bridegroom. Each mile will take me further from the sea, further from the path home.

I look inland, towards the rolling, mist-shrouded hills that disappear into the growing darkness. Somewhere beyond those hills waits my destiny—a pale prince, a crown, a life I cannot yet imagine. The mist parts for a moment, and I glimpse a hint of gold on the horizon. Not the sun—it is too late for that—but perhaps the last reflection of light on some distant cloud. I choose to see it as an omen.

"I am ready," I tell Doña Elvira in Spanish, the words a declaration as much to myself as to her.

As the litter bears me away from the shore, I do not look back at the ship. I look forward, into the grey English evening, and I will the sun to appear. I will it with the same fierce determination my mother showed when she planted the cross on the towers of the Alhambra. This is my conquest, fought not with swords but with patience, not with armies but with faith.

The cold has not lessened. If anything, it seems to grow more bitter as we leave the sea behind. But I no longer shiver. I am learning already—a princess of Spain may feel the cold, but she does not show it. A future Queen of England must be as constant as the northern star, as enduring as these ancient stones.

The litter sways gently as we begin the long journey inland. Through the thin curtains, I can hear the English voices of our escort, foreign sounds that I must learn to love. Behind us, the sound of the sea fades. Ahead lies England, grey and waiting.

I close my eyes and try to summon the sun.

Chapter 2

The Frail Prince

The journey inland is a slow procession through a world of green and grey. For a month, we travel, my retinue and I, an exotic caravan moving through the English countryside. The autumn rains have turned the roads to rivers of mud that suck at the wheels of our carts, slowing our progress to a crawl. My Spanish ladies huddle together in their litter, dark eyes wide with dismay at this waterlogged land. They whisper prayers and complaints in equal measure, their voices a comfort of familiar sounds in this alien landscape.

We are met at each stage by nobles who bow low and speak their carefully rehearsed Latin welcomes. The Earl of Surrey at Dorchester, Lord de la Warr at Salisbury—a parade of pale faces and calculating eyes. They lodge us in the finest houses available, but even these seem damp and cheerless compared to the sun-drenched palaces of my youth. At the Old Deanery in Exeter, I wake to find frost patterns on the inside of the window glass, delicate as Venetian lace but cold as death itself.

The anticipation builds with every league we travel. Soon I will meet him. Soon my life's purpose will be given a face. My ladies speak of it constantly, their chatter like birds before a storm. They speculate about his appearance, his manner, whether he will be charmed by Spanish graces or prefer English ways. I let them talk, but I keep my own thoughts locked behind the fortress of my heart.

Today, I am being dressed in red silk, the finest gown in my trousseau. The fabric was woven in Valencia, dyed with the precious cochineal that makes the color burn like flame even in this grey English light. My ladies fuss with the heavy brocade, adjusting the fall of the skirt, the set of the sleeves. The bodice is stiff with gold embroidery, pomegranates and roses intertwined— Spain and England united in thread if not yet in flesh.

"He must see the blood of Spain," I tell my reflection in the polished silver mirror. The color of passion, of strength, of the dynasty that my mother and father forged from fire and faith. Let him see that I am no weak northern princess, but the daughter of warriors who drove the Moors from Granada after seven hundred years.

We are at a manor in a place called Dogmersfield, a property of the Bishop of Winchester. The great hall has been prepared for our meeting, hung with tapestries that cannot quite disguise the moisture stains on the walls. The air is thick with the smell of roasting meat and woodsmoke, and underneath it, that perpetual English dampness that clings to everything like a second skin.

A commotion in the courtyard sends my ladies rushing to the windows. Horses, many horses, and the sound of English voices raised in greeting. My chief lady, Doña Maria de Rojas, turns from the window with eyes wide. "Your Highness, the King comes! The King himself!"

My stomach tightens. This is not the plan. We were to have more time, more ceremony. The meeting was to be orchestrated, controlled. A message arrives moments later, delivered by Don Pedro de Ayala, my father's diplomat, his face flushed with indignation. The King, Henry VII, and the Prince are riding to meet us now, this very day. When Don Pedro protested that Spanish custom forbids a bride to be seen by her groom before the wedding, the King's reply was swift and sharp: the King of England will not be dictated to in his own kingdom.

A tremor of unease passes through me. This is a court that does not value our traditions. They will expect me to bend, to yield, to become English. But I am Castilian steel, not English clay. I can be shaped by fire, perhaps, but I will not be molded by their cold hands.

Doña Elvira is scandalized, her thin face pinched with disapproval. "It is not proper, Your Highness. You should refuse to see them. Let them understand that a Princess of Spain—"

"Will show them Spanish grace," I interrupt, my voice steady though my heart races. "We are not in Spain now, Doña Elvira. We must choose our battles wisely."

I wait in the great hall, arranged like a painting—the Infanta surrounded by her ladies, a vision of Iberian elegance in this rough English setting. The minutes stretch into an hour. The fire in the great hearth does little to warm the vast space, and I can feel the cold seeping through my silk slippers. But I do not shift, do not show discomfort. I am a statue of royal composure.

Then, the chamber door opens.

The King enters first, and I understand immediately why they call him the Winter King. Henry VII is a lean, watchful man with eyes that seem to miss nothing and give nothing away. His face is all angles and calculation, carved by years of struggle and suspicion. He greets me with formal courtesy, his Latin precise and cold as a legal document. This is a man who counts costs before kindnesses, who weighs every word before he speaks it.

And then he steps aside, and I see my future.

This is the Prince of Wales? My heart, which I have kept so carefully guarded, stutters in my chest. Arthur stands before me, and the word that comes unbidden to my mind is not prince but boy. He is tall, yes, taller than his father, but it is the height of a plant grown too quickly in insufficient light—stretched and pale and fragile. His hair is reddish-gold, catching the firelight in a way that should be handsome but only emphasizes the unhealthy pallor of his skin. His eyes, when they meet mine, are small and uncertain in a face that carries the shadow of sickness.

Dios mío, grant that he is merely shy. Grant that this tremor in his hand as he reaches for mine is from nerves, not weakness. I search his face for signs of the strength that must be there, must be hidden beneath this unpromising exterior. He is the heir to England's throne. Surely there is steel beneath this velvet, surely there is fire beneath this ash.

He bows, and I see the delicate frame beneath the heavy velvet of his doublet. The fabric seems to weigh him down, as if he is a child playing at being a man in his father's clothes. When he straightens, there is a moment where he sways slightly, catching himself with a hand on his father's arm. The King's face remains impassive, but I catch the flicker of something—concern? Calculation?—in those cold eyes.

"My lady," Arthur says, and his voice is another disappointment—thin and reedy, lacking the resonance of authority. "You are most welcome to England."

The absurdity of our situation becomes immediately apparent. We both speak the Latin of scholars, but his English pronunciation grates against my Castilian, rendering the language of Cicero and Virgil a clumsy tool of misunderstanding. When I respond with my carefully prepared greeting, I see confusion flicker across his face. We must speak through interpreters, a bishop for him and Father Alessandro for me, our words filtered through the caution of churchmen.

"His Highness says that your beauty exceeds all reports," the English bishop translates, though I heard no such poetry in Arthur's halting Latin.

"Her Highness is grateful for His Highness's kind welcome," Father Alessandro responds on my behalf, though my actual words were a careful inquiry about the Prince's health after his journey.

It is a dance of mistranslation and misunderstanding, and through it all, I study the boy who will be my husband. He stands slightly behind his father, as if seeking shelter from the weight of attention. His hands, I notice, are long and thin, with prominent veins—the hands of a scholar, perhaps, but not a warrior. Not a king.

A prince's strength is in his lineage, not his limbs, I remind myself firmly. His blood is royal, as is mine. Together, we will forge an empire. I will be his strength. I will be the rock upon which the House of Tudor builds its future. This is my new duty, revealed to me in this hall of forced festivity.

The feast that follows is an ordeal of awkwardness disguised as celebration. I am seated beside Arthur, close enough to hear the slight wheeze in his breathing, to see the way he picks at his food rather than eating it. The King watches us from his place at the high table, those calculating eyes moving between his son and me like a merchant assessing goods.

"Do you enjoy hunting, Your Highness?" I ask Arthur through our interpreters, seeking some common ground.

The translation comes back: "The Prince says he prefers his books to the field."

Books. Of course. I think of my brothers, Juan and Alfonso, how they lived in the saddle, how they trained with swords from the time they could lift them. This pale prince prefers his books. But perhaps this is not entirely bad—my mother values learning above all things. A learned king can be a great king, even if he is not a warrior king.

"What books does His Highness favor?" I pursue, hoping to find some spark of passion in those uncertain eyes.

"Theology," comes the answer. "And philosophy. The Prince is most devoted to his studies of the Church fathers."

The Church fathers. Not even poetry or history, which might stir the blood, but the dry debates of long-dead theologians. I force a smile, inclining my head as if this is the most fascinating thing I have ever heard.

Later, there is music. The English musicians play their strange, melancholy airs that sound to my ears like wind through empty houses. My ladies and I are asked to dance, and we perform a formal Spanish measure, our steps precise and proud. The pavane is a dance of dignity, of control, each movement deliberate and meaningful. We are showing them Spanish cultivation, Spanish grace.

Arthur is prompted to dance with an English lady, a Lord Guildford's wife whose name I do not catch. He moves with a careful grace, but there is no fire in it, no strength. He performs the steps as if reciting a lesson, correctly but without passion. When the dance ends, I see him lean briefly against a pillar, his face pale with exhaustion from even this small exertion.

Madre de Dios, what have they sent me? This is the heir to England's throne? This is the prince who will father a dynasty? I think of the portrait they sent to Spain, showing a robust young man with strong features and confident bearing. Either the artist was a masterful liar, or Arthur has declined greatly since it was painted.

The King approaches me as the evening wears on, his movements silent as a cat's. "I trust Your Highness finds the Prince to your liking?" he asks in French, which we both speak, though mine is coloured by Spanish pronunciation.

What can I say? That his son looks like a breath of wind could topple him? That I fear my wedding night will kill him? I meet those cold, calculating eyes and speak the only truth I can.

"His Highness seems most learned and gentle," I reply carefully. "Qualities much to be valued in a Christian prince."

The King's thin lips twitch in what might be a smile. "Indeed. And your father, I trust, will be pleased that the alliance proceeds as planned? The remainder of your dowry will arrive promptly?"

Ah. There it is. The true concern. Not whether I find his son suitable, but whether my father's gold will flow into England's coffers. I am not a bride but a transaction, and Arthur is not a bridegroom but a seal on a contract.

"My father honors all his commitments," I say, allowing a touch of steel into my voice. "As I shall honor mine."

The King nods and glides away, leaving me with the distinct feeling that I have been weighed and found... adequate. Not valuable, not cherished, but adequate for his purposes.

As the feast draws to a close, Arthur approaches me one more time. Without the interpreters, we attempt to communicate directly. His Latin is actually quite good when I concentrate on understanding his pronunciation, and I realize with surprise that he is trying to quote Virgil to me—something about duty and destiny.

"*Fata viam invenient*," he says softly. "The fates will find a way."

For a moment, I see something in his eyes—intelligence, perhaps even kindness. But also fear. He is as frightened as I am, this fragile prince. We are both pawns in our fathers' games, both bound by duties we did not choose.

"*Audentes fortuna iuvat*," I reply. Fortune favors the bold.

He smiles then, a genuine smile that transforms his thin face. "Then we must both be bold, my lady."

But even as he says it, I see the exhaustion creeping back into his features. Bold. This boy who can barely stand after an evening of ceremony. How can he be bold when he lacks the strength even to be?

The feast ends. I watch Arthur walk away, his shoulders slumped slightly in his heavy robes. His father's hand is on his elbow, guiding him, supporting him in a way that tries to look casual but is clearly necessary. A feeling of immense, unexpected responsibility settles upon me like a lead cloak.

I came here to be a wife, to bear children, to cement an alliance. But I see now that I will need to be so much more. I will need to be the strength that Arthur lacks, the fire that he does not possess. If there are to be heirs, if this alliance is to mean anything, I will have to carry more than my share of the burden.

My ladies cluster around me as we retire to our chambers, their voices an anxious flutter of Spanish.

"He is very pale, Your Highness," Doña Maria ventures carefully.

"He is very learned," I reply, my tone ending the discussion.

But later, alone in my chamber with only the sound of English rain against the windows, I kneel before my portable altar. The Madonna's face is serene in the candlelight, untouched by doubt or fear.

"Holy Mother," I whisper in Spanish, the language of my heart, "give me strength enough for two. Make me the rock on which this fragile dynasty can build. Let my womb be fruitful even if his seed is weak. Let my will be strong enough to carry us both."

The candle flickers, casting shadows that dance across the Madonna's face. Outside, the English wind howls through the manor's ancient stones. Somewhere in this great house, my future husband—that pale, trembling boy—is perhaps saying his own prayers, seeking his own strength.

Tomorrow, we will continue the charade. We will smile and dance and pretend that this is the great romance our fathers have sold to their kingdoms. But tonight, in the darkness of this foreign place, I allow myself one moment of pure, cold truth.

I am alone. Whatever comes, whatever this marriage brings, I will face it alone. Arthur will be my husband in name, perhaps even in affection if we are fortunate. But he will never be my partner in the way I had dreamed, the way my mother and father are partners.

The responsibility is mine. The burden is mine. The future of this alliance, this kingdom, this dynasty—it all rests on my shoulders, not his.

I rise from my knees, my decision made. If God has given me a weak vessel for a husband, then I will be the strength. If He has given me a sick prince, then I will be the health. I will be whatever England needs me to be, whatever this poor, pale boy needs me to be.

This is my vow, made not before witnesses but before God himself. I will not fail. I cannot fail.

The fire in the hearth burns low, casting long shadows across the chamber. I lie in the great bed, pulling the heavy English covers up to my chin. Tomorrow, we continue the journey toward London, toward my wedding, toward whatever future awaits.

But tonight, I close my eyes and try to transform that fragile, frightened boy into the king he must become, if only in my imagination. I try to see past the pale skin and trembling hands to the soul beneath.

Fata viam invenient. The fates will find a way.

They must. For all our sakes, they must.

Chapter 3

The Welsh Winter

The wedding is a blur of statecraft and spectacle. On a raised platform in the great cavern of St. Paul's Cathedral, where all of London can witness the union of Tudor and Trastámara, I make my vows. I am dressed in white satin, a Spanish *verdugado* that makes me appear to float rather than walk, my hair loose beneath a veil glittering with gems that catch the November light streaming through the high windows. At my side, leading me to the altar, is not my husband-to-be, but his younger brother, Henry, Duke of York—a boy of ten with hair like burnished copper and a confident smile that belongs on a much older face. His hand on my arm is steady, assured, so different from Arthur's tentative touch. This second son walks like a young lion, all contained energy and nascent power, making his older brother seem even more fragile by comparison.

Arthur waits for me at the altar, looking small and overwhelmed beneath the great stone arches that soar toward Heaven. The Bishop of London speaks the sacred words, but they seem to echo strangely in the vast space, as if the cathedral itself questions what we do here. When Arthur takes my hand for the blessing, his fingers are cold despite the warmth of the packed cathedral, and I can feel them tremble slightly against mine.

That night, the ritual of the bedding ceremony is performed with solemn precision, as dictated by the King's mother, the Lady

Margaret Beaufort—a woman whose piety is as sharp as a blade and twice as dangerous. She oversees every detail with her hawk's eyes, ensuring that all is done according to ancient tradition. The bed is blessed with holy water, we are escorted by our respective attendants, and the witnesses are positioned to observe us being put to bed. And then, finally, mercifully, we are left alone.

The silence that falls when the door closes is absolute. Arthur sits on the edge of the great bed, his thin shoulders hunched beneath his nightshift. In the candlelight, he looks even younger than his fifteen years, a child dressed in a bridegroom's costume. When he turns to me, I see naked fear in his eyes.

"I—" he begins, then stops, his face flushing red. "I know my duty, my lady."

His duty. Not his desire, not his joy, but his duty. I think of the songs the troubadours sing, of passion and fire and the meeting of souls. There is none of that here. There is only a frightened boy and a girl far from home, both trapped by the expectations of kingdoms.

"We are both tired from the day's ceremonies," I say gently in my careful Latin. "Perhaps we should rest."

The relief that floods his face is almost painful to see. We lie side by side in the great bed, not touching, like carved figures on a tomb. I can hear his breathing in the darkness, shallow and slightly labored. Once, he coughs, trying to muffle the sound in his pillow.

The next day, I hear the whispers among my ladies, their voices carrying from the outer chamber. The Prince, they say, called for ale upon emerging from the bedchamber, boasting to his gentlemen that he had spent the night "in the midst of Spain." The words, repeated with barely suppressed giggles, make my stomach turn. I know the truth—that Arthur's boasts are the desperate fiction of a boy trying to appear a man. We did not consummate the marriage. We barely touched.

But I say nothing to correct the tale. Let him have his fiction. Let the court believe what it needs to believe. I know, and God knows, and Arthur knows the truth of our wedding night—that it was as fragile and incomplete as everything else about this union.

In December, we journey west to Ludlow Castle, on the border of a wild land called Wales. The King had wished for me to remain in London, safe in the comfort of Richmond Palace, while Arthur took up his duties as Prince of Wales. But I insisted. "My place is with my husband," I told the King, meeting those cold, calculating eyes without flinching. I saw him weigh the cost of my maintenance against the political value of appearing to have a united, fruitful marriage. The scales tipped in my favor, barely.

The journey is cold, the landscape growing bleaker with every mile. We travel through forests where the trees stand like skeletons against the grey sky, through valleys where mist clings to the ground like the breath of buried giants. The further we go from London, the more foreign England becomes. If London felt alien, this Welsh borderland feels like the very edge of the world.

The castle, when we finally arrive after days of bone-jarring travel, is even bleaker than the journey. Ludlow Castle squats on its hill like a great grey toad, its towers disappearing into the low-hanging clouds. It has been long uninhabited, and the dampness of the Welsh winter weeps from its stone walls like tears. Ice forms on the inside of the windows. The great hall's fireplace, massive though it is, cannot begin to heat the vast, hollow spaces.

Our apartments are in the eastern range, a series of chambers that might have been grand once but now feel like elegant tombs. The tapestries, sent ahead from London, do little to warm the walls. They hang limp and already smell of mildew. My Spanish braziers, packed so carefully in Castile, provide small islands of warmth, but they cannot fight the cold that seems to emanate from the very stones.

My fingers, numb with cold, trace the gilded lettering of my Spanish book of hours. The illuminated pages, painted in the warm scriptoriums of Castile, seem like windows into another world—a world of gold and blue and crimson, where the saints stand in gardens of eternal summer. It is my only warmth in this place. The only other sound is the wind screaming outside the narrow window, rattling the old glass in its leading, and from the next chamber, separated from mine by only a single door, a faint, dry cough.

This is not a palace. It is a stone tomb at the edge of the world. My ladies and I huddle by the fire, our Spanish chatter a small defiance against the oppressive silence. We speak of home, of the Christmas celebrations that will be happening in Castile, of the orange trees that will be blooming in Seville despite the season.

But our words seem to freeze in the air, falling like dead things to the cold floor.

I find an unexpected friend in Lady Margaret Pole, the wife of Arthur's chamberlain. She is a woman of quiet strength and deep faith, with sad, intelligent eyes that have seen too much sorrow. She is of royal blood herself—the daughter of the Duke of Clarence, a Plantagenet princess reduced to a gentlewoman. She understands what it is to be displaced, to be royal yet powerless.

"Your Highness must find Wales very different from Spain," she says one afternoon as we sit by the inadequate fire, our needlework in our laps.

"Different, yes," I reply carefully. "But every place has its own beauty."

She looks at me with something like pity. "You are kind to say so, Your Highness. But Ludlow in winter has little beauty to offer. It is a place of duty, not pleasure."

Duty. That word again. Everything here is duty—Arthur's duty to be Prince of Wales, my duty to be his wife, our mutual duty to produce an heir. But how can life spring from such cold? How can a dynasty be born in this tomb?

The cough from Arthur's chamber grows more persistent as the days pass. At first, it comes only at night, a dry, hacking sound that echoes through the stone walls. Then it begins to interrupt his days as well. I see him at dinner, pushing food around his plate, his face grey with exhaustion. The Welsh damp has settled in his chest like an unwelcome guest.

"It is merely a winter fever," he insists when I express concern. "It will pass."

But I see the truth in the hollow beneath his eyes, in the way he grips the table when he stands, in the slight sheen of fever-sweat on his brow even in the cold hall. This is not a passing ailment. The Welsh winter has caused a corruption of his humours that consumes him from within.

I tell myself it is a winter fever, nothing more; he was never strong. He needs Spanish sun, not this endless Welsh rain that falls like a curse upon the castle. Even when it is not raining, the mist creeps in through every crack and crevice, making the air itself feel wet and heavy in our lungs.

I send for my physician, Dr. de La Sa, a learned man from Salamanca who traveled with me from Spain. He examines Arthur with grave courtesy, but I see the concern in his eyes when he emerges from the Prince's chamber.

"The climate does not suit His Highness," he tells me in Spanish, his voice low. "His constitution is delicate. He needs warmth, dry air, strengthening food."

"Then we must provide these things," I say firmly.

But how can we provide what does not exist here? The kitchens produce heavy English fare—great joints of meat swimming in grease, thick puddings, ale and more ale. When I request broths, tisanes, the light foods that might tempt an invalid's appetite, the cooks look at me with blank incomprehension. The Welsh servants speak little English and no Latin at all. They are like shadows in the castle, sliding along the walls with downcast eyes.

Miserere mei, Deus. Have mercy on me, God. The prayer rises unbidden to my lips as I kneel in the castle's small, cold chapel. Why this test? Why here, in this cold, forgotten place? Is my faith not strong enough? Have I failed in some duty?

I think of my mother, conquering Granada, riding while pregnant to the siege lines. She would not be defeated by cold and damp and a husband's weakness. She would find a way to triumph. But my mother had the sun of Spain at her back and the armies of Castile at her command. I have only my prayers and my few loyal ladies in this Welsh wilderness.

The castle seems to grow colder as Christmas approaches. Ice forms inside our chambers now, delicate fernlike patterns that would be beautiful if they were not so terrible. My ladies and I wear all our gowns at once, layer upon layer, but still the cold penetrates. We have taken to sleeping three to a bed for warmth, abandoning Spanish propriety for survival.

Arthur barely emerges from his chambers now. When he does, for the obligatory appearance at dinner or to receive some local Welsh lord come to pay homage, he moves like an old man, each step careful and considered. The coughing is constant now, a sound that has become part of the castle's ambient noise, like the wind and the dripping of water from ancient stones.

One night, I can bear it no longer. I leave my chambers and knock softly on Arthur's door. His gentleman, a kind-faced young man named Griffith ap Rhys, opens it, his expression grave.

"Your Highness should not—" he begins, but I push past him.

Arthur is propped up in his bed, struggling for breath. In the candlelight, his skin has a terrible translucence, as if he is already half-ghost. When he sees me, he tries to smile, but it transforms into another coughing fit that wracks his thin frame.

"Katherine," he whispers when he can speak again. It is the first time he has used my Christian name. "You should not be here. If you become ill—"

"Hush," I say, moving to his bedside. I take a cloth and dip it in the basin of water beside his bed, pressing it to his burning forehead. "Save your strength."

We sit in silence for a while, the only sounds his labored breathing and the eternal wind outside. Then he speaks again, his voice barely audible.

"I am sorry," he says. "Sorry I am not the husband you deserve. Sorry I am not the prince England needs."

"You have nothing to apologize for," I tell him, though my heart breaks a little at his words.

"I do," he insists. "You came so far, gave up so much, for this—" He gestures weakly at himself, at the cold chamber, at the whole miserable situation. "For a weak boy in a cold castle."

I want to tell him he is wrong, that he is strong, that he will recover. But the lies die on my lips. Instead, I take his hand—so thin now I can feel every bone—and hold it gently.

"We do not choose our trials," I say softly. "We can only choose how we face them."

He squeezes my hand weakly. "You have your mother's courage," he says. "I have heard the stories. Isabella the Catholic, the warrior queen."

"And you have your father's wisdom," I reply, though we both know it is a gentle fiction.

We sit together through the long night, not as husband and wife but as two young people far from home, facing a fate neither of us chose. I sing to him softly in Spanish, lullabies my nurse sang to me in the Alhambra, songs of orange blossoms and warm winds. He does not understand the words, but the melody seems to calm him.

As dawn breaks—another grey, Welsh dawn that brings no real light, only a lessening of darkness—he sleeps fitfully. I return to my chambers, my ladies fluttering around me with concern and disapproval.

But my prayer is shattered by a sound from behind Arthur's door—a violent, racking fit of coughing that seems to tear the very air apart. It is different from before, wet and terrible, as if he is drowning in his own lungs. I hear running feet, shouted orders, the terrible urgency of crisis.

I begin a desperate, whispered Pater Noster. *Our Father, who art in heaven, hallowed be thy name. Thy kingdom come, thy will be done...*

But even as I pray, I know with a cold certainty that settles in my stomach like a stone: God's will is being done. And His will is that I should be tested in this cold place, with this dying boy, at the very edge of the world.

The coughing stops. The silence that follows is more terrible than any sound.

I close my eyes, the leather of my prayer book cool against my cheek, and I continue my prayer. But now it is not for Arthur's recovery. It is for his soul, and for my own strength to face what comes next.

Outside, the Welsh wind howls through the valley, and somewhere in the castle, a door slams shut with terrible finality.

CHAPTER 4

THE WIDOW'S WEEDS

A single candle gutters by the bedside, its flame a fragile, struggling thing in the thick, stale air of the chamber. The wax has pooled at its base, threatening to drown the wick entirely—a small death that mirrors the larger one unfolding before me. I hold a damp cloth to Arthur's forehead, my face a mask of exhausted vigilance, though beneath it my mind races with prayers and pleas and desperate bargains with God.

For days, I have sat here, listening to the rasp of his breath, a sound that has become the rhythm of my life. Each inhale is a mountain climbed, each exhale a valley crossed. The spaces between grow longer, more terrible. I count them sometimes—one, two, three, four—my own breath held until his chest rises again.

I, too, have felt the fever's grip, a weakness in my limbs that I refuse to acknowledge. My ladies whisper that I should rest, that I risk my own health, but I wave them away with increasing irritation. I will not succumb. I am the Princess of Wales. More than that, I am the daughter of Isabella of Castile, who gave birth on campaign, who held court while ill, who never yielded to weakness of the flesh. This Welsh sickness may claim Arthur, but it will not claim me.

His eyes flutter open, but they do not see me. They are fixed on some point beyond the canopy of the bed, beyond the cold stone walls of this castle. I have seen this look before, in Granada, when the old soldiers who had fought in the wars would lie dying. It is the look of one who sees not this world but the next.

His lips move, but no sound comes out. I lean closer, straining to hear, but there is nothing—only the slight movement of air, less than a whisper, less than a sigh. He is trying to speak, perhaps to pray, perhaps to say goodbye. I will never know.

And then, there is a final, shallow sigh, like wind through an empty room. The rasping stops. The terrible, familiar rhythm that has governed my days and nights is broken. The silence that follows is absolute, a roar that fills my ears and empties my soul.

He is gone. April the second, 1502. Five months a wife, and now this.

I sit frozen for a moment that stretches into eternity. Then, with movements that feel disconnected from my will, I reach out and close his eyes. They close easily, as if grateful for the rest. His face, released from the struggle of living, looks peaceful in a way it never did in life. He looks, finally, like the portrait they sent to Spain—noble, serene, every inch a prince. Death has given him the dignity that life denied.

"Your Highness." The voice comes from behind me. Dr. de La Sa, my physician, has entered silently. He does not need to examine Arthur to know the truth. The stillness in the room speaks louder than any diagnosis.

"How long?" I ask, my voice strange and distant in my own ears.

"Perhaps an hour past, Your Highness. The fever—"

"Leave me," I interrupt. I do not want to hear about the fever, about the weakness of constitution, about all the things that might have been done differently. None of it matters now.

When I am alone with Arthur's body, I allow myself one moment of pure, raw honesty. Five months a wife, and now this. With him dies my purpose. My vow. *Madre de Dios*, my mission is shattered.

The marriage that was to unite England and Spain, to create a dynasty that would rival the Habsburgs, to fulfill the destiny written in my stars since birth—it lies as dead as the boy in this bed. Am I to be sent back in disgrace? A failed bride, a barren widow, my dowry a source of bitter dispute? The thought is a physical pain, sharper than any fever.

No. I force myself to stand, to straighten my spine. I am the Dowager Princess of Wales. That, at least, is my anchor in this storm. My title. My legal standing. It is all I have left.

The news travels on the fastest horses to London. I can picture the scene as clearly as if I were there: the messenger, mud-spattered and grim, kneeling before the King in his presence chamber. The careful words, the formal phrases that cannot soften the blow. "His Highness the Prince of Wales has been called to God."

I hear later of their grief, delivered in carefully worded letters from the court. How my mother-in-law, Queen Elizabeth, had to comfort her husband before collapsing into her own sorrow. How the King had aged a decade in a day. Their grief is for a son, the heir they had such hopes for, the future of their still-fragile dynasty. Mine is a different, colder thing. It is the grief of failure.

They watch me now, these English courtiers who have traveled from London to manage the aftermath. Their faces are masks of appropriate sorrow, but their eyes calculate. They watch my body with particular attention, waiting for a sign, a swelling of the belly that would mean a Tudor heir still lives. Each morning, Lady Margaret Pole helps me dress, and I see her quick, assessing glance at my unchanged figure. Each month that passes will be another confirmation of my uselessness.

But my womb is as empty as my future. The marriage was never consummated, though I will never speak that truth aloud. Let them wonder. Let them calculate. The truth lies buried with Arthur in Worcester Cathedral, where they will inter him with all the ceremony due to a Prince of Wales.

I am not permitted to attend the funeral. Widows, they tell me, do not attend such ceremonies. It is not seemly. So I remain at Ludlow while they take his body away, watching from my window as the funeral cortege winds down the hill and disappears into the Welsh mist. The castle bells toll seventy times—once for each day of our marriage that was not a marriage.

A carriage draped in black is sent to bring me back from Ludlow. It arrives on a day when, miraculously, the sun breaks through the Welsh clouds. The light seems wrong somehow, too bright, too cheerful for this grim business. My Spanish ladies pack our things in silence. There is not much to pack—so many of my belongings were never fully unpacked, as if some part of me knew this was always temporary.

Lady Margaret Pole comes to bid me farewell. She takes my hands in hers, and I see tears in her eyes—genuine tears, not the calculated sorrow of the court.

"Your Highness has shown great courage," she says softly. "Your mother would be proud."

Would she? Would Isabella of Castile be proud of a daughter who failed in her first duty, who could not even keep her husband alive for half a year? But I merely nod and thank her for her kindness.

The journey back to London is slow, a funeral procession for my dead dreams. We stop at the same great houses where we stayed on my bridal progress, but now I am received with awkward formality rather than celebration. The same nobles who rushed to pay homage to the future Queen of England now greet the Dowager Princess of Wales with careful courtesy and visible relief when I continue on my way.

Back in London, I am given chambers at Richmond Palace, but I am no longer at the heart of the court. I am a problem to be solved, a loose end to be tied up. The King receives me once, briefly, his cold eyes assessing me like a merchant evaluating damaged goods.

"You are young," he says, which seems to be meant as comfort. "Your father and I will come to some arrangement."

An arrangement. As if I am a shipment of wine that has gone bad and must be returned or exchanged. I curtsey and say nothing. What is there to say? I am entirely at the mercy of two kings who care nothing for me, only for what I represent—a failed alliance, a questionable investment.

One evening, a lady brings me my mourning clothes. The widow's weeds. The fabric is a heavy, lusterless black wool that seems to absorb light rather than reflect it. It smells of age and sorrow, as if it has dressed other widows before me, other women whose lives ended before they properly began.

I stand before the polished silver mirror as my ladies dress me in this new uniform. The transformation is complete and terrible. The girl who arrived in Plymouth in crimson silk, the bride who stood at the altar in white satin—she is gone. In her place stands a figure from a morality play, the Young Widow, dressed in the color of night and despair.

I look at my reflection in the polished silver mirror. The pale, black-clad woman staring back is a stranger. She is sixteen years old, but her eyes are ancient. Where did the Infanta of Spain go? Where is Catalina, who danced in the gardens of the Alhambra, who listened to her mother plan the conquest of kingdoms? She is as dead as Arthur, buried in the cold ground of Wales.

I touch the unfamiliar fabric, feeling its rough, solid weight against my skin. It is ugly, graceless, designed to render the wearer invisible, to declare to the world that this woman's life is over, that she exists now only as a memorial to the dead. This is my new armor.

But armor can protect as well as conceal. Behind this black wall, I can think, plan, survive. I am no longer the radiant bride, the center of attention and speculation. I am the forgettable widow, and in that forgetting, perhaps, lies my salvation.

That night, I kneel before my portable altar, the one that traveled with me from Spain. The Madonna's face is unchanged—serene, compassionate, eternal. She has seen me in my glory and now sees me in my disgrace, and her expression does not alter.

"Holy Mother," I whisper in Spanish, "I have failed in my first mission. But I am still alive. I still have royal blood in my veins. I still have purpose, even if I cannot yet see it. Show me the way. Show me how to rise from this death."

The candle flickers, casting shadows that dance across the Madonna's face. Outside my chamber, I can hear the sounds of the court—laughter, music, life continuing as if nothing has changed. For them, perhaps, nothing has. One prince is dead, but another lives. Young Henry, that confident boy who led me to the altar, will be the new Prince of Wales. The succession is secure, even if the Spanish alliance is not.

I think suddenly of that boy, Henry. How different he was from Arthur—all fire and strength where his brother was ash and weakness. He will be king one day, a true king, not a pale shadow. The thought comes unbidden, treacherous: what if I had been betrothed to him instead? What if God's plan is not yet complete?

I push the thought away, horrified at my own mind's betrayal. It is too soon for such thoughts, perhaps too impossible. I am the widow of his brother. There are laws, canonical and natural, against such things.

But the thought, once born, will not die. It sits in the corner of my mind like a small, patient spider, spinning its web of possibility.

For now, though, I must mourn. I must wear these widow's weeds and play the part of the grieving wife, though what I grieve for is not the boy who died but the future that died with him. I must be patient, careful, clever. I must survive whatever comes next.

I rise from my prayers and go to my writing desk. I must write to my parents, tell them of my situation, beg for their intervention. But what can I say? That their daughter is a failure? That the great alliance they sought is dust? That I am now a burden rather than an asset?

I dip my quill in ink and begin:

"To their Most Catholic Majesties, my most beloved parents, Your dutiful daughter commends herself to you and begs your blessing. It has pleased God in His infinite wisdom to call my husband to His glory..."

The words are formal, empty, saying everything and nothing. I write of my grief, of my faith, of my trust in their wisdom. I do not write of the cold fear in my belly, of the English courtiers who look through me as if I am already gone, of the terrible possibility that I might be sent back to Spain in disgrace.

When the letter is finished, sealed with black wax and my seal—still the pomegranate of Granada, though I have no right to it now—I give it to my most trusted messenger. It will take weeks to reach Spain, weeks more for a reply. In that time, my fate may already be decided.

I return to my mirror, studying the stranger in black who stares back at me. This is my new armor, yes. But it is also my chrysalis. Inside this dark shell, I must transform. I must become something new, something that can survive in this cold, calculating English court.

The widow's weeds are meant to signify that my life is over. But I am sixteen years old. I am the daughter of Isabella and Ferdinand. I have the blood of warriors and saints in my veins.

My life is not over. It is paused, suspended, waiting. And I will wait with it, patient as stone, constant as the northern star, until God reveals His true purpose for me.

The candle burns low, casting long shadows across my chamber. Outside, the English rain begins again, that eternal, mournful sound that will be the music of my waiting. I close my eyes and listen to it, and slowly, carefully, I begin to build my fortress—not of stone but of will, not of armies but of faith.

I am the Dowager Princess of Wales. It is a title of failure, of ending, of death.

But I am still alive. And while I live, I will not yield.

Chapter 5
The Gilded Cage

The years that follow are a long, grey twilight. Seven of them. Seven years in which I age not seven but seventy, each day a small death, each month a fresh humiliation. They move me to Durham House, a palace on the river that belongs to the Bishop of Durham, though he never resides here. It sounds grand when they tell me of it—a palace on the Thames, with gardens stretching to the water, with rooms enough for a proper household. In my innocence, I dare to hope.

But Durham House, when my small retinue arrives on a grey September morning, is a mockery of its promise. The gardens that stretch to the Thames are overgrown with weeds that reach to my waist, brambles that catch at my skirts like grasping fingers. The topiary, once shaped into fantastic beasts and heraldic devices, has grown wild, transforming into misshapen monsters. The fountains are dry, their basins filled with dead leaves and stagnant rainwater that breeds mosquitoes in the summer heat.

The palace itself is worse. The tapestries are faded, their once-bright threads now the color of dust and disappointment. A damp chill clings to the corridors even in summer, as if the very walls weep with the Thames's moisture. The great hall's roof leaks in three places—I count them during the endless meals where I preside over my shrinking household. The painted ceiling, which must once have shown the glory of Heaven, is now stained and peeling, its angels transformed into lepers by neglect.

It is a house of decay and stagnation, a perfect mirror for my life.

I am a pawn in a game played by two parsimonious kings: my father-in-law, Henry VII, and my own father, Ferdinand. My dowry is the chessboard upon which they move me back and forth, each seeking advantage, neither willing to yield. Half was paid upon my marriage to Arthur, but the other half—100,000 crowns—remains in Spain. King Henry refuses to support my household until the rest is sent. My father refuses to send it until my future is secured. And so I am left in the middle, a princess forced to beg.

I sit at my table in what was once a fine chamber but now serves as my office, my dining room, my reception hall—I cannot afford to heat more than a few rooms. Before me lie the household accounts, each entry a fresh wound to my pride. I meticulously count out a few silver coins, my brow furrowed in concentration that would better suit a merchant's wife than a princess.

There is not enough to pay the butcher. There has not been enough for three months now. He extends credit because he still hopes—poor fool—that one day the Princess of Wales's household will pay its debts. But his patience wears thin. Yesterday, he sent his boy to demand payment, and I had to send him away empty-handed, my cheeks burning with shame that a tradesman's apprentice should see a daughter of Spain brought so low.

My Spanish ladies, the few who have remained loyal, grow thin. Their gowns, like mine, are frayed at the cuffs, the hems muddy and re-hemmed so many times the fabric barely holds. Doña Maria de Rojas, once so proud and elegant, now carefully patches her single remaining court dress by candlelight, her fingers working with the desperate efficiency of poverty. We have learned skills no lady of Spain should know—how to turn a collar to hide the worn edge, how to clean velvet with stale bread, how to make one candle last three evenings.

I have been forced to sell my silver plate piece by piece, a slow bleeding of my dignity. First the great serving dishes, then the chalices, finally even the small personal items—the pomander my mother gave me, the jeweled eating knife that was part of my trousseau. Each piece carried to the goldsmith's is another part of my identity melted down into coins that disappear like water into sand.

The goldsmith, a man named Thomas Wyatt, is kind enough to pretend he does not know who I am, though of course he does. All of London knows of the Spanish princess moldering in Durham House, selling her patrimony for bread. He gives me fair prices, more than fair, and never asks questions. It is a kindness that cuts deeper than cruelty would.

I write letters to my father, letters filled with carefully worded desperation. I have become a master of the diplomatic phrase, the gentle suggestion that masks urgent need. "I choose what I believe, and say nothing," I tell him, my quill scratching across the precious paper—even that is rationed now. "For I am not as simple as I may seem."

The words are a code he will understand. I am not weak. I am not broken. But I am drowning, and I need him to throw me a rope. I plead for him to intervene, to uphold the honor of his house. I remind him, with subtle allusions that cost me greatly to write, that his daughter's poverty reflects upon the glory of Spain itself.

His replies, when they come after weeks of waiting, are full of promises and delays. He is negotiating, he says. He is concerned for my welfare. He is working to secure my future. But he expects King Henry to provide for me in the meantime—am I not the widow of his son? King Henry expects the same of him—is not the unpaid dowry sufficient cause to withhold support?

Between them, I starve.

My ladies suffer more than I do, for they suffer in silence. They came to England as part of my household, young women of good Spanish families who expected to make brilliant marriages at the English court. Instead, they are prisoners of my poverty, unable to return home without funds for passage, unable to marry without dowries. I watch them age before their time, hope dying in their eyes like candles guttering out.

Doña Elvira Manuel, my duenna, maintains her stern Castilian dignity even as her cheeks hollow with hunger. She rules over our small household with an iron hand, stretching each penny, maintaining standards that become more impossible each day. "We are Spanish," she says when the younger ladies weep. "We do not surrender."

But we are surrendering, slowly, inexorably. We are surrendering our health to cold and hunger, our dignity to patches and darns, our hope to the endless, grinding passage of days without change. The worst comes in winter. The Thames freezes, and with it seems to freeze the very blood in our veins. We cannot afford enough wood to heat even the small chambers we inhabit. We huddle together like animals, Spanish ladies who once danced in the gardens of the Alhambra now sharing beds for warmth in a frozen English palace.

One terrible January night, the youngest of my ladies, Isabella de Vargas, falls ill with a fever. We have no money for a physician. I nurse her myself, using the knowledge my mother insisted I learn—a queen must know healing as well as ruling. But knowledge without resources is merely the ability to watch disaster unfold. She needs warmth, nourishing broth, medicine. We have none of these things.

She dies on Candlemas, the feast of the Purification. We cannot afford a proper burial. The parish priest, taking pity, allows her to be interred in the churchyard, but in the section reserved for paupers. A Spanish lady of noble blood, laid to rest in a pauper's grave in a foreign land. I stand at her graveside in a black gown so worn it has turned grey, and I feel something harden in my chest, something that might be my heart turning to stone.

That night, I write again to my father, and this time I do not couch my words in diplomacy. "Your daughter's servants die of want," I write. "Is this the honor of Spain?"

There is no reply for two months. When it comes, it contains only more promises, more delays, and the suggestion that perhaps I might consider entering a convent. A convent. As if I were some surplus daughter to be tidied away, not the Princess of Wales, not the daughter of Isabella of Castile who conquered kingdoms.

But I will not beg the English king. I sit in his city, under his theoretical protection, and I will not give him the satisfaction of seeing me kneel. My ladies starve and my gowns fray, but I will not beg. I am the daughter of Isabella. My dignity is worth more than all the gold this miser King hoards in his cellars. I will endure this. This is another test.

God has not forgotten me, even if the kings of the earth have. He tests me as He tested Job, stripping away all worldly comforts to see if my faith remains. It does. It must. It is all I have left.

There are whispers at court, ugly rumors that float to me through the few English servants who remain. The King, a widower now since the good Queen Elizabeth died in childbirth trying to give him another son, considers marrying me himself. The thought is grotesque—that cold, calculating man with his suspicious eyes and grasping hands, old enough to be my father, seeking to bed his son's widow.

But even this grotesque possibility is preferable to some of the alternatives. At least as Queen of England, I would have dignity, purpose, position. I would rather marry the Devil himself than return to Spain in disgrace or rot away entirely in this Thames-side tomb.

Then, suddenly, the wind shifts. A formal betrothal is announced —not to the old King, thank God, but to the new Prince of Wales, young Henry. A papal dispensation is sought and granted, setting aside the canonical impediments of my marriage to his brother. For a moment, there is hope, brilliant and blinding as Spanish sun. I am summoned to court for the betrothal ceremony. My ladies and I spend three days preparing my single remaining court gown, cleaning and pressing and praying that the worn spots will not show in candlelight. I stand before the court, Prince Henry beside me—taller now, grown into a young man of remarkable beauty and presence. He takes my hand for the ceremony, and his touch is warm, strong, alive in a way Arthur's never was.

"My lady," he says, and his voice is rich with possibility, "I have long admired your grace and patience in adversity."

For a moment, I dare to hope. This golden prince, this young lion —perhaps this was God's plan all along. Perhaps the years of suffering were merely preparation for this greater destiny.

But it is a false dawn. On the eve of his fifteenth birthday, the prince is made to publicly repudiate the contract. He stands before witnesses in the Bishop of London's palace and declares that the betrothal, made when he was a minor, is invalid, that he does not consent to it, that he considers himself free of all obligation to me. I am not present for this betrayal—I learn of it second-hand, from a tearful lady who heard it from a servant who was there. But I can picture it perfectly: the golden prince speaking the words his father has put in his mouth, denouncing me as publicly as possible, ensuring all of Europe knows that Katherine of Aragon is rejected, unwanted, a burden to be shed.

It is another turn of the screw, another humiliation designed to put pressure on my father. The Kings continue their chess game, and I am not even a pawn now—I am merely the board on which they play.

Late at night, alone in my chamber, I sit by a single candle. The great house is silent around me, empty rooms echoing with the ghosts of the household I can no longer afford to maintain. I take up my needle and, with small, precise stitches, I carefully mend a tear in the sleeve of one of my own velvet gowns.

The work is delicate, requiring all my concentration. My mother insisted I learn these domestic arts. "A queen must know how to rule," she said, "but she must also know how to serve. You may command a thousand seamstresses, but you should be able to mend your own shift if needed."

She could not have imagined it would be so literally needed. My fingers are deft, practiced now in the art of making do, making last, making something from nothing. Each tiny stitch is an act of defiance, a refusal to surrender to despair. The thread is Spanish silk, one of my last spools, and it gleams in the candlelight like a thin line of gold.

This is my rebellion—not with armies or treaties, but with a needle and thread, with the simple refusal to unravel. They can take my gold, my servants, my status. They can lock me in this gilded cage and forget I exist. But they cannot take my skills, my knowledge, my will.

I think of Penelope, weaving and unweaving, waiting for Odysseus. But she waited for a husband she knew would return. I wait for a destiny I can no longer see, for a purpose that seems to recede with each passing year. Still, I weave. Still, I mend. Still, I endure.

The candle burns lower, and I work by its dying light until my eyes water and my fingers cramp. When it finally gutters out, I sit in the darkness for a long moment, feeling the weight of the empty house around me. Seven years. Seven years of this purgatory, this living death.

Tomorrow, I will rise. I will dress in my mended gown. I will preside over my ghost of a household with all the dignity of a true queen. I will write more letters that will go unanswered, pay visits that will be barely acknowledged, maintain the fiction that I am still someone who matters.

But tonight, in the darkness of Durham House, I allow myself one moment of pure truth: I am forgotten. I am abandoned. I am alone.

And yet, I am not defeated. That is the miracle, the thing that even I do not fully understand. Seven years of this grinding poverty, this slow erasure, and still something in me refuses to yield. It is not pride—pride would have killed me long ago. It is not hope—hope is a luxury I can no longer afford.

It is something deeper, something that was forged in the furnaces of the Reconquista, hammered on the anvil of my mother's will. It is the simple, implacable refusal to cease existing. I am. Despite everything, I am.

I will not unravel.

CHAPTER 6

THE AMBASSADOR

The seventh year of my widowhood announces itself not with a shift in seasons, but with a deeper settling of the damp that has become the defining quality of my existence. It rises from the Thames in a miasma of rot and river-stench, creeping through the ill-fitting window frames of Durham House, infusing every tapestry, every garment, every breath with its signature chill. The palace, once a bishop's pride, is now my gilded cage, its grandeur a mocking testament to my slow decay. The plaster on the ceiling of my presence chamber has begun to peel away in great leprous sheets, revealing the skeletal laths beneath. The gardens are a wilderness where nature reclaims its territory with a savage indifference to the pruned and ordered elegance of my Spanish youth. I am a ghost haunting the ruins of my own life, a princess whose title is an ache in my soul, a memory of power that my body still feels.

My days are a litany of small humiliations. I spend my mornings poring over the household accounts, a task that would have been beneath a minor lady-in-waiting in my mother's court. Here, it is my primary occupation. The numbers mock me, a relentless calculus of lack. The butcher's bill, three months unpaid. The baker, threatening to cut off our supply of bread. The chandler, refusing to extend more credit for the candles we burn to ward off the oppressive gloom. My ladies, the few who remain, have grown thin, their once-proud Castilian faces etched with a hunger that is not just for food, but for hope. We mend our own gowns, turning collars and patching hems until the fabric is a mosaic of its former self. We eat pottage and black bread, a diet that would shame a peasant, and we do it with the rigid formality of a state banquet, a small, desperate act of defiance against the encroaching squalor. Each meal is a performance, a play we enact for ourselves to remember who we are, or who we were meant to be.

Tonight, the despair is a physical weight in my chest. Doña Elvira, my duenna, watches me across the flickering candlelight, her face a stern mask that cannot quite hide her own weariness. We have eaten our meager supper of stewed rabbit—a rare treat, a gift from a sympathetic gamekeeper—and now the silence of the great, decaying house presses in.

"Your Highness should rest," she says, her voice as brittle as the dry twigs crackling in the hearth.

"Rest is a luxury for those with peaceful minds, Elvira," I reply, my gaze fixed on the accounts ledger. "My mind is a battlefield of debts and deficiencies."

Seven years, my heart cries out. *Seven years of this living purgatory.* I came to England a bride, the jewel of two kingdoms, my dowry meant to cement an empire. Now I am a beggar, a bargaining chip in a game played by two parsimonious kings: my father, Ferdinand, who refuses to send the remainder of my dowry until my future is secure; and my father-in-law, Henry, who refuses to secure my future—or even my present—until the gold is in his coffers. Between their pride and their avarice, I starve.

I think of my mother, Isabella, my guiding star, my constant measure. What would she have done in this situation? My mother would not have waited. She would not have endured. She rode in armor, she governed kingdoms, she bent popes and princes to her will. She would have seen this not as a humiliation to be borne, but as a problem to be solved, a knot to be cut. For seven years, I have prayed. I have been patient. I have been the dutiful daughter, the grieving widow. But my mother's blood runs in my veins, and it is beginning to boil. The piety of my youth is being tempered by the harsh realities of my womanhood, forged into something harder, sharper. Something that might pass for steel.

The letter arrives on a wet March morning that promises nothing but more of the same cold misery. It is carried by a royal messenger, his horse fresh, his livery crisp, a stark contrast to the shabby state of my own household. The very sight of him, a symbol of the world from which I am excluded, sends a tremor of nervous energy through me. I break the heavy wax seal—my father's seal—with fingers that tremble, not from weakness, but from the sudden, terrifying surge of possibility.

I read the Latin script once, twice, a third time before the meaning can penetrate the fog of my despair. My father, seeing the diplomatic stalemate dragging on, has made a move of startling boldness. He has dismissed his ambassador, the cautious, ineffectual de Puebla. And in his place, he has named me.

Ego, Catherina, Principissa Vidua Walliae... I, Katherine, Dowager Princess of Wales, am to become the accredited ambassador of the Crown of Aragon to the Court of England. The words leap from the page, charged with a power I have not felt in years. It is unheard of. A woman as ambassador? The first in the history of Europe. It is a desperate move, a sign of my father's frustration. But it is also a declaration of his faith in me. After seven years of treating me as a liability, he has finally chosen to see me as an asset.

The commission is written in the formal language of law and legitimacy. It invests me with powers no woman has ever held: to negotiate, to treat, to bind my father's kingdom to agreements of my making. It is a title. It is a responsibility. But more than that, it is a weapon, handed to me in the darkest hour of my siege.

For seven years, I have been a ghost. Now, suddenly, I am a presence. I am a voice. I am a power to be reckoned with. The transformation is immediate and intoxicating. It is a draft of strong wine to a starving woman, and it rushes to my head, clearing away the cobwebs of despair.

My first act is one of defiance against my own poverty. I summon my last remaining lady of the wardrobe. "We will need new gowns," I declare, my voice ringing with an authority it has not held in years. "Not the finery of a princess. The sober, dignified attire of a diplomat. Black still, as befits my widowhood, but it will be black silk and fine velvet, not this worn wool."

My ladies stare at me as if I have gone mad. We have no money for such things. But I know that to wield power, one must first look the part. I will sell the last piece of my personal plate if I must, but I will not present myself to the English court as a beggar. I will present myself as an ambassador.

When the day comes for my first official act—the reception of my new assistant—I dress with the care of a general preparing for battle. Doña Elvira helps me, her hands surprisingly steady, her eyes bright with a light I have not seen in years: pride.

"You look like your mother," she says softly, adjusting the severe white ruff that frames my face, a stark contrast to the deep black of the velvet. "When she held court in the military camps, before a battle."

My mother. Yes. The thought gives me strength. She too transformed herself as needed—from princess to queen, from queen to general, from general to saint. Now I must transform from abandoned widow to political power. The metamorphosis is not easy. My hands shake as I pin the heavy brooch bearing my father's arms to my breast. It feels heavier than any jewel, weighted with the fate of nations.

The man sent to assist me is a Castilian nobleman named Don Gutierre de Fuensalida. I receive him in the least damaged of Durham House's formal chambers, seated in a chair of estate I have had dragged from storage and dusted, my cloth of state hanging behind me, a tattered but defiant symbol of my rank.

He enters with a sweep of his traveling cloak and a gust of cold air, a man full of his own importance. His eyes, quick and dismissive, take in the shabby surroundings in a single glance—the peeling ceiling, the faded tapestries, the single chair upon which I sit. I see his assessment in that glance: this is a posting of no importance, and I am a woman of no consequence.

His bow is a perfunctory dip of the head, an insult delivered with practiced ease. He sees what everyone at the English court sees: a woman isolated and impoverished, clinging to meaningless titles. He addresses me in Spanish, his tone that of a man speaking to a child, or a simpleton.

"Your Highness must understand," he begins without preamble, not even waiting for me to grant him leave to speak, "that His Majesty your father has sent me to manage the delicate negotiations regarding your situation. It is a complex matter, requiring a man's grasp of politics. You are to provide me with any information I require and, of course, present a suitable appearance at court when requested, but the actual diplomatic work—"

"Will be conducted by me," I interrupt. My voice is quiet, level, yet it cuts through his arrogant speech like a blade through silk. "I am the accredited ambassador of the Crown of Aragon. You, I believe, Don Fuensalida, are described in your commission as my assistant."

His face flushes a deep, unbecoming red. He is not accustomed to being contradicted, especially by a woman he has already dismissed. "Your Highness perhaps does not understand the complexities of the situation. The English court is a viper's nest. King Henry is a famously difficult and parsimonious man—"

"Sit," I command.

The word is so unexpected, so contrary to the role he has assigned me, that he obeys without thinking. He sits, heavily, on the small stool my ladies have placed for him. And in that moment, as he is forced to look up at me, the balance of power in the room shifts, irrevocably.

He thinks me a helpless girl, a weeping widow who has spent seven years embroidering her sorrows. He forgets that I listened at my mother's knee as she governed a nation, as she bargained with popes and kings. He forgets that I was educated not in the womanly arts alone, but in theology, in law, in history, in the brutal calculus of power. He forgets that for seven years, I have not been idle. I have survived in this hostile court with no resources but my wit. He forgets that necessity has been my greatest and most ruthless teacher.

He recovers his composure and launches into his plan, a strategy so clumsy and ill-conceived it is almost laughable. He speaks of kings and armies, of treaties and alliances. His great idea, it seems, is to bully King Henry. He will threaten him with my father's displeasure. He will demand my dowry be returned in full if the marriage to Prince Henry is not immediately confirmed and celebrated. He speaks of ultimatums and firm lines, the talk of a man who understands force but not finesse.

I listen patiently, my hands folded demurely in my lap, my face a mask of serene attention. I let him lay out his entire strategy, a map drawn by a child, full of dragons and grand pronouncements but with no understanding of the actual terrain. His confidence grows with each word, mistaking my silence for agreement, or perhaps for feminine incomprehension. When he is finished, he sits back with a satisfied smile, a man who has just demonstrated his brilliance to a simpleton and now expects applause.

"An interesting approach," I say mildly, my voice soft. "Tell me, Don Fuensalida, what do you know of King Henry's current secret negotiations with the Emperor Maximilian regarding a marriage for his younger daughter, Mary?"

His smile falters. "The Emperor? That has no bearing on this. Our instructions concern the Princess of Wales and the Prince of Wales."

"Everything has bearing," I say, my voice still soft, but with an edge he cannot miss. "And are you aware of the recent shifts in the wool trade with Flanders? The King's council is deeply divided. The Merchant Adventurers are proposing new tariffs that would harm the Staplers. The King's personal investments are with the Adventurers. He is therefore vulnerable to pressure from the Staplers, who control much of the raw wool that Spain so desperately needs."

His mouth opens slightly, but no sound emerges.

I lean forward, my mask of demure attention dropping away to reveal the cold, hard face of my mother's daughter. "You see, Don

Fuensalida, while you have been traveling, I have been here. For seven years. I have not been weeping in my chambers. I have been watching. Listening. Learning. I know that the King's treasurer, Sir Thomas Lovell, is a cautious man who fears any disruption to trade. I know that Bishop Fox of Winchester resents the rise of the Howard faction and will oppose any policy they champion. I know every member of the King's council, their loyalties, their weaknesses, their ambitions, their prices. I know which merchants have the King's ear, which bishops he trusts, which lords he fears. I know the name of his current mistress and the precise size of his debts to the Frescobaldi bankers."

I rise from my chair, a slow, deliberate movement that forces him to crane his neck to look up at me. "Your plan is a disaster. It would play directly into King Henry's hands. He *wants* my father to threaten him. It gives him the perfect excuse to break off all negotiations, declare the treaty void, and keep the half of the dowry he has already been paid. What we need is not threats, but enticement. We do not storm the castle walls, Don Fuensalida. We find the secret gate and bribe the guard. We need to make him believe that confirming my marriage to Prince Henry is his idea, his own brilliant triumph against his enemies."

I move to the wobbly table where I have laid out my own documents, spreading them out with a practiced efficiency that belies my trembling hands. "The key is not Spain's strength. It is England's fear. And King Henry fears one thing above all others: a French alliance with Scotland. We will not threaten. We will hint.

We will let a rumor, a whisper, reach the King's ears through the Venetian ambassador, a man who cannot keep a secret if his life depended upon it. A rumor that my father, frustrated with English delays, might be willing to support French claims in Italy in exchange for a new marriage alliance. Perhaps for me. Perhaps for another of his line."

Fuensalida is staring at me now, his mouth agape, his arrogance evaporating like morning mist in the face of this cold, hard reality.

"Meanwhile," I continue, tapping a list of names, "we court the London merchants. Not the King. The merchants. They are the real power behind the throne, for the King depends on their loans. I have maintained relationships with several of their wives, Spanish connections through the wool trade. We will emphasize the value of secure Spanish markets, the danger of French competition. Let them pressure the King from below, from his counting-houses, while we apply gentle, almost invisible, pressure from above."

I turn back to him, my voice now imbued with the tone of absolute command I learned at my mother's knee. "You will handle the official communications, of course. It would not do for a woman's hand to be seen. But you will show every dispatch to me before it is sent. You will make no approaches, no commitments, no promises without my express approval. And you will never, ever, presume to tell me again what I do or do not understand. Is that clear?"

He stares at me for a long moment, his face cycling through a kaleidoscope of emotions—shock, anger, humiliation, calculation, and finally, a grudging, astonished respect. He scrambles to his feet and bows, properly this time, a deep, formal bow of deference from a subordinate to his commander.

"I... I beg Your Highness's pardon," he says, his voice quite different now, stripped of its condescending warmth. "I have... misjudged the situation. And you. I see that His Majesty my king chose his ambassador with great wisdom."

"His Majesty," I reply coolly, "recognized that his daughter has spent seven years earning an education in English politics that no university could provide. It is an education that has been paid for in hardship and humiliation. I do not intend to waste it." I gesture for him to sit once more, a small but significant reassertion of my authority. He sits, a chastened man. "Now," I say, my voice softening slightly, for a tool must be sharpened, not broken, "shall we discuss actual strategy, or do you need more time to adjust your assumptions?"

We spend the next hour refining the plan I have laid out. Beneath his arrogance lies a competent mind; he is a tool, and like any good tool, he is most effective when wielded by a skilled hand. My hand.

But there is more to be done. My own position is still precarious, my household starves while the kings of Spain and England haggle over my dowry. My new authority is a weapon, but a weapon is useless if the hand that holds it is too weak from hunger to strike.

Later that week, after we have set our initial plans in motion by letting a carefully constructed "secret" slip to the wife of the Venetian ambassador's secretary, I summon Don Fuensalida again. I receive him not in the formal chamber but in my private study, a smaller room where the leaking roof is less obvious and a fire offers a semblance of warmth. The accounts for my household lie open on the table, a silent, powerful testament to my poverty.

"Don Fuensalida," I say, my voice now full of warmth and confidence, as if we are old, trusted allies. "Your work has been excellent. The whispers we planted have taken root faster than I had hoped. The Venetian ambassador spoke of it at supper last night. He is convinced that France seeks to encircle England by forging a new alliance with Scotland."

"Indeed, Your Highness. He was most agitated. He believes my king is on the verge of abandoning the English treaty."

"A useful belief," I say, tapping the accounts book with a single, elegant finger. "But agitation in a Venetian is not action in an English king. We must give King Henry a reason not just to fear France, but to value Spain. To value *me*."

I rise and walk to the window, looking out at the grey, weeping sky, adopting an expression of thoughtful innocence, as if an idea has just that moment occurred to me. "I was thinking… it is a small matter, perhaps, but these subtle currents can turn the great tides of diplomacy. You are writing to my father soon, are you not? With your full report?"

"Of course, Your Highness. It will detail the success of our initial gambit."

"Good. In your report," I say, my back still to him, my voice casual, as if the thought were a passing fancy, "perhaps you should mention something I have heard. A piece of servants' gossip, nothing more. You know how these things are." I turn back to him, my eyes wide with feigned earnestness. "The French ambassador has had two private meetings with the Bishop of Durham. A minor detail, I'm sure."

Let him think this is my idea, born of the moment. Let him feel he is part of a grand strategy against France. He is a pawn, but a proud pawn who must believe he moves of his own accord. His pride is now my instrument.

"They spoke, I hear from one of my ladies who has a cousin in the Bishop's household, of the young princesses of France. And of Scotland. It will certainly be a coincidence... a mere discussion of hypotheticals... but King Henry is such a suspicious man. A man who counts his pennies with such care. Such news, if it were to leak back to him through my father's diplomats in Flanders, where the English merchants would surely hear of it... it might make him... more desirous of showing his solid alliance with Spain. It might make him see that the cost of maintaining his son's intended bride is far less than the cost of losing Spain as an ally."

Let Fuensalida think this is a brilliant move against France. It is a desperate move against my own poverty. Henry VII fears a Franco-Scottish alliance more than he loves his own gold. He fears being encircled by his two greatest enemies more than he fears God. A whisper of trouble on his northern border, a hint that Spain might be entertaining other options if England does not treat its princess with the honor—and the funds—she is due, will loosen his purse strings faster than a thousand pitiful pleas for my upkeep. This is not about statecraft. It is about survival. It is about having enough money to pay the butcher and to show the English court that the Spanish ambassador is not a pauper.

Fuensalida's eyes light up with an understanding that is both complete and completely wrong. He sees a brilliant, multi-layered diplomatic chess move. He does not see the desperate gamble of a woman who has not eaten a proper meal in a week and whose ladies are mending their own stockings.

"Your Highness's intuition is remarkable," he says, his voice filled with genuine, unfeigned admiration. "To use a rumor of a French marriage for the Scottish king to frighten Henry... it is a masterstroke. It makes our earlier whisper seem like a confirmation of a larger French design. He will be desperate to confirm your marriage to Prince Henry and finalize the treaty. He will shower you with favor to ensure my father does not look to France."

"One must use the tools God provides," I say humbly, lowering my eyes as if embarrassed by his praise. "And God, in His wisdom, has provided us with King Henry's paranoia."

The scene concludes with Fuensalida bowing low, his mind racing with the implications of the "grand strategy" I have laid before him, full of admiration for my "political intuition." He never comprehends the deeper, more personal game I am playing. He leaves to draft his dispatch, a willing and eager instrument of a strategy he believes is aimed at Paris but is in fact aimed squarely at the English treasury. I remain at my desk, outwardly the humble and pious princess, but inwardly a queen who has just learned how to command armies not of men, but of whispers. The weapons are different, but the war for survival is the same. And for the first time in seven years, I have the scent of victory in my nostrils. I have just won my first battle.

Chapter 7
The Sun Rises

The old king is dying. The news comes in whispers at first, carried on the March wind of 1509 like seeds of change. Then in urgent, secret messages passed between those who still remember I exist. For weeks, Henry VII has been secluded at Richmond Palace, his illness—a consumption of the lungs, they say—hidden from the court with the same calculating secrecy that has marked his entire reign.

I sit in my chamber at Durham House, a letter from Fuensalida trembling in my hands. The King refuses all visitors save his closest advisors. His physicians speak in hushed tones of days, perhaps hours. The vultures gather, though they dress as mourning doves—courtiers positioning themselves for the new reign that must surely come.

I wait, my heart a turmoil of prayer and desperate hope. For seven years I have waited in this purgatory. Seven years of poverty, humiliation, and uncertainty. Seven years of being moved like a chess piece between two kings who valued gold over honor. Now, perhaps, the board itself is about to be overturned.

Pater noster, qui es in caelis... I pray, but the words tangle with my racing thoughts. If the King dies, everything changes. The new king will be Henry, that golden boy who once led me to marry his brother, now grown into a man of seventeen years. What will he make of me? Will he honor the betrothal made and broken in his youth? Or will he send me back to Spain, a final embarrassment to be disposed of?

Then, on the twenty-first day of April, in the year of our Lord 1509, the whispers cease. The King is dead.

For two days, his council keeps his death a secret, securing the Tower, moving their gold, making their preparations. I learn of it from a merchant's wife who trades in Spanish wool—the markets know before the court, as they always do. I dress in my finest remaining gown, though it is still black for my widowhood, and I wait. Whatever comes next, I will meet it as a princess of Spain, not as a beggar.

My first thought when the death is confirmed is a prayer for the old king's soul. For all his coldness, his calculation, his miserly treatment of me, he was God's anointed. My second thought is a surge of hope so fierce it frightens me. It rises in my chest like a fire too long banked, suddenly given air.

The new king is Henry, the boy to whom I was once betrothed and who was then forced to renounce me. He is seventeen, on the cusp of his eighteenth year, and he is everything his father was not: where the old king was winter, this Henry is summer; where the father was a miser, the son spends gold like water; where Henry VII trusted no one, Henry VIII embraces the world with the confidence of one who has never known defeat.

Within days of his father's death, he sends for me.

The messenger who arrives at Durham House is no minor functionary but the Duke of Buckingham himself, one of the greatest nobles in England. He bows low, lower than anyone has bowed to me in seven years.

"Your Highness," he says, and his voice carries genuine respect, "His Majesty the King commands your presence at Greenwich Palace."

Commands. Not requests, not suggests, but commands. There is something thrilling in that word, a recognition of my status that has been so long denied.

I arrive at Greenwich as the sun is setting, painting the Thames gold. The palace, which I last saw as a place of cold formality, has been transformed. Music spills from every window, courtiers laugh in the gardens, and everywhere there is the sense of a new beginning, a renaissance after the long winter of the old king's reign.

I am shown not to some antechamber but directly to the presence chamber. And there he is.

Henry VIII stands before his throne, and for a moment I cannot breathe. This is not the boy who escorted me to my wedding eight years ago. This is a young god descended to earth. He is tall—taller than any man in the room—with shoulders broad as a wrestler's and a natural grace that makes every movement seem choreographed. His hair catches the light like burnished copper, his skin glows with health, and his eyes—those small blue eyes that in his father were cold and calculating—in him sparkle with intelligence and unmistakable interest.

He sees me and strides forward, ignoring all protocol. Kings do not approach; they are approached. But this king makes his own rules.

"Katherine," he says, and his voice is rich and warm as Spanish wine. "My lady Katherine. How poorly you have been treated."

The sympathy in his voice undoes me more than seven years of hardship. Tears spring to my eyes before I can stop them. He takes my hand—his is warm, strong, alive with vitality—and raises it to his lips.

"It was my father's dying wish," he announces, loud enough for the entire court to hear, "that I right the wrongs done to this noble lady. That I honor the alliance with Spain as it should always have been honored."

I search his face, looking for the calculation that must be there. This is politics, surely. The need for Spanish alliance against France. But in his eyes I see something else, something that makes my heart race in a way it hasn't since I was a girl in Granada. I see genuine admiration, even desire.

"Your Majesty is most gracious," I manage, my voice steady despite the tumult in my chest.

"I am not gracious," he replies, still holding my hand. "I am determined. You have been a princess in name only for too long. It is time you became a queen in truth."

The court gasps. The meaning is unmistakable. He intends to marry me.

"Your Majesty," I begin, propriety demanding some show of surprise, of maidenly hesitation.

But he interrupts me with a laugh, young and confident and infectious. "I know what you will say—that you were my brother's wife, that there are impediments. But the Pope himself granted dispensation years ago. The marriage was never consummated—" here he looks at me with a question in his eyes, and I nod, just slightly, confirming what he has chosen to believe, "—and therefore no true marriage at all. You are as free to marry as any maiden."

Deus ex machina. God from the machine. The thought comes unbidden. God has not sent a boy, but a lion. This was the true plan all along, the long winter of my widowhood merely a test of my faith before the spring.

He is no longer the shy boy who escorted me to my first wedding. He is a king, and his eyes, when they look at me, are full of an admiration that feels like salvation. All the years of waiting, all the prayers whispered in the cold chapel at Durham House, have led to this moment.

He draws me aside, away from the listening courtiers, to a window that overlooks the river. The setting sun turns the water to molten gold.

"I have watched you," he says softly. "All these years, I have watched how you bore your trials with dignity, how you never complained, never surrendered. You have the heart of a true queen."

"Your Majesty—"

"Henry," he corrects. "In private, I am Henry to you."

The intimacy of it makes me blush like a girl. "Henry," I say, tasting the name. "You honor me beyond my deserving."

"No," he says firmly. "I honor you exactly as you deserve. My father was a good king but a cold man. He saw only the gold, the dowry, the alliance. I see the woman."

And in his eyes, I realize with a start, I see the boy still—not the ten-year-old who walked me to the altar, but a young man in the flush of his first real passion. He is not merely honoring his father's supposed wish or securing a political alliance. He is, in his way, in love with me. Or in love with the idea of me—the patient princess, the woman wronged, the lady he can rescue and thereby prove himself the chivalrous king he dreams of being.

"We will be married as soon as possible," he declares. "I will not have you spend another night wondering about your future. You have wondered long enough."

"The court... the council..." I murmur, thinking of the obstacles that surely remain.

"The court will rejoice to have a true queen again," he says. "And the council will do as I command. I am not my father, Katherine. I do not fear my own shadow or count every penny twice. I am King of England, and I will have the queen I choose."

The confidence in his voice is intoxicating. After seven years of careful calculation, of weighing every word, of never knowing what tomorrow might bring, his certainty is like strong wine.

"And you choose me?" I ask, needing to hear it clearly, needing to be sure this is not another dream that will shatter with the morning.

He turns to face me fully, taking both my hands in his. "I have chosen you since I was ten years old and first saw you in your wedding dress. You were the most beautiful thing I had ever seen. You still are."

Mi Rey, mi corazón. My King, my heart. The Spanish words rise unbidden, though I do not speak them aloud. Not yet.

"Then I choose you as well," I say in English, meeting his eyes steadily. "Not because you are King, not because I have no choice, but because I see in you the prince I was always meant to marry."

It is not entirely true—I was meant for Arthur, prepared for Arthur, sent across the sea for Arthur. But Arthur is dead, has been dead for seven years, and this vital, passionate young man before me is so magnificently alive. Perhaps this is revision of history, but what is history but the story the survivors choose to tell?

He smiles, and it transforms his face from handsome to truly beautiful. "Then we understand each other perfectly."

That night, there is a feast in my honor. I am seated at the high table, in the place where a queen would sit. The courtiers who have ignored me for seven years now press forward with congratulations. The same lords who would not lend me a penny now compete to offer their services. It should disgust me, this sudden change, but I am too happy to care.

Henry leads me in the first dance, and I feel the strength in his arms as he guides me through the steps. This is no fragile Arthur, no pale prince who might break at a touch. This is a man in the full flower of his youth and power, and he has chosen me.

"You dance beautifully," he murmurs as we turn.

"Your Majesty is kind."

"I am honest," he corrects. "And soon you must stop calling me 'Your Majesty.' We are to be married, Katherine. Equals before God."

Equals. The word is sweeter than honey. For seven years I have been less than nothing. Now I am to be equal to a king.

The evening continues in a blur of music and congratulations. I am introduced to the men who will form the new king's inner circle—young men, most of them, full of energy and ambition. Thomas More, brilliant and witty; Charles Brandon, Henry's closest friend, handsome and martial; Thomas Wolsey, ambitious and clever, already positioning himself as indispensable.

"Your Highness," Wolsey says with an elaborate bow, "permit me to say that England has waited too long for such a queen."

I note the calculation in his eyes even as I accept the compliment. This one bears watching. But tonight, I cannot bring myself to care about court politics. Tonight, I am alive again.

As the feast ends, Henry walks me to my chambers—not at Durham House, he insists, never again at Durham House, but here at Greenwich where I belong.

"These will be your rooms until the wedding," he says. "After that..." He grins, young and slightly wicked. "After that, you will share mine."

The implication makes me blush, but also sends a thrill through me. After eight years of cold beds and colder prospects, the promise of warmth, of passion, of genuine human connection is almost overwhelming.

"I must send word to Spain," I say. "My parents—"

"Your father," he corrects gently. "I am sorry, Katherine. The news came while my own father was dying. Queen Isabella is dead."

The words hit me like a physical blow. My mother. Dead. And I did not know, was not told, was not even allowed to mourn. The tears come then, sudden and unstoppable.

Henry pulls me into his arms, and I sob against his chest, feeling the solid warmth of him, the steady beat of his heart. He does not try to comfort me with words, does not tell me not to cry. He simply holds me, strong and sure, until the storm passes.

"She would be proud," he says finally. "To see her daughter become Queen of England. To know that all your suffering led to this triumph."

Would she? I think of my mother, that indomitable woman who conquered kingdoms and never compromised. Would she see this as triumph or merely survival? But she is gone, and I must make my own judgment now.

"Thank you," I whisper against his doublet.

"For what?"

"For saving me."

He pulls back to look at me, his hands gentle as he wipes the tears from my cheeks. "You saved yourself, Katherine. You endured. You survived. All I did was recognize your worth."

We are married on the eleventh of June, 1509, in a private ceremony in the church of the Observant Friars at Greenwich. It is a quiet affair, not a state pageant—Henry insists we have been made to wait long enough. I wear a gown of virginal white, my hair loose beneath a golden circlet, a bride again at twenty-three.

He is magnificent, dressed in cloth of gold that makes his hair shine like fire. When he speaks his vows, his voice is clear and strong, each word a promise not just to me but to himself—to be the king he dreams of being, the husband he believes a queen deserves.

That night, there is no awkwardness, no childish fumbling as there was with Arthur. He comes to me not as a boy fulfilling a duty, but as a man claiming his wife. His touch is sure but gentle, passionate but respectful. He has had mistresses—I know this, the court whispers of everything—but tonight he makes me feel as if I am the first woman he has ever truly seen.

"My Katherine," he whispers against my hair afterward, holding me close in the great bed. "My queen. My wife."

Mi Rey, mi corazón, I whisper back in Spanish, and he smiles even though he doesn't understand the words.

"Teach me," he says. "Teach me to speak your language. I want to know every part of you."

In his arms, warm for the first time in seven years, I am no longer the Dowager Princess of Wales, no longer a political pawn or a problem to be solved. I am Katherine, Queen of England. I am his wife. The vow is sealed, not just in law, but in love.

Outside our window, the summer night is warm and full of promise. Somewhere in the gardens, a nightingale sings. The sound follows me into sleep, where I dream not of cold castles and empty treasuries, but of golden princes and the children we will make together, the dynasty we will build on foundations stronger than stone—on love, on passion, on the choice we have made to save each other.

God's plan, revealed at last, is perfect.

Chapter 8

Our Coronation

The twenty-fourth of June is Midsummer's Day, the feast of St. John the Baptist, and it is the day of our coronation. The sun, for once in this uncertain English summer, shines with Mediterranean brilliance, as if God himself has decreed that this day shall be golden. I stand robed in the Tower of London, where tradition demands we spend the night before the ceremony, waiting for the procession to begin.

For two days, we have observed the ancient customs here. Henry has created eighteen new Knights of the Bath, young men who will forever mark their rise from this moment, this reign, this new beginning. The Tower, usually a place of dread and imprisonment, has been transformed into a palace of celebration. Every chamber rings with music and laughter, every courtyard blooms with banners and cloth of gold.

I feel the weight of the embroidered cope on my shoulders, heavy with gold thread and pearls that catch the morning light streaming through the windows. Each pearl was sewn by my own ladies—Spanish women who have endured seven years of poverty with me and now see their patience rewarded. The weight is substantial, but I find it comforting, not burdensome. This is the weight of my destiny, finally settled upon me after so many years of weightlessness, of being nobody and nothing.

"Your Majesty," Doña Elvira says, and I hear the tremor of emotion in her usually controlled voice. "You are ready."

I look at my reflection in the great mirror they have brought. The woman who looks back is neither the frightened girl who arrived in Plymouth nor the desperate widow of Durham House. She is a queen. The cloth-of-gold robe blazes in the sunlight, the ermine trim pristine white against the gold. My hair, still auburn despite my twenty-three years, flows loose down my back in the tradition of a queen at her coronation—a virgin bride of the realm, though I am a virgin no longer.

The procession from the Tower to Westminster is a river of color and sound that flows through London's ancient streets. The city has been preparing for weeks, and now it unveils itself like a bride. Every building is hung with priceless tapestries—some borrowed, some gifted, some hoarded for generations and brought out for this singular moment. Cloth of gold shimmers from every window, catching the sun and throwing it back multiplied, until the very air seems to sparkle with golden light.

The streets have been cleaned and strewn with herbs—rosemary for remembrance, lavender for devotion, roses for love. The scent rises with each step of the horses, creating a perfumed path through the city. At every corner, tableaux have been erected—living pictures of classical virtues, biblical scenes, allegories of good governance. Children dressed as angels sing from constructed clouds. Wine flows freely from the public fountains, turned red with dye to represent the blood of Christ blessing this union.

The crowds are a roaring sea of jubilant faces, their cheers washing over us in waves that seem to have physical force. "God save the King! God save the Queen!" they cry, and I hear my name taken up like a song: "Katherine! Katherine! Queen Katherine!" They press forward, reaching out to touch the hem of my robe as it trails from the litter, their faces alight with a joy that mirrors my own.

Henry rides ahead on a magnificent charger, a destrier as white as snow, its mane braided with golden thread. He is a vision in crimson velvet and ermine, his doublet so encrusted with jewels that he seems to be wearing captured starlight. The crown of England sits on his auburn head as if it were forged for him alone. He is not merely playing the part of a king—he is kingship incarnate, the very ideal of monarchy made flesh.

He turns in his saddle to look back at me, and his smile is brighter than his jewels. He raises his hand in salute, and the crowd roars louder, understanding the gesture—the King honors his Queen before all his people.

I follow in a litter drawn by white palfreys, their harnesses jingling with silver bells that ring out a crystalline counterpoint to the crowd's cheers. I wear a gown of embroidered white satin that took fifty seamstresses three weeks to complete. Every inch is covered with Tudor roses and Spanish pomegranates worked in gold thread, our two houses united in silk and precious metal. My auburn hair flows free, crowned only with a coronet of gold and precious stones—the great crown waits for me at Westminster.

Beside my litter walk the greatest nobles of England, the men who have served the old king and now serve the new. But today they serve me as well, these proud dukes and earls, walking as my escort, my guards of honor. The Duke of Buckingham carries my train, the Earl of Surrey bears my crown on a velvet cushion, visible to all, a promise of what is to come.

I am a bride again, but this time I am marrying not just a man, but a kingdom.

Westminster Abbey, when we finally arrive after the slow, triumphant procession, is transformed beyond recognition. Thousands of candles flicker from every surface, their light multiplied by mirrors and cloth of gold until the ancient stones seem to glow from within. Incense hangs sweet and heavy in the air—frankincense and myrrh, the gifts of the Magi, the scent of holiness itself. The light streams through the high stained-glass windows, painting the stones in sapphire and ruby, emerald and topaz, as if we walk through the very treasury of Heaven.

The Archbishop of Canterbury, William Warham, presides in vestments so heavy with gold thread that he moves slowly, carefully, like a man carrying sacred relics. Which, in a way, he is—the oil for anointing was blessed in Jerusalem, the coronation regalia dates back to Edward the Confessor, each piece heavy with the weight of centuries.

The ceremony is conducted according to the ancient rites of the Liber Regalis, unchanged since the Plantagenet kings. Each word, each gesture, has been performed before, connecting us to the great chain of monarchy that stretches back into the mists of England's beginning. But it feels new, fresh, unprecedented—as if we are the first king and queen ever crowned, as if we are inventing majesty itself.

I watch as Henry is anointed with holy oil, the sacred chrism placed on his head, breast, and hands. The Archbishop's voice rings out in Latin, calling on God to bless this king, to grant him wisdom and strength, justice and mercy. The heavy crown of St. Edward is placed upon his head—so heavy that he will wear it only for this moment before it is exchanged for the lighter state crown.

"Vivat Rex! Vivat Rex! Vivat Rex!" The shout echoes to the vaulted ceiling, taken up by every throat in the abbey. Long live the King! The sound is overwhelming, a physical force that seems to shake the very stones.

Then it is my turn.

I kneel before the altar, feeling the cold stone through the thick fabric of my gown. The Archbishop's hands, when he anoints me, tremble slightly—whether from age or from the weight of the moment, I cannot tell. The oil is cool on my skin, its scent sharp and sacred. I feel it like a seal, a mark invisible but indelible.

"Receive the crown of glory, honor and joy," the Archbishop intones, and I feel the weight of St. Edith's crown settle on my head. It is smaller than Henry's, more delicate, but its weight is still substantial. I think of all the queens who have worn it before me —Eleanor of Aquitaine, Isabella of France, Margaret of Anjou— strong women, difficult women, women who shaped kingdoms with their will. I am joining their company now.

The scepter and rod are placed in my hands, cold metal warmed quickly by my grip. I rise, and the assembly erupts again: "Vivat Regina! Vivat Regina!" Long live the Queen!

My internal monologue is a single, profound prayer of thanks. *Deo Gratias. Deo Gratias.* Thanks be to God. I am where God intends me to be. I am England's Queen. The wife of the most noble king in Christendom. All the years of waiting, all the prayers whispered in the cold chapel at Durham House, all the humiliations and poverty and despair—they have led to this moment. They were not punishment but preparation. God was tempering me like steel, making me strong enough for this crown.

I think of my mother, dead now these five years, and I know with absolute certainty that she sees me from Heaven. She who wore armor and led armies, who united kingdoms and expelled the Moors—she sees her daughter crowned Queen of England, and she is proud.

The Mass that follows is a blur of Latin and incense, of bells and genuflection. Henry and I sit enthroned side by side, his throne slightly higher than mine as protocol demands, but close enough that our hands can touch. And they do, throughout the service, our fingers intertwining in the folds of our robes where no one can see. Each touch is a promise, a reassurance—we are in this together, united not just by ceremony but by choice.

When we take communion, the Archbishop himself serves us, the Body and Blood of Christ placed on our tongues with trembling reverence. This is the final seal, the ultimate sanction—God Himself has blessed our union, our reign, our future.

Later, at the great banquet in Westminster Hall, the celebration reaches heights of magnificence that even I, raised in the splendor of Spanish courts, have never seen. The hall has been transformed into a golden cavern, every surface gleaming with plate and jewels. The high table where we sit is raised on a dais, covered with cloth of gold, our chairs—thrones, really—placed so that all can see us.

The feast is a spectacle of royal wealth, each course more elaborate than the last. Swans roasted and re-dressed in their feathers, their necks gracefully curved. A subtlety of sugar and marzipan depicting our coronation, accurate down to the tiny jeweled crowns. Peacocks with their tails displayed, ships of confection sailing on seas of blue jelly, towers of fruit from every corner of the kingdom and beyond—oranges from Spain, a gift from my father, their scent a sudden, poignant reminder of home.

But I barely taste any of it. I see only him, my golden king, my rescued rescuer. At one point, amidst the noise and celebration, our hands find each other and clasp together beneath the table. He turns to me, his face illuminated by the torchlight, and he smiles at me with an expression of pure love and pride.

"My queen," he says, low enough that only I can hear. "My Katherine. Are you happy?"

"Beyond any happiness I imagined possible," I answer truly.

"Good," he says, squeezing my hand. "Because this is only the beginning. We will have such a reign, Katherine. We will have sons, many sons. We will unite Europe through our children. We will be remembered as the greatest king and queen England has ever known."

Sons. Yes, sons will come. They must come. It is the only shadow on this golden day—the knowledge that my crown, secure as it feels in this moment, depends ultimately on my womb. But I am young, he is young, we are healthy and passionate. The sons will come.

"We will be remembered," I agree, "as a king and queen who loved each other."

"Is that not the same thing?" he asks, and his innocence, his absolute conviction that love and greatness are synonymous, makes my heart swell with protective tenderness.

The celebrations continue deep into the night. There is dancing—Henry leads me in the first measure, and we move together as if we have been partners all our lives. There are masques and pageants, musicians from across Europe, jesters and acrobats and players. Wine flows like water, and the laughter of the court rises to the rafters.

But the greatest moment comes at the end, when Henry rises and calls for silence. The great hall gradually quiets, all eyes on their king.

"My lords and ladies," he says, his voice carrying to every corner of the vast space. "Today you have seen a king and queen crowned. But I would have you know that you have seen more than that. You have seen a wrong righted. You have seen patience rewarded. You have seen love triumphant."

He turns to me, taking my hand and raising it for all to see.

"This noble lady endured seven years of unjust suffering. Seven years of poverty and humiliation that would have broken a weaker spirit. But she endured with grace, with dignity, with faith. She is not just my queen by right of coronation. She is my queen by right of her noble heart, her constant soul, her unconquerable spirit."

The tears come then, impossible to stop. The court erupts in cheers, but I hear them only distantly. All I can see is Henry, my Henry, publicly acknowledging what I suffered, publicly honoring not just what I am but what I survived to become.

"To Queen Katherine!" he shouts, raising his goblet. "Long may she reign!"

"Queen Katherine!" the court roars back. "Long may she reign!"

I stand, though protocol does not require it, and curtsey deeply to my husband, to my king. When I rise, I speak, my voice clear and carrying.

"To King Henry," I say, raising my own goblet. "Who has brought summer after winter, joy after sorrow, love after loneliness. Long may he reign!"

The cheers are deafening now. Henry pulls me into his arms, there before the entire court, and kisses me with a passion that sets the assembly to stamping and whistling. It is not proper, not protocol, but it is perfect. We are young, we are in love, we are king and queen. The world is ours.

Later, much later, when the feast finally ends and we retire to our chambers, Henry dismisses all the attendants. We stand alone in the royal bedchamber, still wearing our crowns, still glittering with jewels, but finally, blessedly alone.

"My queen," he says softly, reaching up to carefully lift the crown from my head. "My wife. My love."

"My king," I respond, reaching up to remove his crown in turn. "My husband. *Mi corazón.*"

We help each other out of the heavy ceremonial robes, laughing as we struggle with the countless buttons and laces. When we are finally free of them, standing in our simple linen shifts, we are just Henry and Katherine, a man and woman in love.

"We did it," he says wonderingly. "We are King and Queen of England."

"We are," I agree. "But more than that—we are ourselves. We chose each other."

"Every day," he says, pulling me close. "I choose you every day."

In this moment, our world is perfect. The future stretches before us, golden with promise. There will be children—sons to inherit, daughters to make great marriages. There will be glory—Henry will win France, I'm sure of it, and our children will rule an empire. There will be love—the kind of love the troubadours sing of, constant and true until death.

We do not know—how could we know?—that this is the summit, the highest point from which all paths lead down. We do not know about the sons who will die, the daughters who will disappoint, the other women who will catch the king's eye. We do not know about the bitter theology that will divide us, the heresy that will tear England from Rome, the day when I will kneel before him in a different court and he will not even look at me.

Tonight, we know only this: we are young, we are crowned, we are in love. God has blessed us, England has accepted us, the future is ours to write.

Outside our window, all of London celebrates. Bonfires blaze in every square, music spills from every tavern, our subjects dance in the streets. The sound rises to us like incense, a prayer of celebration from an entire kingdom.

"Listen," Henry says. "They love us."

"They love you," I correct.

"They love us," he insists. "Their golden king and his constant queen."

Constant. Yes, I will be that. Whatever comes, I will be constant. It is my nature, my gift, my curse. I am Katherine, daughter of

Isabella, Queen of England. I have sworn my vows before God and man. I will keep them.

The crown sits on a cushion nearby, catching the candlelight. Tomorrow I will wear it again, and the next day, and all the days of my life. It is heavy, but I am strong enough to bear it. I have been made strong by suffering, by patience, by faith.

This is my coronation, not just as Queen of England, but as myself —Katherine, complete and victorious. The vow is made. Now I must keep it.

Chapter 9

A Son for England

My first duty as queen, the duty for which I was born and bred, is to provide an heir. My body, which for so long was a symbol of political stalemate, a contested territory between warring kings, is now the vessel of a kingdom's hope. Every morning when I wake beside Henry, every night when he comes to me with passion that has not dimmed since our wedding night, the unspoken prayer hangs between us: let this be the time. Let this be the seed that grows into England's future.

The first pregnancy ends in sorrow, though it begins in such joy. I know almost immediately—my body tells me in a dozen small ways. The food that turns my stomach, the tenderness in my breasts, the bone-deep exhaustion that strikes without warning. I wait a month to be certain, then another to be absolutely sure, before I tell Henry.

I choose my moment carefully, waiting until we are alone in the privy garden at Greenwich, the September roses still blooming around us. He is reading dispatches from France, his brow furrowed with concentration, already dreaming of the wars he will fight, the glory he will win.

"My lord," I say softly, taking his hand and placing it on my still-flat belly. "Your son grows here."

The transformation in his face is miraculous. The dispatches fall forgotten to the ground as he drops to his knees before me, pressing his ear to my stomach as if he might hear the child's heartbeat.

"Truly?" he asks, looking up at me with an expression of such naked hope it makes my heart ache.

"Truly," I confirm. "By summer, England will have its prince."

He leaps to his feet and lifts me in his arms, spinning me around until I am dizzy with laughter and have to beg him to stop, mindful of the precious burden I carry. The entire court knows within the hour—Henry cannot contain his joy, announcing it to everyone he meets. Preparations begin immediately for a royal nursery, for a christening that will rival our coronation in magnificence.

But God has other plans.

The child comes too early, in the cold of January, after a labor that is mercifully brief but terribly wrong. A daughter, the midwife tells me, her face grave. Born still and silent, never drawing breath. They wrap her in cloth of gold—Henry insists on it, this child who lived only in my womb deserves royal honors—and she is buried quietly at Westminster.

Henry comes to me in my chamber of recovery, and we weep together, this young king and queen brought low by a grief neither of us expected. "We are both young," he says, his voice thick with unshed tears. "If it was a daughter this time, by the grace of God the sons will follow."

His words are a balm, and his faith shores up my own. He does not blame me, not yet. The failure is God's will, mysterious but not malicious. We pray together, and we try again.

Soon, God is merciful. By April, I know I am with child again. This time, I guard the secret more carefully, waiting until the quickening to be sure before I tell Henry. This time, I carry the baby to term, feeling it grow strong and active within me, kicking with such vigor that Henry laughs when he feels it through my skin.

"A warrior," he says proudly. "Like his father."

"Like his mother," I counter, thinking of Isabella riding to war while pregnant.

As the new year of 1511 dawns, I take to my chamber at Richmond Palace for my lying-in. The room has been prepared according to all the ancient traditions—the windows covered with heavy tapestries to keep out harmful light and air, blessed relics placed around the bed, my ladies maintaining a constant vigil of prayer. The walls are hung with tapestries depicting the lives of female saints, their patient suffering and ultimate triumph meant to inspire and comfort.

My ladies pray around me, their voices a constant murmur of Ave Marias and Pater Nosters. My own thoughts are a single, desperate, silent prayer, a litany of one word repeated like a heartbeat: son, son, son.

The labor is long, longer than the first, as if this child is reluctant to leave the safety of my womb for the uncertain world. The pain comes in waves that threaten to drown me, each one lifting me up and casting me down like a ship in a storm. I bite down on the leather strap they give me, tasting blood from my own lips, and I think of Christ on His cross, suffering for the salvation of the world. This is my cross, my salvation—to bring forth the heir England needs.

The final pains of labor tear through me with a violence that seems to split me in two. I hear my own voice, screaming words in Spanish I don't remember choosing—prayers, curses, pleas to God and His mother. And then, finally, blessedly, in the early hours of New Year's Day, a cry.

A strong, healthy cry that fills the chamber like a trumpet's call.

"It is a prince!" the midwife announces, her voice triumphant. "A perfect prince!"

Gloria in excelsis Deo! Glory to God in the highest! A wave of joy so profound it feels like divine grace washes over me, washing away the pain, the fear, the memory of that small, still daughter. I have done it. I have given my king a son. The dynasty is secure. My place is secure. My vow is fulfilled.

They clean him quickly and bring him to me, this perfect, tiny creature wrapped in fine linen embroidered with Tudor roses. He is red-faced and squalling, his tiny fists waving in indignation at being thrust into the cold world. But to me, he is beautiful beyond description. He has Henry's nose already, and wisps of reddish hair that promise to be like his father's.

"Henry," I whisper, the name we have already chosen. "Henry, Duke of Cornwall."

When they bring my husband to see his son, the King of England falls to his knees beside my bed, tears streaming down his face. He takes the baby with hands that tremble, holding him as if he were made of spun glass and dreams.

"My son," he says wonderingly. "My boy. My heir."

The celebrations that follow are beyond anything I have ever witnessed, surpassing even our coronation in their exuberance. A great tournament is held at Westminster, a pageant of chivalry and splendor where Henry, my glorious husband, jousts in my honor. He has never been more magnificent—his armor polished to mirror brightness, his horse dancing beneath him, his lance never missing its mark.

He wears my favor, a sleeve of cloth-of-gold embroidered with pomegranates and roses, and before each course, he salutes me where I sit in the gallery with our son in my arms. The crowd roars its approval—their king is victorious in war and love, their queen has proven fruitful. England's future is assured.

I watch from the gallery as Henry holds our son up to the cheering court. The nobles and ambassadors press forward, eager to see the future of England. The French ambassador looks sick—this child represents the end of their hopes to exploit a succession crisis. The Imperial ambassador smiles—this child is half Spanish blood, a potential ally for the Empire. But I see only my husband and son, the two Henrys who are my whole world.

Henry's face is alight with a joy so pure it brings tears to my eyes. He has never looked at me with more love, more gratitude. In this moment, I am not just his wife; I am the mother of his heir, the woman who has secured his legacy. I have never loved him more, this golden king who holds our golden future in his arms.

The child thrives for fifty-two days. Fifty-two days of perfection, of watching him grow stronger, hearing his cries grow louder, feeling his grip grow firmer around my finger. The wet nurse reports that he feeds vigorously. The rockers say he sleeps peacefully. The physicians declare him the healthiest prince ever born to England.

I spend hours in the nursery, a luxury queens are not supposed to indulge in. I should leave him to his attendants, maintain the royal distance. But I cannot stay away. I hold him, sing to him in Spanish—the same lullabies my mother sang to me. I tell him about Granada, about the Alhambra where his blood comes from, about the greatness that flows in his veins from both sides.

"You will be a greater king than your father," I whisper to him one afternoon as weak February sunlight streams through the windows. "You will unite all of Europe through wisdom and strength. You will be Henry IX, the greatest Henry of all."

He gurgles and waves his fist, and I choose to take it as agreement. Henry visits the nursery daily, sometimes twice daily, unable to stay away from this miracle we have created. He brings gifts—a silver rattle from the London goldsmiths, a tiny suit of armor commissioned as a jest but crafted with serious skill, a pony so small and gentle it's almost a large dog.

"He'll ride before he walks," Henry declares. "He'll joust before he's ten. He'll conquer France before he's twenty."

"Let him learn to hold his head up first," I laugh, but I love his grand dreams for our boy.

On the evening of February 21st, I retire early, exhausted from the celebrations that seem never to end. There is to be another feast tomorrow, another pageant. The Venetian ambassador has commissioned a masque in the prince's honor. The Emperor has sent gifts that have not yet arrived. The King of France has sent grudging congratulations that fool no one.

I kiss my son goodnight, pressing my lips to his soft forehead, breathing in his sweet milk scent. "Sleep well, my prince," I whisper. "Tomorrow, you will be adored by all of London."

I am woken in the depths of night by a sound that freezes the blood in my veins—not a sound, actually, but the absence of sound. The nursery, which should echo with the soft noises of a sleeping baby, with the whispered conversations of his attendants, is silent.

The frantic knocking on my chamber door comes moments later. I see the face of one of my ladies-in-waiting, Lady Margaret Pole, pale with a terror that needs no words.

No. No. God would not be so cruel.

I run to the nursery barefoot, my nightshift billowing behind me, my loosened hair streaming like a banner of despair. The cold February air bites at my skin, but I don't feel it. I feel nothing but the terrible certainty growing in my chest.

The nursery is full of people—physicians, ladies, servants—but they part before me like the Red Sea, their faces masks of grief and fear. In the center of the room, the cradle that only hours before held the future of England is still occupied, but the small body within it does not move.

I fall to my knees beside the cradle, my hands reaching for him, but they stop me.

"Your Majesty must not—" someone says, but I strike their hands away.

I lift my son from his cradle, and I know immediately. The weight is wrong—too heavy, too still. The warmth is gone. His perfect face is pale as wax, his lips tinged blue. The physicians flutter around me, murmuring about a sudden flux of the stomach, about God's mysterious will, but their words are meaningless noise against the deafening silence of my grief.

He is dead. My perfect prince, my Henry, Duke of Cornwall, heir to England, hope of the Tudor dynasty—dead at fifty-two days old.

What sin have I committed? What flaw in me has displeased Him? The questions hammer at my soul as I hold my dead child, rocking him as if motion might bring back life. Is it because my first marriage was consummated after all, despite my denials? Is it punishment for my moment of joy when Arthur died, freeing me to marry Henry? Is it Spain's sins visited upon me, the blood of Moors and Jews crying out for vengeance?

I hear a sound, a terrible sound—a woman keening like an animal in pain. It takes me a moment to realize it's coming from my own throat. The sound brings Henry running, and he bursts into the nursery like a warrior charging into battle, as if he can fight death itself.

He sees me holding our son, sees the truth in my face, and something breaks in him. Not just his heart—something fundamental, something that will never fully heal. He takes the baby from my arms with gentle hands, holding him against his chest, and for a moment, we are just two parents united in the most terrible grief imaginable.

"Why?" he asks, not to me, not to the physicians, but to God himself. "Why give us this gift only to snatch it away?"

There is no answer. There is never an answer.

We bury our son with full royal honors in Westminster Abbey. The tiny coffin, covered in cloth of gold, looks absurd in the vast space. The Archbishop speaks of God's plan, of children called home to be angels, but his words are dust in my mouth. I don't want an angel. I want my son.

The days that follow are a waking nightmare. The court, which so recently celebrated with us, now tiptoes around us in their mourning clothes. The magnificent tournament pavilions are dismantled in silence. The nursery is closed, its door sealed. No one speaks of the prince who was, only of the princes who might yet be.

Henry comes to me less frequently in those first weeks. When he does, he holds me, but his grief is different from mine. Mine is the primal sorrow of a mother for her child, a physical ache in my breasts that still expect to nurse, in my arms that still expect to hold. His is laced with something else, something I have never seen in him before: anxiety.

He looks at me, and for the first time, I see not a husband sharing my pain, but a king counting his losses. He has lost a son. But he has also lost the security of succession, the proof of God's favor, the validation of his reign. He needs an heir, and now he knows—we both know—that I can fail in providing one.

Weeks later, I find myself standing alone in the silent nursery. I convinced a servant to unlock it, pressing coins into her hand and swearing her to secrecy. The room is exactly as it was left, as if the attendants expected the prince to return at any moment. His cradle still holds the indentation of his small body. His toys are arranged on a table, waiting for hands that will never grasp them.

The scent of milk and linen still hangs in the air, a ghostly reminder of life. I pick up the silver rattle Henry gave him, feeling its weight, hearing its gentle chime. Such a small sound in such a large silence.

The door opens, and Henry stands there. He doesn't speak, doesn't reproach me for being here. He simply stands beside me, looking at the empty cradle with an expression of profound, anxious disappointment.

"There will be others," he says finally, but it sounds like a question.

"Yes," I answer, making it a certainty through will alone. "There will be others."

But we both know something has changed. The innocence of our love, the certainty of our future, the conviction that God smiles upon us—all of it lies as dead as our son. We are still young, still in love, but now we know that love alone cannot protect us from tragedy.

The quest for a son is not over; it has merely been suspended in tragedy. And when it resumes, as it must, it will carry with it the weight of this loss, the fear that God might be telling us something we don't want to hear.

I place the rattle back on the table, careful not to let it chime again. We leave the nursery together, and I hear the door being locked behind us. But I know I will carry this room with me forever—not just the grief of it, but the brief, perfect joy of those fifty-two days when I was the mother of England's prince.

In my prayers that night, I do not ask why. I only ask for strength—strength to bear another child, strength to survive if that child too is taken, strength to remain the queen Henry needs even if I cannot be the mother England requires.

The Madonna on my altar seems to weep in the candlelight, or perhaps it is only my tears reflected in her painted eyes. She too lost a son, I remind myself. She too knew this grief. But her son's death saved the world.

What will my son's death save? What purpose could God have in taking him?

I will never know. But I will continue. I will try again. I will break my body and my heart as many times as necessary to give England its heir.

This is my vow, remade in the ashes of loss: I will not surrender. I will not despair. I will be constant as the northern star, even when all other lights go out.

Chapter 10

The Empty Cradle

The joy of those fifty-two days now feels like a dream from which I have been violently awakened. Each morning I wake expecting to hear his cry, only to be met with silence that presses against my ears like water, threatening to drown me. The nursery at Richmond Palace has been sealed on Henry's orders, but I know it remains exactly as it was—the tiny shirts laid out for dressing, the silver apostle spoons waiting for a hand that will never grasp them.

Three weeks pass before I am strong enough to leave my chambers. When I do, the court greets me with such careful, pitying kindness that I want to scream. They bow and curtsey deeper than before, their eyes sliding away from mine as if grief were contagious. Even my Spanish ladies, usually so forthright, speak to me in whispers, handling me like a piece of Venetian glass that might shatter at a touch.

But it is Henry's presence—or absence—that cuts deepest. He comes to my chambers each evening as duty requires, but he is different. The easy joy that once defined him has been replaced by something watchful, calculating. He still calls me his beloved wife, still kisses my hand with courtly grace, but his eyes, when they meet mine, hold questions he doesn't voice.

Tonight, he sits by my fire, a cup of wine untouched in his hand. The flames cast shadows that age him, showing me the king he will become rather than the golden boy he was.

"The physicians say you are recovered," he says carefully, as if testing ice on a frozen pond.

"My body is recovered," I answer truthfully. The bleeding has stopped, my strength has returned. But there are other wounds that do not show.

"Then we must... that is, we should..." He stops, unable to speak the words.

"We must try again," I finish for him. "Yes, my lord. We must."

The relief in his face is painful to see. This is what I am to him now—not just Katherine, his love, but a vessel that has proven it can fail. A investment that might not yield the expected return.

He comes to me that night with a desperation that has replaced passion. There is no joy in our coupling, only determination and unspoken fear. When he leaves, I lie awake in the darkness, my hand on my flat belly, praying to feel the quickening of new life. Praying that this time, God will be merciful.

A month passes. Then two. My courses come with terrible regularity, each one a fresh failure. Henry says nothing, but I see him watching me at meals, noting what I eat, whether I seem tired or ill. The entire court watches my body for signs, and I feel their eyes like hands, examining, assessing, judging.

By summer, the whispers have begun. They think I don't hear them, these English courtiers who smile to my face and sharpen their knives behind my back. "The Queen is barren," they murmur. "The Spanish woman cannot give us an heir." "Perhaps the King should look elsewhere for England's future."

One afternoon, I am walking in the gardens with my ladies when we come upon a group of younger courtiers. They don't see us at first, hidden as we are by the high hedges. I am about to announce our presence when I hear Anne Stafford's voice, clear and cutting.

"They say she's cursed. That God is punishing the King for marrying his brother's widow."

"Hush," another voice warns. "You speak treason."

"I speak what everyone thinks," Anne continues. "One dead prince and nothing since. How long will the King wait?"

I step into view, and the group falls silent, their faces draining of color. Anne drops into a deep curtsey, but I see no apology in her eyes, only a speculative interest. She is young, beautiful, with the kind of vitality that draws men's eyes. She looks at me and sees not a queen but an obstacle.

"Your Majesty," she says smoothly. "We did not hear you approach."

"Evidently," I reply, my voice cold as Spanish steel. "Perhaps you should be more cautious. Walls have ears, and tongues that wag too freely might find themselves cut out."

She pales at the threat, but I see something else in her expression —excitement. She enjoys this danger, this dancing on the edge of disaster. I make note of her name. Enemies should be watched closely.

That evening, I find Henry in his study, surrounded by maps of France. He is planning his war, the great campaign that will win him glory and prove his manhood to all of Europe. When I enter, he looks up with an expression of barely concealed impatience.

"Katherine. Is something amiss?"

"The court gossips," I say bluntly. "They say I am cursed. They say our marriage displeases God."

His face darkens. "Who says this? Give me names, and I will have them in the Tower before nightfall."

"Half the court says it in whispers," I reply. "You cannot imprison shadows."

He sets down his quill with such force that ink spatters across his careful plans. "Then I will give them something else to gossip about. My victories in France will silence them. When I return with French gold and French territory, no one will dare question God's favor."

"And if I am not with child before you leave?"

The question hangs between us like a blade. He looks at me, and for a moment I see not my husband but my judge, weighing my worth against my failures.

"You will be," he says finally. "You must be."

But I am not. September comes with its harvest of grain and disappointment. October brings the red and gold of autumn leaves and the red of my courses, regular as moonrise. By November, Henry's preparations for war are complete, and my womb remains empty.

The night before he sails for France, he comes to my chambers. We have tried so many times, with such desperate determination, that the act has become almost mechanical. But tonight is different. Tonight he holds me afterwards, his arms tight around me as if he could press his heir into existence through will alone.

"When I return," he whispers against my hair, "I will be a conqueror. And you will be pregnant with my son. God will reward our faith."

"Yes," I agree, though the word tastes of ash. "God will provide."

But as his fleet sails from Dover, I stand on the white cliffs and wonder if God has already given His answer. The wind whips my veil across my face, and for a moment I cannot breathe, cannot see, can only feel the terrible emptiness where my children should be.

No. No. God would not be so cruel.

I return to Greenwich to rule in Henry's absence, throwing myself into the work of governance with desperate energy. If I cannot be a mother, I will be a queen. I will prove my worth through wisdom if not through fertility.

But everywhere I look, I see reminders. The young wives of courtiers, their bellies rounding with promise. The peasant women in the villages, surrounded by broods of healthy children. Even the cats in the palace kitchens nurse their squirming litters. The whole world is fertile except for me.

What sin have I committed? What flaw in me has displeased Him? The questions hammer at my soul as December snow begins to fall. I spend hours in the chapel, my knees aching from the cold stone, my fingers bleeding from the pressure of my rosary beads. I fast until my ladies fear for my health. I give alms until my personal treasury is empty. I pray in Latin, in Spanish, in the wordless language of desperation.

Miserere mei, Deus. Have mercy on me, God.

One night, I dream of the nursery. But in my dream, it is not empty. Three children play there—two boys and a girl. They have Henry's golden hair and my dark eyes. They laugh and chase each other around the cradle where their brother once lay.

"Mother," the eldest boy says, turning to me with a smile that breaks my heart. "Why do you weep? We are all here, waiting."

"Where?" I ask, reaching for them. "Where are you waiting?"

"In God's hands," the girl says. "He holds us until the time is right."

I wake sobbing, my pillow soaked with tears. The dream felt so real I can still smell them—that sweet milk scent of babies, the sunshine in their hair. But the chamber is dark and empty, and I am alone.

Lady Margaret Pole finds me the next morning, still in my nightshift, standing at the window that overlooks the Thames. She says nothing at first, simply stands beside me as we watch the ice forming on the river's edges.

"Your Majesty is grieving," she says finally. It is not a question.

"I grieve for what never was," I reply. "For the children who die before they live. For the sons England needs and I cannot provide."

"God's time is not our time," she says gently. "I have borne five children, Your Majesty. But I buried two before their first birthdays. The pain never fully heals, but it... changes. Becomes bearable."

"And if there are no more children? If the prince was my only chance?"

She is quiet for a long moment. "Then Your Majesty will find another purpose. God does not create us for only one task."

But what other purpose can a queen have if not to bear heirs? I am not like my mother, who ruled in her own right. I am a consort, valuable only for what my body can produce. Without children, I am nothing but an expensive ornament, a failed investment, a mistake to be corrected.

As Christmas approaches, a letter arrives from Henry in France. His campaign goes well, he writes. He has taken several towns and expects to be home by spring, victorious. He asks after my health with words that try to sound casual but carry weight. "I trust God has blessed us in my absence," he writes.

I stare at the letter for a long time before I reply. What can I say? That my womb remains as empty as the nursery? That I have failed him again?

I write instead of court business, of the preparations for his return, of my prayers for his safety. I do not mention my body at all. Let him hope a little longer. Let him have his victories in France before he must face this defeat at home.

But that night, alone in the chamber we once shared with such joy, I allow myself to speak the truth that I cannot write, cannot say aloud, can barely think.

"I am afraid," I whisper to the darkness. "I am afraid that God has abandoned me. That my marriage is cursed. That I will never give England an heir."

The darkness offers no comfort, no contradiction. Only silence, as empty as my womb, as vast as my fear.

I think of the tiny prince in his golden coffin, those fifty-two perfect days that now seem like a lifetime ago. Was he my only chance? Did I have one perfect child and will never have another?

The candle gutters and dies, leaving me in absolute darkness. But I do not call for another. I sit in the black silence and feel the weight of the empty cradle pressing down on me like a stone.

Tomorrow, I will rise. I will dress in my royal robes. I will hold court and sign documents and be the Queen of England. I will write to Henry of victories and hopes and prayers answered.

But tonight, in this darkness that mirrors the darkness in my womb, I mourn not just for the son who died but for all the children who will never be born, all the princes and princesses who exist only in my desperate dreams.

The cradle is empty. And I am beginning to fear it always will be.

Chapter 11
Queen Regent

The grief for my lost son sits in my chest like a stone, heavy and cold, but duty is a stern physician that allows no time for wallowing. In the year of our Lord 1513, Henry makes his decision to pursue his claim to the throne of France. The council chambers ring with talk of war, of glory, of England's ancient rights across the narrow sea. My husband's eyes shine with the fever of it, seeing himself as the new Henry V, conqueror of Agincourt.

"I will win such glory," he tells me one night, his hands sketching battles in the air between us, "that all of Europe will know God smiles upon England. Upon us."

Upon us. As if military victory could heal my barren womb. As if French gold could replace an English prince. But I nod and smile, playing the supportive wife, even as part of me rejoices at his leaving. In his absence, I will not have to see the disappointment in his eyes each month when my courses come.

But Henry does more than leave me behind as a grieving, failed mother. He names me Queen Regent and Governess of England, Wales, and Ireland, bestowing upon me the full power to raise armies, issue warrants, and command his treasury. The great seal of England is placed in my hands with more ceremony than our wedding rings.

"Katherine's honor, excellence, prudence, forethought and faithfulness," he declares in the official letters patent, read aloud before the full court, "could not be doubted."

His faith in me is a balm to my wounded heart. If I cannot be the mother of his children, I can be the guardian of his kingdom. If my womb fails him, my wisdom will not.

I stand at Dover to see him off, the June wind whipping my veil as his fleet prepares to sail. He is magnificent in his armor, every inch the warrior king he dreams of being. When he kisses me farewell, it is a public performance of marital devotion, but in his whispered words I hear genuine affection still.

"Keep my kingdom safe, my Katherine. I trust no one as I trust you."

"Return to me victorious and safe," I reply. "England needs her king."

"And her prince," he adds, his hand briefly touching my belly in a gesture that looks like blessing but feels like accusation. "When I return, surely..."

"When you return," I agree, letting him keep his hope a while longer.

As his ship disappears into the channel mist, I turn back to land with a strange lightness in my chest. For the first time in two years, I have purpose beyond my failing body. I am not just a womb waiting to quicken. I am the Queen Regent of England.

I return to London and immediately summon the council. I sit at the head of the King's table, in his chair, wearing the severe black that has become my armor since our son's death. The lords look at me with barely concealed skepticism—Norfolk, Suffolk, the bishops and earls who serve Henry but do not think a woman, a Spanish woman, can rule.

I unroll a map of the Scottish border, my movements precise and deliberate.

"My lords," I begin, my voice carrying the authority my mother taught me, "while the King wins glory in France, we must guard against the serpent to the north."

"Your Majesty surely does not suggest the Scots would dare—" Norfolk begins.

"I suggest nothing," I interrupt. "I know. My sources tell me James IV mobilizes his forces. He will strike while England's strength is across the sea. The 'Auld Alliance' with France demands it."

They exchange glances, these English lords who thought to test a woman. They have found a queen.

Isabella's blood flows in my veins. I remember watching her manage the logistics of war, her mind as sharp as any general's blade. She taught me that war is won not on the battlefield alone but in the counting houses, the supply trains, the careful marshaling of resources. While my husband fights for honor abroad, I shall guard his kingdom at home. This is a duty I understand. This is a grief I can master.

I issue orders with the crisp efficiency of my mother's campaigns. The Earl of Surrey, a veteran of the old wars, is summoned from his estates to lead our forces. Ships are commandeered to patrol the eastern coast. The arsenal at the Tower is inventoried, and I personally inspect the great guns that will travel north.

"Your Majesty," the Master of Ordnance stammers as I examine the cannon they call the Seven Sisters, "surely such matters are beneath your attention."

"Nothing that defends England is beneath my attention," I reply, running my hand along the cold iron. "These guns killed Scots at Flodden in my father-in-law's time. They will do so again."

The expected blow comes in August. James IV, my husband's own brother-in-law, crosses the border with the largest army Scotland has ever fielded. The council panics. Messages fly to Henry in France, begging him to return. But I remain calm. This is what I was born for, bred for, trained for. My mother's daughter knows how to face an enemy.

I do not remain in the safety of London. Though pregnant again —a fragile hope I dare not embrace too fully—I know I must be the visible heart of England's resistance. I establish my headquarters at Buckingham, a central point from which to manage the war effort, and order a reserve army to muster nearby.

"The men must see their queen," I tell them. "They must know that England does not fear."

Though I do not ride to the border myself, I order my personal banners and standards to be sent north with the Earl of Surrey's army, a symbol of my presence with them. I think of my mother, riding to the siege of Granada while carrying my brother Juan. If

Isabella could conquer kingdoms while pregnant, her daughter can defend one.

I address the reserve troops at Buckingham, my voice carrying across the assembled thousands as I sit astride my horse, wearing not armour, but a gown of royal purple with a steel gorget at my throat. The speech I have prepared is in English, carefully practiced to minimize my accent. These men must hear their queen, not a foreign princess.

"Men of England," I call out, standing in my armor with the royal standard flying above me, "you do not fight for conquest or glory in foreign lands. You fight for your homes, your families, your own soil. The Scots come as invaders, breakers of sacred peace. But you are Englishmen, and this is England. Remember Agincourt! Remember Crécy! Remember that English courage has never failed when England itself is threatened!"

The roar that greets my words shakes the very ground. These men, who might have doubted a Spanish queen, see instead a warrior sovereign. They see the spirit of England itself, swollen with new life but unbowed by danger.

From my headquarters, I coordinate supplies, manage communications, and act as the visible heart of England's resistance. Every dispatch from the north comes to me first. Every order bears my seal alongside the King's.

On the ninth of September, at a place called Flodden Field, our armies meet. The battle is bloody and brutal, fought in rain that turns the field to mud, but English bills and English courage prove stronger than Scottish spears and Scottish pride. By nightfall, the flower of Scottish nobility lies dead in the mud, and among them, King James himself.

The Earl of Surrey sends me James's blood-soaked coat, torn from his body on the field. I hold it up, this gory trophy, and feel not triumph but grim satisfaction. This is what comes of threatening England. This is what comes of testing a daughter of Isabel.

I write to Henry in France, sending him the news of victory—for I call it his victory, knowing his pride demands it—along with a piece of the dead Scottish king's coat to use as a banner.

"I had wished to send the body itself," I write, allowing myself this one moment of dark humour, "as my mother once sent the heads of her enemies, but our Englishmen's hearts would not suffer it."

In truth, I ordered James's body to be treated with royal honors. He was a king, after all, and my husband's sister's husband. But Henry need not know the full extent of my mercy.

When I stand before my victorious troops to give thanks, I feel a surge of profound purpose unlike anything since holding my living son. For this moment, I am not merely Henry's wife. I am England's queen, in command and utterly respected. The men kneel before me, muddy and bloodied from battle, and in their eyes I see not the pity that has followed me since my son's death, but genuine admiration.

"Your Majesty," Surrey says, his grizzled face glowing with pride, "England owes you a debt that can never be repaid. You have saved the realm."

"I have done my duty," I reply, but inside, my heart sings. This is what I am capable of when freed from the narrow confines of wife and mother. This is the queen I could be if given the chance.

But even in this moment of triumph, my body reminds me of my primary purpose. A cramp seizes me, sharp and sudden, and I have to grip the table to keep from crying out. Not now. Please, God, not now.

That night, in my chambers at Buckingham, the child comes too early. Another son, the midwives tell me through their tears. Another prince who never draws breath. I hold his tiny, perfect body and feel the cruel irony of it—I can defend England from invasion, but I cannot carry a child to term.

When Henry returns from France in October, full of his own victories—though they pale beside Flodden—he finds me changed. I am thinner, harder, marked by loss but also by triumph. I have tasted power, real power, and found it sweet.

"You have been magnificent," he tells me, genuine admiration in his voice. "All of Europe speaks of the Queen of England who destroyed the Scottish threat."

"I did what was necessary," I reply.

"And our child?" The hope in his voice is painful.

"Lost," I say simply. "The stress of the campaign, perhaps. I am sorry, my lord."

His face falls, the familiar disappointment settling over his features. But then he surprises me.

"You saved England," he says. "That matters more than—" He stops, unable to finish the lie. Nothing matters more than an heir, we both know it.

But for a brief, shining moment, I was more than a failed mother. I was a true queen, a defender of the realm, my mother's daughter in deed as well as blood. I have proven that I am more than my womb, even if Henry cannot see it.

That night, alone in my chambers, I unfold the piece of James's coat I kept for myself. The blood has dried to brown, stiff and strange. I think of my mother, sending the heads of Moorish kings to my father. She understood that sometimes a queen must be harder than any king.

I fold the cloth carefully and place it in my jewel box, beside the ribbon from my dead son's christening gown. Tokens of triumph and tragedy, intertwined like the threads of my life.

Tomorrow, I will return to being Henry's wife, trying and failing to give him sons. But today, for this one golden autumn moment, I was Katherine the Queen Regent, victor of Flodden, defender of England.

It is a memory no one can take from me. And in the dark years to come, when my worth is measured only in my empty womb, I will remember that once, I was magnificent.

Chapter 12
My Jewel, Maria

After the triumph of the regency, my body betrays me again with terrible predictability. A son, born prematurely in the autumn of 1513, never draws breath. His tiny body, perfect but too small, fits in Henry's two hands as he holds him up to the light from the window, as if sunshine might wake him. Another stillbirth follows in 1514, this time a boy who lived long enough in my womb for me to feel his movements, to know his patterns, to believe this time would be different. The court whispers grow louder with each loss, though they silence themselves when I pass. The king's anxiety deepens like lines carved in stone, permanent now on his face that was once so unmarked by worry.

My own heart is a landscape of grief, cratered by losses, punctuated by fervent, desperate prayer. I have become intimate with every saint who protects mothers and children. St. Anne, mother of the Virgin, who knew the pain of barrenness before God's blessing. St. Margaret of Antioch, patron of childbirth. St. Gerard Majella, protector of expectant mothers. Their names are a litany I recite with each movement of my rosary beads, worn smooth now from constant handling.

Then, in the spring of 1515, God grants me hope once more. I am with child again, and this time, something feels different. The morning sickness is stronger, lasting well into the afternoon. The quickening comes earlier and more vigorously. This child moves constantly, a restless swimmer in my womb, as if eager to enter the world.

I guard my body with fierce vigilance. I follow every prescription, every superstition, every piece of advice from physicians and midwives alike. I eat only white meats. I avoid cold air and strong emotions. I have my chambers painted in soft yellows, supposedly beneficial for the child's temperament. I wear an eagle stone bound against my belly, said to prevent miscarriage. I am desperate enough to try anything, everything.

When news comes that my father Ferdinand has died, Henry and the council conspire to keep it from me. But I know. I see it in the careful way people speak around me, the letters from Spain that suddenly cease, the black-clad Spanish ambassador who will not meet my eyes. My father is dead, and I am not permitted even to mourn him properly lest the shock bring on early labor.

I mourn in private, tears falling silently as I embroider tiny shirts for the child I carry. Ferdinand was not a warm father—he used me as a chess piece from the moment of my birth—but he was my last link to Spain, to my mother, to the girl I once was. Now I am truly alone, an orphan as well as an exile, with no powerful family to protect me if this child, too, fails to thrive.

As my time approaches in February of 1516, I take to my chamber at Greenwich Palace. The rooms have been prepared with obsessive care. Every surface is draped in the finest linen. Holy relics ring the bed—a piece of the Virgin's girdle, said to ease labor pains; a splinter of the True Cross; the finger bone of St.

Margaret. The air is thick with the scent of rose oil and burning herbs meant to purify the space.

I clutch a crucifix, my prayers a frantic mix of pleas for a safe delivery and for a male child. "Please," I whisper to the carved Christ, His face serene in suffering. "I have given You my grief, my humiliation, my failures. Give me this one mercy. A son. A living son."

The fate of the dynasty, the happiness of my husband, the very meaning of my life—it all rests on this moment.

Labor begins at sunset on the seventeenth of February, as if the child wants to be born between day and night, between hope and fear. The pains are different from before—stronger but more regular, purposeful rather than chaotic. My body knows this dance now, has practiced it too many times, and performs its part with grim efficiency.

"The child comes well," the midwife murmurs, her hands gentle but sure. "Your Majesty is doing perfectly."

Perfectly. If only she knew how imperfect I feel, how my faith wavers with each wave of pain, how I bargain with God even as I doubt His mercy.

The labor stretches through the night. I bite down on leather to keep from screaming, aware that the entire court waits beyond these doors, listening for signs of success or failure. Henry paces in the presence chamber, I'm told later, wearing a track in the Turkish carpet, snapping at anyone who approaches.

Then, as dawn breaks on the eighteenth of February, after a final, tearing push that feels like it splits me in two, my child is born.

The silence that follows stops my heart. Not again. Please, God, not again.

Then—a cry. Strong, angry, very much alive.

"A princess, Your Majesty," the midwife announces, and I hear the apology in her voice. "A healthy, perfect princess."

A girl.

Relief and disappointment war in my chest. Alive. My child is alive. But not a son. Not the prince England needs, that Henry demands, that would secure my position forever.

They clean her quickly and bring her to me, this tiny, furious creature who has survived what her brothers could not. She is red-faced and squalling, her small fists waving in indignation. But to me, she is beautiful beyond description. She has my nose, distinctive already, and wisps of reddish hair that might darken to my auburn or brighten to Henry's gold.

"Mary," I whisper, the name we had chosen for a daughter. "Mary, after the Virgin, and after Henry's beloved sister."

When Henry enters the chamber, I search his face for disappointment. It is there, flickering like a shadow, but it is quickly replaced by wonder as he looks at his daughter. She is the first of our children he has seen alive, moving, breathing.

"She's perfect," he says, taking her with careful hands. "Look at her, Katherine. She's perfect."

"But not a prince," I say, needing to voice the failure before he does.

"We are both young," he replies, the same words he said after our son died, but with less certainty now. "If it was a daughter this time, by the grace of God the sons will follow."

The Venetian ambassador, Sebastian Giustinian, comes to offer his congratulations. Henry receives him with royal graciousness, but his words reveal the truth of his heart. "We are both young," he tells the ambassador, that phrase becoming a refrain, a prayer, a desperate hope. "If it was a daughter this time, by the grace of God the sons will follow."

But I see the calculation in the ambassador's eyes, the message he will send back to Venice: The Queen of England has produced only a daughter. The succession is not secure.

In private, though, Henry dotes on Mary. He carries her through the palace, showing her off to courtiers like a merchant displaying his finest ware. "She never cries," he boasts, though this isn't quite true. "She has the Tudor spirit already. See how she grips my finger? Strong as a boy."

Strong as a boy. Even in his love for her, the comparison wounds. She must be measured against the son she is not, will always be found wanting simply by virtue of her sex.

But to me, she is perfect. She is enough. She must be enough.

She is my jewel, this serious, watchful child who seems to study the world with eyes too knowing for an infant. When I hold her, I whisper to her in Spanish, the language of my heart, telling her the stories my mother told me—of Isabella the Catholic, who ruled kingdoms and led armies, who proved a woman could be as strong as any man.

"You are the granddaughter of the greatest queen who ever lived," I tell her as she nurses, her small hand splayed against my breast. "*Hija mía*, you carry the blood of warriors and saints."

Mary thrives in a way her brothers never did. Each day she grows stronger, more alert. By three months, she holds her head steady. By six months, she sits unassisted. Each milestone is a tiny miracle, a rebuke to death that tried so hard to claim her.

My last pregnancy comes in 1518, ending, once again, in the stillbirth of a daughter. After that, my body is barren. The monthly hope and disappointment cease. At thirty-three, my childbearing years are over, though we don't acknowledge it aloud. Henry still comes to my bed, but less frequently, and with a mechanical determination that has replaced passion.

The physicians examine me with increasing desperation. They prescribe herbs, special diets, pilgrimages to shrines. But I know, with a woman's certainty that needs no physician's confirmation, that there will be no more children. My womb, which quickened so readily but could not sustain life, has closed its doors forever.

One evening, I sit alone with Mary in her nursery. She is two years old now, speaking in a mixture of English and Spanish that only I fully understand. She plays with a set of silver bells, arranging them by size with the methodical precision that marks everything she does.

"Mama," she says, looking up at me with those serious eyes, "why does Papa look sad when he sees me?"

The question is a dagger to my heart. How do I explain to a child that her father loves her but wishes she were someone else? That her very existence is both a joy and a disappointment?

"Papa loves you very much," I say carefully. "Sometimes grown people look sad because they think of complicated things."

She considers this with the gravity of a judge. "I will make him not sad," she declares. "I will be very good."

I pull her into my arms, crushing her against me with a fierceness that makes her squirm. "You are already perfect, *mi amor*. Never think otherwise."

But I know she will spend her life trying to be the son she isn't, trying to earn the love that should be hers by right. I see it already in the way she practices her letters with desperate concentration, the way she tries to please her father with perfect curtseys and carefully rehearsed Latin phrases.

That night, after Mary is asleep, I stand over her bed watching the gentle rise and fall of her chest. She clutches a small wooden doll, a gift from her father, though she prefers the books I read to her, the maps I show her, the lessons I have already begun.

She is my jewel, the living proof of my valid marriage, the one perfect fruit of our union. But I know what the court whispers, what Henry thinks but doesn't say: one daughter is not enough. England needs sons. Without them, what is to prevent the realm from falling into civil war when Henry dies? The memory of the

Wars of the Roses is still fresh, when the lack of clear male succession tore the country apart.

I look down at her small, peaceful face and my heart fills with a love so fierce it is almost painful. It is a love mixed with fear—fear for her future, fear of what will happen to her if Henry sets me aside for a woman who can give him sons.

I lean down and whisper in Spanish, the language of promises and prayers: "*Hija mía*, you will have to be stronger than any son. You will have to be twice as good, twice as wise, twice as faithful. The world will tell you that you are not enough because you are not male. But you are the daughter of Katherine of Aragon and the granddaughter of Isabella of Castile. You are enough. You are more than enough."

She stirs in her sleep, murmuring something unintelligible. I smooth her hair, noting how it has darkened to a rich auburn like mine. She will not be the golden princess Henry might have preferred, but she will be something better—a woman of substance, of intelligence, of faith.

I think of my mother, who had me and my sisters before she finally bore a son. But she never made us feel lesser for our sex. She educated us as thoroughly as any prince, made us understand that queens could rule as well as kings. If only she were here to teach Mary what she taught me. If only Mary could grow up in a world that valued daughters as much as sons.

But this is England, not Spain, and the Tudor dynasty is too new, too fragile, to risk a female succession. Mary will have to fight for every scrap of recognition, every acknowledgment of her worth.

A sound from the doorway makes me turn. Henry stands there, having entered silently. He looks at me, then at Mary, and for a moment his face is unguarded. I see love there, genuine love for this child we made together. But I also see sorrow, disappointment, the weight of dynastic necessity.

"She looks like you when she sleeps," he says softly.

"She has your determination when she's awake," I reply.

He enters the room and stands beside me, looking down at our daughter. "If she were a boy..." he begins, then stops.

"But she is not," I say firmly. "She is Mary, and she is perfect as she is."

He looks at me then with an expression I cannot read. Is it pity? Regret? Or something harder, colder—calculation?

"There will be no more children, will there?" he asks, though it isn't really a question.

"God has given us Mary," I say. "Perhaps He means for her to be enough."

"Perhaps," he says, but I hear the doubt, the fear, the beginning of thoughts that will lead us down dark paths.

He leaves without kissing me goodnight, and I am left alone with our daughter, our only living child, our jewel who must somehow be enough to hold a kingdom together.

I kneel beside her bed and begin to pray, not for sons now—that prayer has been answered with silence too many times—but for Mary. For her safety, her future, her happiness in a world that will demand she be something other than what she is.

"Make her strong," I whisper to the Virgin, mother to mother. "Make her wise. Make her faithful. And if her father abandons us both for the sake of sons, make her remember that she was loved, completely and fiercely, by her mother."

The candle flickers, casting shadows on the wall. In the dancing light, I can almost see them—the ghosts of the children who were never born, the princes England needed, the sisters Mary will never have. They crowd the room with their absence, these phantom babies, making the one living child seem even more precious, even more alone.

Tomorrow, the court will whisper. The King will fret about the succession. The councilors will hint at solutions too terrible to speak aloud.

But tonight, there is just a mother and her daughter, the only fruit of a love that is already beginning to sour, the living proof that I am not entirely a failure, even if I am not entirely a success.

Mary. My jewel. My triumph. My perfect inadequacy.

She is all I have to show for seven years of marriage, years of pregnancy and loss, hope and heartbreak. One small girl against the weight of England's need.

It will have to be enough. She will have to be enough.

And if the worst happens—if Henry puts me aside, if he names me adulteress or worse to free himself for another wife—then Mary will be my only legacy, the only proof that I was ever Queen of England, ever loved, ever mattered.

I touch the small cross at her throat, a gift from me at her baptism. "You are a princess of England and Spain," I whisper. "Never forget. Never let them make you forget."

In her sleep, she smiles.

It is enough to break my heart and mend it, all at once.

Chapter 13

The Shadow in the Gallery

The years pass in a semblance of peace, though peace is perhaps too generous a word for the careful dance Henry and I perform around the crater of our losses. I am the Queen, respected and secure in my position—or so it appears to those who do not look too closely. Henry is still a loving husband in public, still visits my bed, though his embraces have become dutiful rather than passionate. His eye wanders, as is the way of kings. There have been mistresses—Elizabeth Blount, who bore him a son he acknowledged and titled, proving to all the world that the fault in our childlessness lies with me, not him. But these affairs are fleeting, discreet. He always returns to me, to his wife and his queen, as a man returns to his home after a journey.

We are at a court festival for May Day, 1526. The air is alive with music and laughter, the great hall at Greenwich transformed into a bower of greenery and silk flowers. Spring has come late this year, but it has come with glory, and the court celebrates with the desperate gaiety of those who have survived another harsh winter.

I watch Henry joust in the tiltyard, though he is thirty-five now, heavier in his armor than in our youth. The athletic grace that once seemed effortless now requires more effort, though he would strike dead anyone who dared suggest it. He rides in my honor, as he always has, breaking his lance against Sir Nicholas Carew's shield and saluting me in the royal box. My heart swells with a familiar pride, tinged now with nostalgia. He is still my king, still magnificent, even if the gold has begun to tarnish.

"Your Majesty's champion rides well," says Lady Salisbury beside me, ever diplomatic.

"His Majesty has lost none of his skill," I reply, though we both hear the slight wheeze in his breathing when he removes his helmet.

Later, there is dancing in the great hall. The younger courtiers perform a masque representing the triumph of love over time, a theme that feels pointed given that most of us are no longer young. Henry leads me in the first measure, as tradition demands. His hand is firm in mine, but his attention seems elsewhere, scanning the room over my shoulder.

"You dance as beautifully as ever, my lady," he says, but the compliment is automatic, worn smooth from overuse.

"Your Majesty is kind," I respond with equal formality.

We are play-acting now, performing the roles of devoted king and queen for an audience that knows better but pretends not to notice. The distance between us is a chasm that widens with each failed pregnancy, each month that passes without the prince England needs.

As we turn in the dance, my attention is caught by a woman standing among my ladies-in-waiting. She should blend into the background—her position demands it—but somehow she draws the eye like a dark star. She is not a great beauty, not in the English style of roses and cream that Henry has always favored. Anne Boleyn is all sharp angles and knowing looks, with dark eyes that hold secrets and a neck so long and slender it seems designed to display jewels.

She is one of the Boleyn girls, the younger sister of Mary, who was once the king's mistress for a time. This one, Anne, has recently returned from the French court, and she carries its fashions and its forwardness with her like an expensive perfume that doesn't quite mask something earthier underneath.

French. That explains the arrogance in the way she holds her head, the calculation in how she positions herself just within Henry's line of sight. The French women have a way of looking at men as if they were prizes to be won rather than masters to serve. They make an art of availability while maintaining the illusion of independence.

I dismiss her from my mind. She is a foolish fancy, nothing more. The King has his appetites—what king does not? They pass like summer storms, all thunder and lightning, then clearing skies. He always returns to me, to the solidity of our marriage, to the woman who has stood beside him for seventeen years.

But later in the evening, I see him lead her in a dance.

It is not the first dance—that would be too obvious. Nor the second or third. But in the fourth dance of the evening, when wine has loosened propriety's stays and the torches burn lower, casting shadows that hide as much as they reveal, I see him take her hand.

The transformation in him is immediate and terrible. The practiced courtesy he showed with me vanishes, replaced by something raw and hungry. He laughs—really laughs, not the political laugh he deploys at council or the indulgent chuckle he grants to courtiers' poor jokes. This is the laugh I remember from our early days, when the world was golden and anything seemed possible.

He leans close to hear what she is saying, and she does not lean away as propriety demands. Instead, she tilts her head, exposing that impossibly long neck, and whispers something that makes him throw his head back with delight. The rest of the court fades for him—the music, the other dancers, the world itself. There is only Henry and this dark-eyed girl who dares to meet his gaze as an equal.

I turn away, my smile fixed in place for the benefit of the court, brittle as spun sugar and as likely to shatter. But a cold, unfamiliar feeling coils in my gut like a serpent waking from hibernation. This is not like the others. This is not simple dalliance of the flesh. Mary Boleyn was pretty and available and forgotten the moment she was out of sight. Elizabeth Blount was a conquest, proof of virility.

This is something different. I see it in the way he watches her even when they are not dancing, his eyes tracking her movement through the hall like a hawk marking prey. I see it in her calculated responses—encouraging enough to keep him interested, distant enough to drive him mad with wanting.

"The Boleyn girl dances well," Lady Salisbury observes carefully beside me.

"All my ladies are accomplished," I reply, my tone ending the discussion.

But my eyes, against my will, return to them. She is teaching him a French dance, something intricate and intimate that requires their bodies to be closer than English propriety permits. Their hands touch, part, touch again. Each contact seems to send lightning through him.

She is younger than Mary, my daughter. Twenty-five to his thirty-five, though she seems both older and younger—old in her knowledge of men's desires, young in her ambitious energy. When she laughs, it is not the tinkling courtesy laugh of a lady-in-waiting. It is something earthier, more genuine, as if she actually finds him amusing rather than merely powerful.

And Henry—my Henry, who has grown careful with his emotions, who has learned to hide disappointment behind kingliness—responds like a flower turning toward the sun. He stands straighter. His voice carries more authority. He is becoming the king he imagines himself to be, reflected in her dark, admiring eyes.

"Your Majesty," she says as the dance ends, dropping into a curtsey so deep it borders on mockery. "You honor me beyond my worth."

"Mistress Boleyn," he replies, and his voice carries across the hall, ensuring everyone hears, everyone knows, "the honor is entirely mine."

The court pretends not to notice, but I feel the shift in attention, the sideways glances, the whispered speculations. A new player has entered the game, and everyone is recalculating their positions.

Later, as my ladies prepare me for bed, I catch sight of myself in the mirror. Forty-one years old, though I have aged more in the last few years than in the decade before. The losses—of children, of hope, of Henry's passionate love—have carved themselves into my face. I am still handsome, I tell myself, still queenly. But I am autumn to her spring, dusk to her dawn.

"Shall I remove the pearls, Your Majesty?" asks Lady Willoughby.

"Leave them," I say. Pearls for tears, the poets say. How appropriate.

That night, Henry does not come to my chambers. It is not unusual—he often works late with his councilors or carouses with his gentlemen. But tonight I know, with the certainty that wives possess, that he is thinking of her. Perhaps writing poetry, as he did for me once. Perhaps lying awake, planning how to win her.

I kneel at my prie-dieu, the wood hard against my knees, and try to pray. But the words tangle in my throat. What can I ask? For God to strike down a silly girl who has caught my husband's eye? For Henry to remember his vows? For my womb to quicken one last time with the son that would solve everything?

Instead, I find myself thinking of my mother, Isabella, who fought wars and conquered kingdoms but never had to fight for Ferdinand's love. Their marriage was a partnership of equals, two Catholic Majesties united in purpose and faith. She never had to watch him look at another woman the way Henry looked at Anne Boleyn tonight.

No, that is not true. There were mistresses, Spanish ladies whose names history has forgotten. But Ferdinand never looked at them in public the way Henry looks at her. He never made my mother's humiliation a spectacle for the court's entertainment.

A shadow has fallen across the sunlit gallery of my life. I tell myself it will pass, as all Henry's infatuations pass. But deep in my heart, in the place where truth lives despite our desperate denials, I know this is different.

This girl, this nobody from Kent with her French graces and her calculated availability, is not just another mistress to be enjoyed and discarded. She is something far more dangerous—a woman who makes the King feel young again, potent again, full of possibility again.

And I am the aging wife who has failed to give him sons, who reminds him with every glance of duty rather than desire, of disappointment rather than delight.

The candle flickers, casting dancing shadows on the wall. In them, I can almost see the future—dark and twisted and terrible. But I push the vision away. I am Katherine of Aragon, daughter of Isabella and Ferdinand, Queen of England. I have survived worse than a husband's wandering eye.

Tomorrow, I will smile. I will be gracious to Mistress Boleyn, kind even. I will show no weakness, no fear, no acknowledgment that anything has changed. I will be constant as the northern star, unmoving and unmoved.

But tonight, alone in my chambers while somewhere in this palace my husband dreams of another woman, I allow myself one moment of pure, cold truth:

The shadow in the gallery has a name, and her name is Anne Boleyn.

And unlike the others, she has not come to warm his bed.

She has come for my crown.

Chapter 14

The King's Scruple

He comes to my private chambers late at night in the spring of 1527, but he does not come to my bed. This, in itself, is not unusual—our marital visits have become increasingly rare, carefully scheduled attempts at conception that have long since ceased to yield fruit. But tonight is different. He carries a heavy, leather-bound Bible, its pages marked with slips of parchment like accusations waiting to be voiced. His face wears an expression I have never seen before—a terrible, feigned piety that fits him as poorly as a hair shirt.

"Katherine," he says, and already I know this will be painful by the way he uses my full name, formal and distant. "I must speak with you on a matter of conscience."

Conscience. The word falls between us like a stone into still water, sending ripples of dread through my chest. I set aside my book of hours, marking my place carefully—Psalm 51, *Miserere mei, Deus*. Have mercy on me, God. How appropriate.

"Of course, my lord," I say, folding my hands in my lap. "I am always ready to hear your concerns."

He paces before the fire, his shadow looming and shrinking on the tapestried walls. He will not meet my eyes, this man who has shared my bed for eighteen years, who has planted his seed in my womb again and again only to harvest grief. He speaks instead to the flames, to the night beyond the windows, to anywhere but my face.

"I have been reading Scripture," he begins, his voice low and strained. "Studying the word of God with learned men. And I have found... that is, it has been brought to my attention... a terrible truth."

He opens the Bible, his finger—heavy with rings including the one I placed there at our wedding—traces a line on the open page. The candlelight catches the gold leaf illumination, making the sacred words seem to burn.

"Leviticus," he says, as if the name itself were an indictment. "Chapter twenty, verse twenty-one. 'If a man shall take his brother's wife, it is an unclean thing: he hath uncovered his brother's nakedness; they shall be childless.'"

The words hang in the air between us, cold and venomous. Childless. As if our Mary, our jewel, is nothing. As if the sons I lost —the ones I carried and birthed and held as they died—were not children but signs of God's wrath. As if my grief were actually guilt.

I feel a cold fury rise within me, but I keep my voice calm, measured, drawing on years of diplomatic training. "My lord, you forget Deuteronomy. Chapter twenty-five, verse five. When brothers dwell together and one dies without a son, his brother shall take the widow to wife and raise up seed for his brother. It is not a sin but a duty."

"That applies only when the marriage was not consummated," he says quickly, too quickly, as if he has rehearsed this response. "And we both know—"

"We both know that my marriage to Arthur was never consummated," I interrupt, my voice steel wrapped in silk. "You know this because I told you truly on our wedding night. You know this because you found me a virgin. You know this because the Pope himself examined the matter and granted dispensation for our marriage."

He flinches at the mention of the Pope, and I see something flicker in his eyes—not doubt about our marriage's validity, but annoyance that I would invoke higher authority than his own conscience.

"The Pope," he says slowly, "is a man. He can err. But God's law, written here in sacred Scripture, cannot err."

"Then what of the twenty years we have lived as man and wife?" I ask, rising from my chair to face him. "What of the vows we made before God? What of our daughter?"

"Our daughter," he repeats, and there is real pain in his voice now. "Our only living child. Don't you see, Katherine? This is God's judgment upon us. We have lived in sin, unknowing but sin nonetheless, and He has punished us with the loss of our sons."

I want to strike him. I want to take that Bible from his hands and throw it into the fire. I want to scream that this is not piety but excuse, not conscience but cowardice. But I see the trap now, laid as carefully as any hunter's snare. If I rage, I confirm his suspicion that I am guilty, defensive. If I weep, I am the weak woman who cannot face truth. I must be cleverer than that.

"My lord," I say, returning to my chair with deliberate calm, "if you truly believe our marriage is invalid, why come to me in the night like a thief? Why not bring this matter before the Church courts, before learned theologians who can examine it properly?"

He pauses in his pacing, and I see I have scored a hit. He doesn't want examination. He wants capitulation.

"I hoped," he says, attempting to sound sorrowful, "that you would see the truth as I have seen it. That you would understand the danger to your immortal soul."

"My soul is in no danger," I reply firmly. "Our marriage was made in Heaven, blessed by the Church, consummated in love. Our daughter Mary is the living proof of that blessing."

"One daughter in eighteen years," he says bitterly, the mask of piety slipping. "While my bastard son thrives. What does that tell you?"

It tells me that Elizabeth Blount was younger, healthier, luckier. It tells me that bearing children is as much chance as divine providence. But most of all, it tells me that this sudden crisis of conscience coincides remarkably with Anne Boleyn's refusal to become his mistress without greater promises.

"It tells me," I say carefully, "that God's will is mysterious but not malicious. That He tests us as He tested Job. That faith means constancy especially in hardship."

He closes the Bible with a snap that echoes like judgment. "You are stubborn."

"I am constant," I correct. "As I vowed to be."

He looks at me then, really looks at me for the first time since entering my chamber. I see him catalog my age—forty-two to his thirty-six. The gray threading through my auburn hair. The lines that map my sorrows across my face. The body that has been broken again and again trying to give him what he needs.

"This matter is not ended," he says finally. "I must examine my conscience further. Consult with learned men. Prayer and study will reveal God's will."

"Yes," I agree. "Prayer and study. I recommend particularly the study of the marriage vows we took. 'For better or worse, in sickness and in health, until death do us part.' They are quite clear."

His face flushes red, and for a moment I see the temper that has grown worse with age, the rage of a man who is never contradicted. But he controls it, barely.

"I bid you goodnight, madam," he says stiffly.

"May God grant you peaceful sleep, my lord," I reply. "And truthful dreams."

He leaves without another word, but his Bible remains on my table. I wait until his footsteps fade before I pick it up. His finger has left a faint smudge on the page, underlining the passage in Leviticus. But I turn to other pages, other truths.

Matthew 19:6: "What therefore God hath joined together, let not man put asunder."

Mark 10:9: "What God has united, man must not divide."

Ephesians 5:25: "Husbands, love your wives, even as Christ also loved the church, and gave himself for it."

The Bible is full of commandments about marriage, about constancy, about faith. But Henry has found the one verse that seems to support what he wants, and he clings to it like a drowning man to driftwood.

I know what this is really about. Anne Boleyn has refused to follow her sister's path, refused to be used and discarded. She holds herself apart, tantalizingly unavailable, driving him mad with desire. And someone—perhaps Anne herself, perhaps her ambitious family, perhaps one of the reformist theologians who cluster around the court like crows—has whispered this poison in his ear.

You are not truly married. Your conscience should trouble you. God himself has shown his displeasure. You are free to take another wife, one who can give you sons.

This is not piety. This is an excuse, a heresy fed to him by his flatterers and by that dark-eyed girl who dares to aim for my crown. This is her poison, whispered in his ear at night, flattering his intellect while she denies him her body, stoking his fears while she stokes his desire.

I close the Bible and hold it against my chest. This book, which should be our salvation, has become a weapon turned against me.

But I know Scripture too. My mother insisted on my education in theology as much as in languages and law. I can match him verse for verse, interpretation for interpretation.

More importantly, I have something he does not—the absolute certainty that I am right. Our marriage is valid. Our vows are sacred. What God has joined, neither man nor king can tear asunder.

He is not attacking me. He is attacking God's holy sacrament. And I must be God's defender.

I kneel at my prie-dieu, the Bible still clutched against my chest, and I pray. Not for Henry to desire me again—that ship has sailed. Not for my womb to quicken—that miracle will not come again. But for strength. For wisdom. For the courage to stand against a king's will armed only with truth.

"Holy Mother," I whisper to the small statue of the Virgin that has traveled with me from Spain, "you who knew sorrow, who watched your son betrayed by those he loved, help me bear this betrayal. Help me stand firm when all the world would have me yield."

Outside my window, I hear the sounds of the palace settling for the night. Somewhere, Henry lies awake, wrestling with his conscience—or what he calls his conscience. Somewhere, Anne Boleyn smiles in the darkness, knowing her poison works its way through his veins.

And here I kneel, Katherine of Aragon, Queen of England, suddenly understanding that I am no longer a wife defending her marriage.

I am a queen defending her throne.

The battle has begun, fought not with swords but with Scripture, not with armies but with arguments. And I will not yield. Not to Henry's manufactured conscience, not to Anne Boleyn's ambition, not to all the theologians and courtiers who would see me erased.

I am the daughter of Isabella of Castile, who conquered kingdoms.

I am the wife of Henry VIII, anointed and crowned.

I am the mother of Mary, Princess of England.

And I will not go quietly into the night of annulment and abandonment.

If Henry wants to end our marriage, he will have to tear down heaven itself to do it.

CHAPTER 15

THE POISONED TEXT

I cannot sleep. The King's words echo in the silence of my chamber, blasphemous and terrible, twisting Scripture into a weapon against our sacred union. I rise from my bed, wrapping a fur-lined robe around my shoulders—even in May, these English nights carry a chill that has settled permanently in my bones. My ladies sleep in the antechamber, their soft breathing a counterpoint to my racing thoughts.

I need answers. I need to understand the depth of this heresy that has infected my husband's mind. The palace is quiet as I make my way to the library, my slippered feet silent on the cold stones. The guards bow but do not question—I am still Queen, still free to walk where I will in what remains my home.

The library at Greenwich is not as grand as the one at Richmond, but it serves. Moonlight streams through tall windows, casting silver light across the reading tables where Henry often studies. His desk draws me like a lodestone—perhaps understanding his mind will help me fight this battle.

On his desk, where he so often labors over state papers and correspondence, lies a collection of theological tracts and legal arguments. My hands tremble slightly as I pick up the first document. The script is that of a scholar, the Latin dense and academic, but I was trained by the finest tutors in Christendom. I can read this as well as any churchman.

"A Treatise on the Invalidity of Papal Dispensations in Matters of Divine Law"

The title alone makes my blood run cold. I read on, my horror growing with every carefully constructed argument. This is not a simple document but a fortress of logic built on foundations of sand. The author argues that even the Holy Father cannot set aside divine law as written in Leviticus, that the papal dispensation for my marriage to Henry was therefore invalid, that we have lived in sin these eighteen years.

Another document: *"Whether It Be Lawful for a Man to Marry His Brother's Widow"*

And another: *"The King's Secret Matter: A Question of Conscience"*

Stack upon stack of them, some in English, some in Latin, some in French. All arguing the same poisonous thesis: that our marriage is an abomination, that God's displeasure is manifest in our lack of male heirs, that the King not only may but must set me aside for the good of his soul and his realm.

This is not a passing scruple, a sudden fit of piety born of too much prayer and fasting. This is a campaign, carefully orchestrated, meticulously planned. He is gathering scholars, lawyers, theologians—men who are willing to twist Scripture to serve his will. Each document is a brick in the wall he is building to imprison me, to bury our marriage beneath the weight of false scholarship.

I sink into his chair, the leather cold beneath me, and continue reading. Some of the authors I recognize—Dr. Wakefield, who once praised our marriage as blessed by God, now argues it is cursed. Bishop Fox, who performed our coronation, now questions whether it was valid. These men who smiled at me, who took my gold and ate at my table, now sharpen their quills against me like assassins' blades.

But it is the marginalia that reveals the most. Henry's own hand has annotated these texts, his distinctive scrawl filling the margins with notes and questions. Here, beside a passage about the invalidity of the marriage, he has written: "A.B. says this is the heart of the matter."

A.B. Anne Boleyn.

So this is her work. I see her hand in it now, her ambition dressed in theological robes. She is not content to be a royal mistress, a passing fancy. She whispers this poison in his ear at night, flattering his intellect, stoking his fears, and dressing his lust in the robes of religious duty.

"Your conscience troubles you," she likely purrs. "As it should, my lord. You are too godly a prince to live in sin."

"But the Pope—" he might protest, still clinging to some shred of orthodoxy.

"The Pope is far away in Rome," she would reply, those dark eyes wide with feigned innocence. "But God sees all. God knows the truth of your suffering."

I can picture it so clearly it makes me sick. She has convinced him that his desire for her is actually God's will, that adultery would be obedience, that breaking sacred vows would be keeping faith.

A sound in the corridor startles me. I should leave, return to my chambers before I am discovered. But I cannot stop reading. Here is a letter from the University of Paris, arguing that Leviticus supersedes Deuteronomy. Here is an opinion from Cambridge scholars, suggesting that the papal dispensation exceeded the Pope's authority.

Page after page of poison, each drop carefully distilled to eat away at the foundations of our marriage.

At the bottom of the pile, I find something that stops my heart. It is a draft letter in Henry's hand, addressed to Pope Clement VII. He is asking His Holiness to examine the validity of our marriage, to convene a court to determine whether we have lived in sin these many years.

The letter is not yet sealed, not yet sent, but its existence tells me everything. This is no longer a matter of private conscience. Henry intends to make our marriage a public trial, to drag our most intimate failures before the world, to humiliate me in the eyes of all Christendom.

I set the letter down carefully, exactly as I found it. My mind races through the implications. If the Pope agrees to try the case, it will not be decided on theology alone. Politics will play its part. My nephew, the Emperor Charles V, is the most powerful monarch in Europe. The Pope will not lightly offend him by declaring his aunt's marriage invalid.

But Henry has never been denied anything he truly wants. And he wants Anne Boleyn with a fever that has burned away reason, faith, even common sense.

"Your Majesty?"

I spin around to find Thomas More standing in the doorway, a candle in his hand casting shadows across his intelligent face. Of all Henry's councilors, I have always respected More the most—a true scholar, a man of genuine faith, a friend who dares tell Henry truths he does not wish to hear.

"Sir Thomas," I say, rising from Henry's chair with as much dignity as I can muster. "I could not sleep. I came seeking... comfort in books."

His eyes take in the documents spread across the desk, and I see understanding dawn in them. His face, always serious, becomes grave.

"Your Majesty," he says carefully, "these are dangerous waters."

"I did not choose to sail them," I reply. "But I find myself adrift nonetheless."

He enters the room fully, closing the door behind him. For a moment, we stand in silence, two souls who understand that the world is about to change in ways neither of us can fully foresee.

"The King seeks opinions," he says finally. "He has asked me for mine."

"And what will you tell him?"

More looks out the window at the night sky, where clouds obscure the stars. "I will tell him that marriage is a sacrament instituted by

Christ himself. That what God has joined, man cannot separate. That conscience must be formed by the Church's teaching, not reformed to suit our desires."

"He will not thank you for such counsel."

"No," More agrees with a sad smile. "He will not. But I took an oath as his councilor to serve his soul as well as his crown. I cannot tell him his sin is virtue, no matter how much he wishes it were so."

"Others have proven more... flexible," I say, gesturing to the pile of documents.

"Others have families to feed, ambitions to serve, fears to calm," More replies. "I do not judge them too harshly. It takes great courage to tell a king he is wrong. Most men do not possess such courage."

"Do I?" I ask, the question escaping before I can stop it.

More looks at me then with such compassion that tears spring to my eyes. "Your Majesty has more courage in her smallest finger than most men have in their entire bodies. You are the daughter of Isabella of Castile. You conquered Scots when the King was in France. You have buried children and remained faithful. If anyone can weather this storm, it is you."

"This storm may sink all of England," I say. "If Henry defies the Pope—"

"Then England will be torn from the body of Christ," More finishes. "Yes. I see that danger. As do others. But the King sees only Mistress Boleyn's eyes and believes them to be windows to Heaven rather than doors to Hell."

The crude honesty of it shocks us both. More colors slightly, but does not retract his words.

"You know this matter is not truly about conscience," I say. It is not a question.

"I know that the King has convinced himself it is about conscience," More replies carefully. "Sometimes that is more dangerous than simple lust. A man who sins knowing he sins may repent. A man who calls his sin virtue will defend it to the death."

We stand in silence again, two people watching a tragedy unfold, powerless to prevent it.

"What should I do?" I ask finally.

"Stand firm," More says without hesitation. "You are his true wife. Your daughter is his legitimate heir. Do not let anyone—not the King, not his councilors, not all the scholars in Christendom—convince you otherwise. Truth does not become false simply because power declares it so."

"Truth without power is mere words," I say bitterly.

"Truth with faith is salvation," he counters. "Your Majesty's faith has sustained you through worse trials than this."

Has it? I have lost children, yes. I have endured poverty and humiliation. But I have never before had to fight for the very foundation of my identity, for the validity of my entire adult life.

"I should return to my chambers," I say, suddenly exhausted.

"As should I," More agrees. "But Your Majesty... be careful. The King's passion has made him dangerous. He will brook no opposition to his will in this matter."

"He is my husband," I say. "He would not harm me."

More's silence is answer enough. The Henry we knew, the golden prince who rescued me from poverty, who crowned me with such joy—that man might not harm me. But this new Henry, this king drunk on his own power and Anne Boleyn's promises, is capable of anything.

I leave the library, my mind full of poisoned texts and bitter truths. As I walk back to my chambers, I pass the gallery where Anne Boleyn has her rooms. No light shows beneath her door, but I know she does not sleep. She lies awake planning, scheming, weaving her web ever tighter around my husband's soul.

This is no longer just a matter of the heart, a husband's infidelity to be endured with prayer and patience. This is a battle for the soul of the king and his kingdom. He is not merely seeking to set me aside; he is seeking to rewrite the law of God itself.

And in this battle, I am not just a wife fighting for her marriage. I am a queen fighting for the true faith against a rising tide of heresy.

The poisoned texts on Henry's desk are weapons in a war I never chose to fight. But fight I must, armed with my own knowledge, my own faith, my own implacable will.

Tomorrow, Henry will continue to gather his false scholars and corrupt theologians. Anne Boleyn will continue to whisper her poison in his ear. The court will continue to watch and whisper and choose sides.

But tonight, I know the truth: This is not about conscience. This is about conquest. Anne Boleyn seeks to conquer my throne, and Henry seeks to conquer the very laws of God.

They will find that Katherine of Aragon does not surrender easily. The battle for my marriage, my crown, and my soul has truly begun.

Chapter 16
The Cardinal's Plea

Cardinal Wolsey is announced on a humid afternoon in July, the air thick with the promise of thunder that will not come. He enters my audience chamber with his usual theatrical flourish, scarlet robes sweeping the floor like spilled blood, his cardinal's cap sitting on his large head like a crown he believes he deserves. Thomas Wolsey, Lord Chancellor of England, Archbishop of York, Cardinal of the Holy Roman Church—and son of a butcher from Ipswich. He has risen higher than any commoner in England's history, and he never lets anyone forget it, especially not those of us born to the purple.

I receive him seated, forcing him to approach me across the long chamber. It is a small assertion of my status, but necessary. Wolsey has grown so accustomed to power that he sometimes forgets he serves the crown, not the other way around. My ladies withdraw at my gesture, though I know they linger just beyond the doors, ears pressed to the wood.

He bows low, but his eyes are insolent, already calculating, already dismissing me as an obstacle to be removed rather than a queen to be served.

"Your Majesty," he says, his voice unctuous as oil, "I come as your friend and spiritual advisor, concerned for your welfare in these troubled times."

"How kind of Your Grace," I reply, my tone making it clear I find it nothing of the sort. "Though I was not aware my welfare was in question."

He settles himself in a chair without invitation, his bulk making the delicate furniture creak. Everything about him is excessive—his girth, his ambition, his pride. He has built himself palaces grander than the King's own, Hampton Court being the jewel in his collection until Henry's envy forced him to gift it to the crown. Even in his submission, Wolsey found a way to display his wealth.

"Your Majesty must be aware," he begins, steepling his fingers like a schoolmaster about to deliver a lesson, "of the King's troubled conscience regarding your marriage."

"I am aware that the King has been reading Scripture," I reply carefully. "Study of God's word is always commendable in a Christian prince."

"Indeed," Wolsey agrees, though his smile is cold. "And his studies have led him to a terrible conclusion—that your marriage, made in good faith though it was, stands in violation of divine law."

"Cardinal Wolsey," I say, allowing steel to enter my voice, "you yourself pursued the papal dispensation that made our marriage possible. You yourself praised it as a union blessed by God. Have you now discovered you were in error?"

A flash of annoyance crosses his fleshy face. He does not like to be reminded of his past positions, especially when they contradict his current convenience.

"I was younger then," he says smoothly, "less learned in theology. We all grow in wisdom, do we not? And wisdom sometimes requires us to acknowledge painful truths."

"And what truth would you have me acknowledge?"

He leans forward, his voice dropping to a confidential whisper, as if we were conspirators rather than adversaries. "That for the good of the kingdom, for the sake of peace and the succession, Your Majesty might consider a compromise."

"What manner of compromise?"

"You might retire to a nunnery," he suggests, the words falling between us like drops of poison. "Take the veil, dedicate your remaining years to God. It is an honorable path, one taken by many noble ladies. You would retain your title, your dignity, your daughter's legitimacy would be... negotiable."

The audacity of it takes my breath away. He dares to lecture me on sacrifice? This butcher's son, draped in silk bought with simony and corruption? He speaks of the things of Caesar as if they were the things of God, politics dressed in piety's robes.

"Tell me, Your Grace," I say, my voice dangerously quiet, "when you take your cardinal's oath, did you swear to uphold the sacrament of marriage or to dissolve it at a king's whim?"

"I swore to serve the Church," he replies stiffly.

"And yet you serve only the King's desires," I counter. "Or perhaps your own. Tell me, what has Henry promised you? The papacy itself? Is that the price of my marriage?"

His face flushes purple, and for a moment I think he might suffer an apoplexy here in my chamber. "Your Majesty goes too far—"

"I go exactly as far as necessary," I interrupt, rising from my chair. He is forced to stand as well, his heavy breathing audible in the sudden silence. "You come here speaking of compromise, of dignity, of honor. But what you really offer is an abomination. You ask me to declare my sacred marriage a sin, my daughter a bastard, and my life a lie."

"I ask you to be reasonable—"

"You ask me to be weak!" The words burst from me with such force that he actually steps back. "You think because I am a woman, because I am aging, because I have failed to produce sons, that I will simply disappear at your command. You forget who I am."

I move closer to him, close enough to smell the perfume he uses to mask the sweat of his ambition. "I am the daughter of Isabella of Castile, who broke the power of nobles greater than you. I am the Queen of England, anointed with holy oil. I am the King's true wife, joined to him by God Himself. You may show yourself out, Lord Cardinal."

"Your Majesty," he tries again, his tone now harder, more threatening, "you must understand the alternative. If you do not cooperate, the King will pursue an annulment through the courts. The process will be... public. Humiliating. Every detail of your marriage, your... failures... will be examined. Is that what you want? For all of Europe to discuss your barren womb?"

The cruelty of it is breathtaking. But cruelty from Wolsey does not surprise me. This is a man who has destroyed anyone who stood in his path—the Duke of Buckingham executed on trumped-up charges, lesser nobles ruined by his tax policies, honest churchmen silenced or exiled.

"Let them examine," I say, my chin raised in defiance. "Let the whole world see. They will find a true marriage, valid in the eyes of God and man. They will find a wife who has been faithful, obedient, and loving for eighteen years. And they will find a king who seeks to break sacred vows for the sake of a dark-eyed witch who has bewitched him."

"You should not speak so of Mistress Boleyn," Wolsey warns.

"Why? Does she frighten you too, Your Grace? The butcher's son and the minor gentleman's daughter, conspiring to bring down a queen. What a pair you make."

His face is now nearly purple with rage, but he controls himself. He is, above all things, a survivor, and he knows that losing his temper here gains him nothing.

"I came in friendship," he says coldly. "I leave in sorrow. Your Majesty has chosen a difficult path."

"I have chosen the only path," I correct. "The path of truth."

He bows, stiffly, minimally, the courtesy of an enemy rather than a subject. "We shall see, Your Majesty, whether truth without power can stand against power without truth."

"We shall see," I agree, "whether a cardinal remembers his God when his king demands he forget."

He leaves without another word, his scarlet robes swishing against the floor like a serpent's retreat. I remain standing until I hear his footsteps fade, then sink into my chair, suddenly exhausted.

Lady Willoughby enters moments later, her face pale with concern. "Your Majesty, we heard raised voices..."

"The Cardinal came to threaten me," I say simply. "He will not be the last."

"What will you do?"

I look at her, this good English lady who has served me faithfully despite the danger it now poses to associate with me. "What I have always done. Endure. Resist. Survive."

"But if the King truly means to pursue this annulment..."

"Then I will fight," I say firmly. "In the courts, in the churches, in the streets if necessary. I will not go quietly into a nunnery. I will not abandon my daughter to bastardry. I will not let that Boleyn woman steal what God has given me."

That evening, I write to my nephew, Emperor Charles V. The letter is coded, hidden in what appears to be a simple family correspondence, but the message is clear: I need his support. Henry seeks to cast me aside. The Cardinal has abandoned justice for ambition. I am alone, save for God and the truth.

As I seal the letter with wax and my signet ring—the pomegranate of Granada intertwined with the Tudor rose—I think of Wolsey's parting words. Truth without power against power without truth. He meant it as a taunt, a declaration of my weakness.

But he forgets that truth has its own power. Every lie Henry tells himself about our marriage, every false scholar he recruits, every bribe Wolsey pays—they are all building on sand. And when the storm comes, as it must, their edifice of lies will collapse.

I may be the daughter of Isabella, but I am also the daughter of the Church. And the Church has stood for fifteen hundred years against kings and emperors who thought their will superseded God's law. Henry and Wolsey and Anne Boleyn are not the first to challenge the sacraments.

They will not be the first to succeed.

The thunder that has threatened all day finally breaks as night falls, rain lashing against the windows like tears from an angry heaven. I kneel at my prie-dieu and pray, not for the storm to pass but for the strength to weather it.

"My Lord Cardinal," I murmur to the crucifix, thinking of Wolsey's bloated pride, "you speak of the laws of men and the needs of kings. I speak of a vow made before Almighty God. My marriage was made in God's eyes. Only He may put it asunder."

The thunder rumbles again, as if in agreement.

Tomorrow, Wolsey will whisper his poison in Henry's ear. Tomorrow, new plots will be hatched, new pressures applied. Tomorrow, the battle continues.

But tonight, I have won a small victory. I have looked corruption in the face and not blinked. I have been offered the easy path and chosen the right one.

I am still Queen. I am still wife. I am still mother.

And I will remain so until God Himself says otherwise. Not Cardinal Wolsey. Not King Henry. Not Anne Boleyn. God alone.

Chapter 17

A Court of Whispers

The world shrinks with each passing day. The palaces that were once my home—Greenwich, Windsor, Richmond—now feel alien and hostile, as if the very stones have turned against me. I walk through galleries where I once presided as undisputed queen, and I feel the eyes upon me, watching, calculating, choosing sides in a war that has not yet been declared but whose drums beat louder with each sunrise.

This morning, I make my way to the chapel for Mass, my Spanish ladies trailing behind me like a small, dark flock of loyal birds. We move through the great gallery at Windsor, our footsteps echoing in the vast space. Two English ladies-in-waiting, girls I have known for years, stand near a window embrasure, their heads bent together in conversation. Lady Anne Parr and Lady Elizabeth Somerset—young women I have favored, whose marriages I helped arrange, whose children I have held.

They fall silent as I approach, dropping into deep curtseys, their eyes fixed firmly on the floor. The silence is more eloquent than any words—they cannot even meet my gaze.

"Good morning, ladies," I say, my voice deliberately warm.

"Your Majesty," they murmur in unison, but they do not raise their heads until I have passed.

As I continue down the gallery, I hear the whispers resume behind me, urgent and excited. They are choosing sides, and few are choosing mine. Their futures depend on the King's favor, and the King's favor now shines only on the Boleyn girl.

At Mass, my usual place remains reserved—the Queen's closet, elevated and separate, where I can observe the service while being observed myself. But the space around me has grown. Where once ladies would compete for the honor of kneeling near me, now there is a careful distance, as if my misfortune might be contagious.

The priest, Father William, reads the Gospel with trembling hands. He has served this chapel for ten years, has heard my confessions, has placed the Host on my tongue countless times. But today he will not look at me directly, his eyes sliding past as if I were already a ghost.

Only my Spanish ladies remain constant—Doña María de Salinas, who came with me from Spain twenty-six years ago; Lady Willoughby, English-born but Spanish in her loyalty; and a handful of others who value truth over convenience. We are a small island of constancy in a sea of shifting allegiances.

After Mass, I hold my usual public audience in the presence chamber. Once, this room would be crowded with petitioners, ladies seeking positions, merchants hoping for royal patronage. Today, there are perhaps a dozen souls, and half of those are here only because protocol demands it.

But there is one unexpected visitor. Lady Margaret Pole enters, her bearing as upright as ever despite her advancing years. She is of royal blood herself—the daughter of the Duke of Clarence, niece to Edward IV and Richard III. She has survived the Wars of the Roses, the fall of her family, the rise of the Tudors. She knows what it is to navigate dangerous waters.

"Your Majesty," she says, curtseying with the perfect balance of respect and dignity.

"Lady Margaret," I reply warmly. "You honor us with your presence."

She approaches, and I see others watching, noting that the Countess of Salisbury still pays court to the Queen. It is a small victory, but I have learned to treasure small victories.

"I come to assure Your Majesty," she says, loud enough for others to hear, "of my continued loyalty and that of my family. Truth does not become false simply because fashion favors lies."

The words are bold, dangerous even. To declare loyalty to me now is to risk the King's displeasure. But Margaret Pole has Plantagenet blood in her veins—she does not bend easily to Tudor whims.

"Your loyalty has never been in question," I reply. "Would that all English nobles possessed your courage."

A small cough draws my attention. Thomas Cromwell stands in the doorway, a man who has risen from even humbler beginnings than Wolsey to become the King's secretary. He is all sharp angles and sharper intelligence, with eyes that miss nothing and reveal less.

"Master Cromwell," I acknowledge coolly. "Have you business with us?"

"I merely wished to pay my respects to Your Majesty," he says with a bow that is precisely calibrated—respectful enough to avoid insult, shallow enough to suggest diminished status.

"How thoughtful," I reply. "And how is your master, the Cardinal?"

"His Grace is much occupied with the King's Great Matter," Cromwell replies, and I notice he does not call it by its proper name—the King's Secret Matter. It is secret no longer. All of Europe knows that Henry VIII seeks to put aside his wife.

"Indeed," I say. "We trust his conscience guides him truly."

Cromwell's thin lips twitch in what might be a smile. "Conscience is a luxury few can afford, Your Majesty. Most of us must make do with survival."

The honesty of it is surprising and somehow refreshing. At least Cromwell does not pretend to piety like his master.

After he leaves, Lady Margaret leans closer. "That one bears watching," she warns. "He is more dangerous than Wolsey because he has no pretensions to virtue. He will do whatever needs doing without troubling himself about right or wrong."

"They multiply," I observe bitterly, "these men who would sell their souls for advancement."

"They see which way the wind blows," Margaret replies. "But winds can change, Your Majesty. They can change suddenly and with devastating force."

That afternoon, I return to my chambers to find them subtly altered. Nothing dramatic, nothing that could be called an insult, but changes nonetheless. The tapestry depicting my coronation has been replaced with one showing the judgment of Solomon—a none-too-subtle message about wise kings making difficult decisions. Several of my ladies' belongings have been moved, their rooms reassigned to newcomers I don't recognize.

"Who ordered these changes?" I demand of the chamberlain.

He fidgets, unable to meet my eyes. "Orders from above, Your Majesty. To make room for new appointments to the household."

"Whose household?"

He mumbles something unintelligible and flees. But I know the answer. Anne Boleyn is building her own court, a shadow court that grows larger and more powerful every day, while mine dwindles like snow in spring.

That evening, I take my supper in my chambers rather than face the great hall where I would have to see her presiding at the King's side—not on the throne, not yet, but close enough that everyone understands the message. My food tastes of ashes, though my cook has prepared all my favorite dishes, trying in his small way to provide comfort.

María de Salinas sits with me, working on her embroidery while I pick at my food. We have known each other since we were girls in Spain, and she reads my moods like a familiar book.

"The Emperor will not allow this," she says quietly. "Your nephew has the Pope's ear. He will protect you."

"Charles has his own troubles," I reply. "The Turks press his eastern borders. The German princes rebel against his authority. He cannot fight Henry for my sake."

"Then what will you do?"

I set down my knife, my appetite completely gone. "What choice do I have? I am a ghost at their feast. They see me, they bow, but they look through me. My husband's court has become a web of whispers, and I am the fly they are all waiting to see devoured."

"You still have supporters," María insists. "Bishop Fisher, Thomas More, the common people—"

"Fisher is one voice against many. More is careful not to speak too boldly. And the common people cannot storm the palace to defend my marriage."

A knock at the door interrupts us. A page enters, bearing a letter on a silver salver. The seal is the King's, and my heart sinks. What new humiliation does he devise now?

I break the seal and read. It is brief, formally worded, but its message is clear. I am commanded to appear before a special legatine court to be convened at Blackfriars to examine the validity of our marriage. Cardinals Wolsey and Campeggio will preside. The King himself will appear as petitioner.

So. It has come to this. Not a private matter of conscience but a public trial. My marriage, my life, my very identity to be dissected before an audience like a corpse in an anatomy theater.

I must trust no one. Only my Spanish ladies, whose loyalty is to me and to the honor of our homeland. Only Eustace Chapuys, the

Emperor's new ambassador, a man of integrity and a lifeline to my nephew. And only God, who sees all and judges truly even when earthly judges are corrupted.

That night, I kneel in my private chapel, a small space that has become my refuge. The altar is simple—a crucifix, two candles, a painting of the Virgin that traveled with me from Spain. But even here, the emptiness is a reproach. Once this chapel would be full of ladies joining me in prayer. Now there are only a handful of faithful souls.

"Holy Mother," I pray, "you who knew sorrow, who watched your son betrayed by those he loved, give me strength. The world becomes smaller each day. Friends become strangers. Protectors become persecutors. But I will not yield. I will not break. I will not go quietly into the oblivion they have prepared for me."

A sound makes me turn. In the doorway stands Jane Seymour, one of my ladies, a quiet girl from Wiltshire with a plain face but kind eyes. She hesitates, uncertain.

"You may enter, Jane," I say gently.

She comes forward and kneels beside me. "Your Majesty," she whispers, "I wanted you to know... not all of us have forgotten our duty to you."

"That is dangerous talk, Jane. Your family will not thank you for loyalty to a falling queen."

"Your Majesty is not falling," she says with surprising firmness. "You are being pushed. There is a difference."

I look at this unremarkable girl and see unexpected steel. "You are kind, Jane. But you must be careful. The King's anger—"

"The King is bewitched," she says bluntly. "Everyone knows it. The Boleyn woman has used French arts to cloud his mind. But spells can be broken. Truth endures."

Her faith is touching, if naive. Anne Boleyn's spell is not witchcraft but something far more potent—youth, availability, and the promise of sons. Against that trinity, what defense does an aging, barren wife possess?

But I do not voice these bitter thoughts. Instead, I place my hand on Jane's head in blessing. "God keep you safe, child. Your loyalty will not be forgotten."

She leaves, and I am alone again with my prayers and my fears. Tomorrow, the court of whispers will continue its work. Allegiances will shift, friends will become strangers, the web will tighten.

But tonight, in this small chapel, I remember who I am. Not the discarded wife they whisper about, not the barren queen they pity or mock, but Katherine of Aragon, daughter of Isabella, Queen of England by right and law and sacred vow.

The whispers will grow louder. The trial will come. Henry will stand before all the world and call our marriage a sin.

But I will answer him. I will speak truth to power, faith to heresy, constancy to betrayal.

And all their whispers will not drown out the voice of righteousness.

Let them whisper. Let them plot. Let them weave their web.

I am no fly to be devoured.

I am the Queen.

And I will not go quietly.

CHAPTER 18

My Daughter's Right

I find refuge from the poisonous atmosphere of court in Mary's chambers at Richmond Palace. Here, at least, is a small island of innocence and warmth in the cold, treacherous sea of the King's Great Matter. My daughter is eleven years old now, small for her age but with a gravity that belongs to someone much older. She has my auburn hair and stubborn chin, but her eyes—those are pure Tudor, small and calculating, seeing everything while revealing little.

She sits at the virginals, practicing a complex piece by Josquin des Prez. Her small fingers move with precise determination across the keys, never missing a note. She does not play for joy—I have rarely seen Mary do anything for pure joy—but with the grim determination of someone who must be perfect because imperfection is not permitted to a princess whose legitimacy is increasingly questioned.

"That was beautiful, *hija mía*," I say when she finishes.

She looks up at me, and for a moment the mask of the accomplished princess slips, revealing the frightened child beneath. "Mother," she asks, her voice barely a whisper, "why is Father angry with you?"

The question is a dagger to my heart. How do I explain this evil to a child? That her own father would make her a bastard to satisfy his lust for another woman? That he would cast aside her mother, his true wife of twenty years, for a black-eyed whore who promises him sons?

I sit beside her on the bench, taking her small hands in mine. They are cold, always cold, as if the chill of this uncertain time has settled in her bones.

"Your father is troubled," I say carefully. "Sometimes grown people become confused about things that should be simple. But his confusion does not change the truth."

"What truth, Mother?"

"That you are the legitimate Princess of England. That I am the true Queen. That our family, though tested, remains valid in the eyes of God."

She considers this with that preternatural seriousness that breaks my heart. "Lady Bryan says there are rumors. That Father means to marry Mistress Boleyn."

Lady Bryan, Mary's governess, should not be repeating court gossip to a child. But then, Mary is no ordinary child. She is a pawn in this terrible game, and perhaps it is better she understands the board.

"People say many things," I reply. "But saying does not make it so. Your father is married to me. That is the law of God and man."

"But if Father says otherwise?"

I look at her face, so earnest and so worried, and I feel my resolve turn from defensive stone to offensive steel. For myself, I might bend. I have endured poverty and humiliation before. I could endure it again. But for this child, the legitimate heir of England, the granddaughter of Isabella of Castile, I will break the world before I yield.

"Then Father would be wrong," I say firmly. "Even kings can be wrong, Mary. Even fathers. Your right to the throne comes not from his whim but from your legitimate birth. You are my daughter, born in lawful wedlock, recognized by all of Christendom. No act of Parliament, no corrupt court, no amount of wishful thinking can change that."

"The Boleyn woman hates me," Mary says suddenly. "When she looks at me, her eyes are cold."

Of course she hates Mary. My daughter is living proof that I am Henry's true wife, that our marriage was real and consummated and fruitful. Every breath Mary takes is a reproach to Anne Boleyn's ambitions.

"You must be careful around her," I warn. "Smile, be courteous, but never trust her. Never be alone with her. And never, ever, acknowledge any title for her save Mistress Boleyn."

"Yes, Mother."

I pull her close, feeling how thin she has become. The strain of this uncertainty is wearing on her. She eats little, sleeps less, studies constantly as if perfect Latin and flawless deportment could somehow secure her position.

"Listen to me, Mary," I say, speaking in Spanish now, the language of secrets and promises. "Dark days are coming. Your father may say terrible things, do terrible things. The court may turn against us. We may be separated."

Her body tenses against mine. "No, Mother—"

"Listen," I insist. "If we are separated, you must remember: you are the true Princess of England. Whatever they call you, whatever they force you to say or sign, in your heart you must know the truth. You are legitimate. You are royal. You are my daughter and your father's only true child."

"What about Fitzroy?" she asks, naming Henry's acknowledged bastard by Elizabeth Blount.

"A bastard, however acknowledged, cannot inherit the throne," I say firmly. "And any children the Boleyn woman might bear would be bastards too, for I am your father's only lawful wife."

She nods, absorbing this like she absorbs everything—seriously, completely, filing it away in that formidable mind of hers.

"I have been learning my history," she says. "About other disputed successions. The Wars of the Roses began because of questions of legitimacy."

My brilliant, tragic daughter. Eleven years old and already understanding that her very existence might spark civil war.

"Which is why you must be strong," I tell her. "England needs you to be strong. You may be the only legitimate Tudor heir."

"I will be strong, Mother. I will be like grandmother Isabella."

"*Sí, mi amor*. Like Isabella. But also like Katherine. Your own person, shaped by these trials into something even stronger than those who came before."

A knock at the door interrupts us. Lady Shelton enters, one of the Boleyn faction, recently appointed to Mary's household over my objections. Her curtsey to me is perfunctory, barely respectful.

"Your Majesty," she says, though the title sounds like mockery in her mouth, "His Majesty requires the Princess's presence in the great hall."

My blood runs cold. Henry has not summoned Mary to his presence in months. What new cruelty does he devise now?

"I will accompany her," I say.

"His Majesty's instructions were for the Princess alone," Lady Shelton replies with barely concealed satisfaction.

I want to refuse, to fight, to demand my right as a mother to protect my child. But I see Mary straighten her small shoulders, lifting her chin in a gesture she has learned from me.

"I will go, Mother," she says with dignity beyond her years. "I am not afraid."

But I see the tremor in her hands as she smooths her skirts. I kiss her forehead, a blessing and a farewell.

"Remember who you are," I whisper.

She nods and follows Lady Shelton out, her small figure dwarfed by the grand doorway but her bearing that of a queen. I wait, pacing her chambers like a caged lioness, until she returns an hour later.

Her face is pale but composed. Lady Shelton does not enter with her, and Mary closes the door firmly before speaking.

"Father asked me about my studies," she says carefully. "He examined my Latin, my French. He seemed... pleased."

But there is more. I wait.

"She was there," Mary continues. "The Boleyn woman. Sitting beside him where you should sit. Wearing jewels I recognize as yours."

My jewels. The ones I was forced to return to the royal treasury, now decorating that creature's neck. The symbolism is crude but effective.

"And?"

"Father asked me if I would welcome a brother." Mary's voice is steady, but I see the hurt in her eyes. "I said I would welcome any child Your Majesty might bear. He said the child would not be yours."

"What did you answer?"

"I said nothing. I curtsied and asked to be excused. He... he looked angry. But also sad. As if he wanted me to say something else but didn't know how to ask for it."

My poor daughter, caught between a father who wants her to legitimize his sin and a mother who needs her to stand for truth. No child should bear such weight.

"You did well," I assure her. "Perfect, in fact. Silence is sometimes the strongest response."

That night, after Mary is asleep, I stand over her bed watching the gentle rise and fall of her chest. In the moonlight, she looks even younger than her eleven years, vulnerable and precious and terribly alone.

She is my jewel, the living proof of my valid marriage, the one perfect fruit of our union. But I know with terrible certainty that she will suffer for that legitimacy. Anne Boleyn will not tolerate a rival to any children she might bear. Henry will pressure Mary to acknowledge his new marriage, to admit her own bastardy, to betray everything I have taught her.

I lean down and whisper in Spanish, a prayer and a promise: "*Hija mía*, you will have to be stronger than any son. You will have to survive things no child should face. But you are my daughter, and Isabella's granddaughter, and you carry in your veins the blood of warriors and saints. They will try to break you, but you will not break. They will try to erase you, but you will endure. And one day, God willing, you will be Queen."

She stirs in her sleep, murmuring something unintelligible. I smooth her hair, noting how it darkens each year, becoming more like mine and less like Henry's. She will not be the golden princess he might have preferred, but she will be something better—a woman of substance, of faith, of implacable will.

Tomorrow, the battle for her legitimacy continues. Letters will be written, arguments made, pressures applied. The King will rage, the Boleyn woman will scheme, the court will whisper.

But tonight, there is just a mother and her daughter, the only fruit of a love that is dying, the living proof that it once lived.

Mary. My jewel. My purpose. My weapon against despair.

If I save nothing else from the wreckage of my marriage, I will save her.

This I swear on my mother's grave, on my own salvation, on the sacred vows that Henry seeks to break:

Mary will survive this. She will remain legitimate in the eyes of God if not of man. And she will remember, always, that she was loved completely and fiercely by a mother who would face Hell itself to protect her.

The moonlight shifts, casting shadows across the room. In them, I can almost see the future—dark, uncertain, full of trials I cannot prevent.

But also, perhaps, ultimate triumph. For Mary has something Anne Boleyn's children will never have: the unbending certainty of her legitimacy, the steel of constancy in her spine, and the knowledge that she is the daughter of Katherine of Aragon, who never yielded.

That may be enough. It will have to be enough.

For if it is not, then all is lost—not just my crown, but England's soul.

Chapter 19
The Emperor's Ear

The hour is late, past midnight, when Eustace Chapuys is shown into a small, hidden room in the oldest part of Greenwich Palace. This chamber, known only to a few, has witnessed secrets since Plantagenet times. Now it serves as my confessional, though the man I meet is not a priest but the Emperor's ambassador, my nephew's voice in this hostile court.

A single trusted Spanish lady, María de Salinas, stands guard at the door. She will cough twice if anyone approaches. The necessity of such precautions would have been unthinkable even a year ago. Now, I am watched constantly, my letters opened, my visitors reported. I am Queen in name but prisoner in fact.

Chapuys bows low, his face grave in the candlelight. He is a small man, neat and precise, with the sharp intelligence of a trained lawyer and the careful manner of a career diplomat. But beneath that cautious exterior beats a heart loyal to the Emperor and, through him, to me.

"Your Majesty," he says, his voice low but fervent, "I bring greetings from His Imperial Majesty, your nephew. He is deeply concerned for your welfare."

"My nephew's concern is appreciated," I reply, "though concern without action is merely sentiment."

Chapuys winces slightly at my directness, but these midnight meetings are too dangerous for diplomatic niceties. "The Emperor is not inactive, Your Majesty. He presses the Pope constantly on your behalf. His armies in Italy ensure His Holiness remembers who his true protectors are."

"And yet the Pope has allowed this travesty of a trial," I counter. "Cardinals sit in judgment of my marriage as if twenty years of sacrament could be undone by lawyers' tricks."

"The trial is a sham," Chapuys agrees. "Cardinal Campeggio has secret instructions from Rome to delay, to prevent any judgment. The Pope will not rule against you while the Emperor's armies are at his doorstep."

"Delay is not victory," I say sharply. "While Rome hesitates, Anne Boleyn strengthens her hold on the King. She has convinced him that his conscience, not the Pope's authority, should guide him. This is not merely about my marriage anymore, Excellency. This is about England's soul."

Chapuys leans forward, his lawyer's mind engaging with the larger implications. "You believe the King would break with Rome?"

"I know he would," I reply with grim certainty. "He has already written theological arguments claiming that no Pope can dispense with divine law. He surrounds himself with reformers and heretics who whisper that he could be Supreme Head of the Church in England. The Boleyn woman encourages these thoughts—she knows it is the only way she can have my crown."

I see the understanding dawn in his eyes. He is a diplomat, trained in the art of compromise and negotiation. He does not yet understand the nature of this fight.

"You must make my nephew understand," I continue, my voice urgent. "This is not a domestic squabble between husband and wife. It is not a simple matter of succession. This is a challenge to the authority of the Holy Father in Rome. It is a challenge to the unity of Christendom itself. If Henry is allowed to defy the Pope and cast me aside, then no sacrament is safe. No royal marriage in Europe is secure. It is an attack on the very foundations of our world."

Chapuys nods slowly, his fingers steepled in thought. "The implications are indeed grave. If England breaks from Rome..."

"England becomes a rogue nation, a heretic kingdom," I finish. "And other princes, seeing Henry's success, might follow his example. The Emperor's own authority, derived from his position as defender of the faith, would be undermined."

"I will write to His Imperial Majesty immediately," Chapuys promises. "But Your Majesty must understand the Emperor's position is delicate. He faces the Turkish threat in the east, the Lutheran princes in Germany rebel against his authority, the French seek any opportunity to weaken him. He cannot simply invade England to defend your rights."

"I do not ask for invasion," I say. "I ask for pressure. Economic sanctions. Diplomatic isolation. Make Henry understand that casting me aside will cost him more than keeping me."

"And if such pressure fails?"

I look at this careful diplomat, this man of compromises and calculations, and I speak the truth that burns in my heart like sacred fire.

"Then I will fight alone if I must. The King is bewitched," I say bluntly. "Not by witchcraft, though some whisper of it, but by his own pride and lust. He is not himself. This heresy has been fed to him by the woman Boleyn and her faction. They seek to sever England from the body of Christ for their own ambition."

Chapuys produces a small leather pouch from his doublet. "The Emperor sends this, Your Majesty. Not openly, of course, but for your... personal needs."

I open it to find Spanish gold coins, enough to sustain my household for months. It is charity, which stings my pride, but necessity overcomes dignity. Henry has already begun to reduce my income, a slow strangulation meant to force my submission.

"Tell my nephew I am grateful," I say, though the words taste bitter. "Tell him also that gold cannot buy what I truly need—justice."

"Justice may come from unexpected quarters," Chapuys says carefully. "The common people of England love Your Majesty. They call Anne Boleyn 'the concubine' and worse. If the King proceeds with this annulment, there could be... unrest."

"I will not have English blood shed for my cause," I say firmly. "I am Queen of England still. These are my people, even if their King has forgotten his duty to them and to me."

"Your nobility of spirit does you credit, Majesty. But nobility without power is mere gesture."

"You sound like Cardinal Wolsey," I observe coldly.

"Heaven forbid," Chapuys says with a slight smile. "But I am a practical man, Your Majesty. You need allies, leverage, strategies beyond simple resistance."

"What do you suggest?"

"Document everything," he says immediately. "Every conversation, every threat, every violation of your rights. We are building a case not just for the Church courts but for the court of European opinion. The Emperor can use such documentation to rally other monarchs to your cause."

"And what of Mary?" I ask, voicing my deepest fear. "If Henry casts me aside, what becomes of my daughter?"

Chapuys's face darkens. "That is the Emperor's gravest concern. The Princess Mary is his cousin, of royal blood. Any attempt to bastardize her is an insult to the Habsburg family itself. The Emperor will not tolerate it."

"Words," I say bitterly. "All words. Meanwhile, that woman already speaks of the children she will bear, the sons who will displace Mary."

"The Boleyn woman may promise sons, but promises are not births," Chapuys observes. "Your Majesty has proven you can conceive. She has proven only that she can refuse the King's bed until he offers marriage."

"She is cleverer than his other mistresses," I admit grudgingly. "She holds herself apart, making him mad with wanting. She has turned his lust into something he believes is love, even destiny."

"All fevers break, Your Majesty. Even the fever of infatuation."

"But will it break before he breaks England itself?"

We sit in silence for a moment, contemplating the catastrophe that looms. Then Chapuys rises, understanding that our time grows dangerous.

"Your Majesty," he says, bowing again, "you have the heart of your mother, Isabella. She faced the assembled might of the Moorish kingdoms and prevailed. You face a different enemy, but the courage required is the same."

"My mother had armies," I reply. "I have only my faith and my certainty that I am right."

"Sometimes," Chapuys says softly, "that is enough. Truth has its own power, Your Majesty. It may take time to prevail, but it does prevail."

He is about to leave when I stop him with a gesture.

"Tell me honestly, Excellency. Does my nephew truly support me, or does he simply use my cause as a diplomatic tool against Henry?"

Chapuys pauses at the door, considering his words carefully. "The Emperor is a practical man, Your Majesty. But he is also a Habsburg, and Habsburgs do not forget family. Your cause serves his interests, yes. But his interests also serve your cause. In this, at least, you are aligned."

It is not the reassurance I hoped for, but it is honest, and I value honesty in this court of lies.

After he leaves, slipping away through the secret passages that honeycomb these ancient walls, I remain in the hidden chamber. The candle burns low, casting dancing shadows that seem like portents of the dark days ahead.

I think of Charles, my nephew, sitting in his palace in Spain or his court in Vienna, moving armies and diplomats like chess pieces across the board of Europe. I am one of those pieces, valuable for my position but expendable if the game requires it.

But I am also my mother's daughter, and Isabella was never anyone's pawn. She made herself a queen through will and faith and implacable determination. I may not have her armies, but I have her blood, her example, her unconquerable spirit.

Tomorrow, Chapuys will dispatch his letters to the Emperor, carefully coded, sent by trusted messengers through circuitous routes. Charles will read them and calculate what my cause is worth in gold, in soldiers, in diplomatic pressure.

But tonight, in this small, secret chamber where English queens have prayed and plotted for centuries, I make my own calculations. Not of power and politics, but of faith and constancy. I count not coins or soldiers but the strength of my conviction, the righteousness of my cause, the power of truth against lies.

The Emperor may be my nephew, but he is not my savior. That role belongs to God alone. Charles can provide gold and diplomatic pressure, but only I can stand before the court and speak truth to power. Only I can show England what constancy means, what faith demands, what honor requires.

The candle gutters and dies, leaving me in darkness. But I am not afraid of the dark. I have lived in it for years now, ever since Henry's love began to cool. I have learned to navigate by faith rather than sight, to find my way by the fixed star of truth rather than the false lights of court favor.

I make my way back to my chambers through the dark passages, my hand trailing along the cold stone walls. Behind me, the secret room returns to its silence, keeping its secrets for another generation of queens who may need a place to plot survival.

Tomorrow, the battle continues. Letters will fly across Europe, gold will change hands, armies will march or threaten to march. The great game of nations will continue, and I will be a piece on that board, moved by hands more powerful than mine.

But I am also a player in my own right, making moves they do not expect, cannot counter. My weapon is not gold or armies but something stronger—the absolute certainty that I am right, that my cause is just, that God Himself stands with me against all the powers of earth that array themselves against me.

Let the Emperor calculate. Let Chapuys negotiate. Let Henry rage and Anne scheme.

I will endure. I will resist. I will prevail.

For I am Katherine of Aragon, and I do not yield.

Chapter 20
The Insult

They come for me in a formal delegation on a grey May morning when the Thames runs high with spring floods. The Duke of Norfolk leads them—Anne Boleyn's own uncle, Thomas Howard, a man whose ambition would sell his soul for a penny's profit. Behind him walks the Duke of Suffolk, Charles Brandon, once my friend, Henry's boon companion who has chosen his master over his conscience. They are accompanied by a phalanx of other lords, men who once knelt before me, now come as executioners of my dignity.

I receive them in my presence chamber at Greenwich, seated in my chair of estate beneath my cloth of state. I will not make this easy for them. They must approach me as supplicants approach a queen, even if they come to unmake me.

"Your Graces," I acknowledge coolly as they bow. Norfolk's bow is perfunctory, barely respectful. Suffolk at least has the grace to look uncomfortable.

"Your Majesty," Norfolk begins, and I hear the slight hesitation before my title, as if he already questions its validity. "We come from the King with a proposal."

"His Majesty has many proposals of late," I observe. "Few of them worthy of consideration."

Norfolk's face flushes, but he continues. "The King, in his great mercy and consideration for your years of service—"

"Service?" I interrupt, my voice sharp as Toledo steel. "I have not served the King. I have been his wife, his queen, the mother of his children. One does not serve in these roles; one lives them, breathes them, bleeds for them."

Suffolk shifts uncomfortably, but Norfolk presses on, his voice hardening. "The King offers you a generous settlement. If you will agree to the annulment, if you will confess that your marriage was invalid from the beginning and retire to a nunnery of your choosing, His Majesty will be... generous."

There it is. The insult wrapped in silk, the dagger presented handle-first as if it were a gift.

"Generous," I repeat, tasting the word like poison. "How generous of the King to offer me the privilege of denying my entire life."

"Your Majesty—" Suffolk begins, but I raise my hand for silence.

"Let me understand this proposal fully," I say, rising from my chair. They must look up at me now, these great lords reduced to supplicants. "The King wishes me to declare that I have lived in sin for twenty years. That I have been not wife but whore. That my daughter Mary is a bastard. That every child I bore and buried was God's punishment for a non-existent crime. Is that the sum of it?"

"The King offers to ensure the Lady Mary is well treated," Norfolk says, and I note how he has already stripped my daughter of her title.

"Well treated," I echo. "As one treats a favored bastard, perhaps? Given some small manor, some insignificant husband, allowed to live in shameful obscurity while the Boleyn woman's spawn inherits what is rightfully hers?"

"Madam, you try our patience—" Norfolk begins, his face purple with rage.

"I try your patience?" My voice rises, filling the chamber with royal authority. "You come to my chambers, into my presence, and ask me to sign my own spiritual death warrant. You ask me to damn my soul with lies to convenience a king's lust. You ask me to betray my daughter, my God, and myself. And you speak to me of patience?"

I move closer to them, close enough to see the sweat on Norfolk's brow, the shame in Suffolk's eyes.

"My lords," I say, my voice now deadly quiet, "you may tell the King that I have received his proposal. You may tell him that I have considered it with all the attention it deserves. And you may tell him this: I am his true wife, married in the sight of God and man. The Pope himself sanctioned our union. I will not defy him, and I will not defy God. If the King wishes to imperil his soul with adultery and heresy, that is his choice. But he will not make me an accomplice to his damnation."

"You speak treason, madam," Norfolk snarls.

"I speak truth, Your Grace. If truth has become treason in England, then England is already lost."

Suffolk steps forward, his voice gentler. "Your Majesty, please consider. The King's mind is set. If you do not accept this offer, he will proceed through the courts. It will be... public. Humiliating.

Every detail of your marriage will be examined, discussed, judged. Is that what you want?"

I look at Suffolk, this man who once danced at my coronation, who named his daughter after me, who now comes as my executioner's assistant.

"What I want," I say slowly, "is for my husband to remember his vows. What I want is for England to remain faithful to Rome. What I want is for my daughter to inherit her rightful place. But since none of these things seem possible, I will settle for keeping my soul intact."

"This is the King's final offer," Norfolk states flatly. "Refuse it at your peril."

"My peril?" I laugh, and the sound is bitter as gall. "What can he do to me that he has not already done? He has taken his love, his presence, his protection. He parades his whore before the court while I am pushed into shadows. He questions my honor, my honesty, my very identity. What more can he take?"

"Your life," Norfolk says quietly, and the threat hangs in the air like a blade.

The chamber falls silent. Even my ladies, listening from the edges of the room, seem to stop breathing.

"If the King wishes to add murder to his list of sins," I say finally, "that is between him and God. But I will not murder myself, spiritually or otherwise, to save him the trouble."

I return to my chair, sitting with deliberate grace. "You may go, my lords. You have your answer."

They stand there for a moment, uncertain. They came expecting tears, hysteria, perhaps a woman's weakness they could exploit. Instead, they found Spanish steel, tempered by suffering but unbroken.

"You will regret this, madam," Norfolk says as they turn to leave.

"I regret many things, Your Grace," I reply. "But standing for truth will never be among them."

They leave, their footsteps echoing through the palace like a retreat. When the door closes behind them, I allow myself one moment of trembling. My ladies rush to me, Maria de Salinas taking my hands, finding them ice cold.

"Your Majesty was magnificent," she whispers.

"I was necessary," I correct. "They sought to break me with insults disguised as mercy. But I am not some merchant's wife to be bought off with gold and promises."

That evening, I learn the full extent of the King's displeasure. My household is to be reduced further. More of my ladies are dismissed, my guard decreased, my income cut to a fraction of what a queen requires. It is a slow strangulation, designed to force me to my knees.

But I have lived through poverty before. Seven years in Durham House taught me how to survive on nothing but pride and faith. I can do it again.

I write that night to Chapuys, encoding my message in the Spanish he reads fluently:

"They came today with the final insult, dressed as an offer. I am to declare myself a whore and my daughter a bastard in exchange for a comfortable cage. I refused. The King will now proceed through the courts, making our private grief a public spectacle. I am prepared. Twenty years of marriage cannot be erased by lawyers' tricks. Truth will prevail, though it cost me everything."

As I seal the letter, I think of the Duke of Norfolk's threat. Would Henry truly go so far? Would he have me killed rather than admit he cannot bend me to his will?

Once, I would have said never. The golden prince who rescued me from poverty, who crowned me with such joy, who wept with me over our dead children—that man would never harm me. But that man is gone, replaced by this stranger who speaks of conscience while planning adultery, who invokes God while defying His church.

This new Henry is capable of anything.

But I am Katherine of Aragon, daughter of Isabella who faced down armies, wife of Henry VIII by true sacrament, mother of Mary, the legitimate heir of England. I have been insulted, threatened, diminished, but I have not been defeated.

Tomorrow, the public trial begins. They will drag my marriage through the mud, question my virginity, debate my worth like merchants haggling over damaged goods. It will be agony.

But I will endure it. I will face their court, their questions, their insults. I will stand before all of England and declare the truth: I am the Queen. I am the wife. I will not go quietly.

The insult they offered today—to buy my acquiescence with false comfort—is the last they will deliver in private. From now on, their attacks must be public, and public attacks can be publicly refuted. They think they have cornered me. They are wrong.

They have freed me.

For now I have nothing left to lose but my life, and I place that in God's hands. Everything else—dignity, honor, truth—I will defend to my last breath.

The battle lines are drawn. The war begins in earnest.

And I will not yield.

CHAPTER 21

THE SUMMONS

It is a quiet afternoon in my chambers at Greenwich, one of those rare moments when the storm seems to pause for breath. I am working on a piece of embroidery with my remaining ladies—a altar cloth depicting the Virgin and Child, each stitch a prayer for strength. The rhythm of the needle through fabric is meditative, almost peaceful. For a blessed hour, I can pretend that nothing has changed, that I am simply the Queen engaged in womanly pursuits.

The illusion shatters with the formal knock at my door.

A court official enters—Sir William Paulet, a man who has served the crown for decades but whose eyes now refuse to meet mine. He carries a rolled parchment heavy with seals, and I know before he speaks what this is.

"Your Majesty," he says, bowing stiffly, his discomfort palpable.

I set aside my needlework with deliberate calm, though my heart begins to race. "Sir William."

He extends the parchment toward me as if it might burn him. "I am commanded to deliver this into Your Majesty's own hands."

I take it, feeling the weight of it—not just the physical weight of parchment and wax, but the weight of what it represents. The great seal of England marks it, along with other seals I recognize: Cardinal Wolsey's, the seal of the Papal Legate, the seal of the ecclesiastical court.

I break the seals and unroll the document. The Latin is dense, legalistic, but the meaning is brutally clear. I am summoned to appear before a special legatine court, to be convened at Blackfriars monastery, to answer the King's petition regarding the validity of our marriage. The date is set: June 18th, 1529.

So. It begins. Not in private chambers with whispered threats and offered bribes, but in public court, before all of London, before all of Christendom. A trial. As if a sacrament can be put on trial. As if twenty-four years of marriage, of shared beds and shared griefs, of children born and lost, can be argued away by lawyers with their dusty books.

"Is there a reply Your Majesty wishes to send?" Sir William asks, clearly desperate to escape.

I look up at him, this man who has eaten at my table, whose wife has served in my household, who now delivers my summons to humiliation as if it were any ordinary correspondence.

"Tell them," I say, my voice steady though my hands tremble slightly, "that I have received their summons."

"Nothing more, Your Majesty?"

"What more is there to say? They have summoned me. I will appear. But not as they expect."

He bows again and retreats hastily, leaving me with the damning document. My ladies cluster around me, their faces pale with concern.

"Your Majesty," María de Salinas ventures, "surely you need not attend. You could send representatives, lawyers—"

"No," I interrupt firmly. "They expect me to hide, to send others to speak for me while I cower in my chambers. But I will face them. I will look Henry in the eye before all the world and make him see what he is doing."

"But the humiliation—" Lady Willoughby begins.

"The humiliation is his, not mine," I reply. "I have nothing to be ashamed of. I was a virgin when I married Henry. Our marriage is valid. Our daughter is legitimate. These are truths that no court can change, no matter how they rule."

I rise from my chair and walk to the window, looking out at the Thames flowing past, carrying its burden of boats and barges, commerce and life continuing as if the world were not about to change.

"They will ask terrible questions," I say quietly. "About my marriage to Arthur, about our wedding night, about the most intimate details of my life with Henry. They will strip me bare before the world, hoping to find some shame that will make me yield."

"It is monstrous," María says fiercely.

"It is desperate," I correct. "Henry knows he has no true grounds for annulment. So he must create them, fabricate them from half-truths and whole lies. But lies spoken in court are still lies. And I will answer them with truth."

That night, I cannot sleep. I kneel in my private chapel, the summons spread before me on the altar like an unholy offering.

The Latin words blur in the candlelight, transforming into older words, sacred words.

"In nomine Patris, et Filii, et Spiritus Sancti..."

I am not afraid. That surprises me. For months, I have dreaded this moment, the formal beginning of the end. But now that it has come, I feel something else: relief. No more waiting. No more uncertainty. The battle is joined.

I think of Christ before Pilate, summoned to answer charges He knew were false, facing a trial whose outcome was predetermined. He did not flee. He did not send others in His place. He stood and spoke truth to power, even knowing it would lead to Calvary.

I am not Christ, but I am a Christian queen, and I will follow His example. I will go to their court. But I will not be a defendant. I will be a witness. A witness for God, for truth, for the sanctity of marriage itself.

The next morning, I summon what remains of my household. They gather in my presence chamber—a pitiful remnant of what a queen's household should be, but loyal souls every one.

"You have heard, I am sure, of the summons," I begin. They nod, their faces grave. "I will attend the trial. But I will not go as a supplicant or a criminal. I will go as your Queen, as England's Queen."

"We will stand with you, Your Majesty," Lady Willoughby declares, and others murmur agreement.

"I know you will," I reply, touched by their loyalty. "But you must understand the danger. To support me now is to defy the King. He will not forget those who stand with me. Your families may suffer. Your fortunes certainly will."

"Your Majesty," says old Lady Pole, Margaret Pole, who has survived so many dangerous reigns, "we have counted the cost. We stand with you not from ignorance but from conviction. Right is right, though all the world say otherwise."

I look at these women, English and Spanish, young and old, who risk everything for principle. "Then we must prepare. They mean this trial to break me. We must ensure it reveals them instead."

Over the following days, I prepare with the same meticulous care I once brought to preparing for war when Henry was in France. I study canon law, though I know it better than most bishops. I review the papal dispensation, though I have memorized every word. I practice my Latin pronunciation, though it has been flawless since childhood.

But most importantly, I pray. Hours upon hours on my knees, not for victory—for I know the court is rigged against me—but for the strength to stand firm, to speak truth, to be the queen God called me to be even if men deny it.

A letter arrives from Bishop Fisher, one of the few churchmen brave enough to support me openly. "Your Majesty," he writes, "remember that you stand not alone. Heaven itself watches this trial. The saints and angels are your true judges, and they have already acquitted you."

Another comes from Thomas More, carefully worded but clear in its support: "Truth has its own authority, Majesty, which no earthly court can overthrow."

But the most unexpected message comes from the common people. As news of the trial spreads, crowds gather outside Greenwich. They do not shout or demonstrate—that would bring the King's guard—but they stand in silent witness, hundreds of them, their faces turned toward my windows.

When I venture out to chapel, they line the path, dropping to their knees as I pass. "God save Your Majesty," they murmur. "God save the true Queen."

Henry must see them from his windows. He must hear their prayers. Does it trouble his conscience, I wonder, to know that his people see through his lies?

The night before the trial, Chapuys comes to me one last time.

"Your Majesty," he says urgently, "the Emperor suggests you might claim illness, avoid the trial altogether. Let it proceed without you, then challenge its legitimacy later."

"And let them paint me as a coward?" I reply. "Let them say I feared to face their questions? No, Excellency. I will attend. I will stand before that court and all the world. I will speak truth even if no one wishes to hear it."

"Your courage is admirable, Majesty, but courage without strategy—"

"Is faith," I interrupt. "I go tomorrow not with strategy but with faith. Faith that truth matters. Faith that God sees all. Faith that history will remember not what the court decides but what actually is."

He bows, accepting my decision. "Then may God go with Your Majesty."

"He always has," I reply. "Even when I walked alone."

That last night before the trial, I do not sleep. I spend it in prayer, in preparation, in gathering every ounce of strength I possess. Tomorrow, I face not just Henry but all the forces arrayed against me—Wolsey's ambition, Anne Boleyn's determination, the court's cowardice, the world's expectation that I will yield.

But I will not yield. I am the daughter of Isabella, who faced the armies of Islam. I am the wife of Henry VIII, truly married whatever he now claims. I am the mother of Mary, legitimate heir to England's throne.

Tomorrow, I will walk into their court with my head high. I will answer their summons not as Katherine the defendant but as Katherine the Queen.

And whatever they decide, whatever lies they tell, whatever verdict they render, I will speak truth.

For truth, in the end, is all I have.

And truth, I believe, is enough.

The summons has been delivered. The trial awaits.

Let them come. I am ready.

CHAPTER 22

THE EVE OF JUDGMENT

The stone floor of my private chapel is cold beneath my knees, as it has been for the past six hours. It is the middle of the night before the trial at Blackfriars, and I have sent even my most faithful ladies away. This vigil is between me and God alone. Tomorrow, the world will watch as my marriage is dissected like a corpse in an anatomy theater, but tonight, I prepare my soul for the ordeal ahead.

My rosary beads, worn smooth from twenty years of handling, pass through my fingers in endless rotation. Each bead is a prayer, a memory, a moment of the life they seek to erase. The first bead: our wedding night, Henry's eyes bright with love and desire. The second: the birth of our son, those fifty-two perfect days before God called him home. The third: standing as regent while Henry fought in France, proving I could be more than a brood mare. On and on, twenty years of marriage reduced to these small spheres of polished wood.

Pater Noster, qui es in caelis... Our Father, who art in heaven...

The Latin comes automatically, but my mind wrestles with deeper questions. Tomorrow, I must stand before men who have already decided my fate. Cardinal Wolsey, that butcher's son in cardinal's robes, who once pursued our marriage with such zeal and now seeks its destruction with equal fervor. Cardinal Campeggio, sent from Rome with secret instructions to delay and obfuscate, a

Italian diplomat more concerned with papal politics than truth. And Henry—my husband, my king, my betrayer—who will sit in judgment of the woman he vowed before God to cherish until death.

My knees ache, sharp pains shooting through them with each slight movement. My back protests the hours of kneeling, muscles cramping and burning. But physical discomfort is nothing compared to the spiritual trial that awaits. Tomorrow, they will ask me about my marriage to Arthur, about those five months in Wales that ended in his death. They will demand to know if I came to Henry's bed a virgin or a wife already used. They will strip bare the most intimate moments of my life, searching for some shame that will justify their predetermined verdict.

I am weak. The admission comes in the darkness, as honest as prayer must be. I am a woman alone in a foreign land that has become hostile to me. My nephew, the Emperor Charles, is far away, fighting his own battles against French aggression and Turkish invasion. He sends letters of support, gold when he can spare it, but no armies will march to defend my marriage. My friends at court have dwindled to a handful—Bishop Fisher, who risks his position daily by supporting me; Thomas More, who walks a careful line between conscience and survival; Lady Margaret Pole, who knows the cost of royal displeasure but stands with me nonetheless.

How can I stand against a king? My own husband, who holds the power of life and death, who has already shown he will destroy anyone who opposes him? The Duke of Buckingham, executed on trumped-up charges of treason. Cardinal Wolsey himself, who even now does not realize that Henry will discard him the moment he becomes inconvenient. What chance does one Spanish woman have against the machinery of English law, English power, English ambition?

But I am not alone. The thought comes like a whisper of warm wind in this cold chapel. You are with me, my Lord. As You were with Daniel in the lions' den, as You were with Susanna falsely accused, as You were with Your own Son standing before Pilate. The innocent have always stood trial before the guilty. Truth has always been judged by lies. This is not new. This is as old as sin itself.

And my mother is with me. I feel Isabella's presence as surely as if she stood beside me, her hand on my shoulder, her voice in my ear. "Hija," she would say, "you come from a line of warriors. We fought the Moors for seven hundred years. We did not yield our faith or our honor to superior numbers then. You will not yield them now."

Her courage flows through my veins. She faced down rebellious nobles who thought a woman could not rule, Moorish armies that outnumbered her forces, even her own husband when he strayed from righteousness. She made herself Queen of Castile through sheer force of will, and she made Spain whole through faith and determination. I am her daughter. I carry her blood, her faith, her implacable will.

I think of tomorrow's trial, and suddenly I see it differently. They expect me to come as a defendant, to answer their charges, to plead my case according to their rules. But what if I refuse? What if I deny their very right to judge what God has joined? What if I speak not to them but to Henry, to history, to God Himself?

I will not prepare a legal defense. That would be to acknowledge their authority over divine sacrament. I will not quote canon law or papal bulls or theological precedents. Those are their weapons, and they have already twisted them to serve their purposes. Instead, I will speak the simple truth of a wife to her husband, of a queen to her people, of a soul to its Creator.

Rising from my knees is agony, every joint protesting the hours of stillness. I move to the small altar where my most precious possessions rest. My mother's cross, carried from Spain, worn smooth by her fingers during her own trials. My wedding ring, which Henry placed on my finger with such joy twenty years ago. A small portrait of Mary, my daughter, my only living child, whose legitimacy hangs in the balance of tomorrow's proceedings.

I pick up the portrait, painted last year when Mary was thirteen. She has my stubborn chin and Henry's sharp intelligence, a combination that will serve her well in the trials ahead. For she too will be tried, my precious daughter. If they succeed in bastardizing me, they bastardize her. If they make me a whore, they make her a bastard. This is not just about my marriage or my crown. This is about her future, her identity, her very soul.

"Be strong, my daughter," I whisper to the painted face. "Whatever tomorrow brings, remember that you are legitimate, you are royal, you are loved. No court can change that truth."

A sound breaks the chapel's silence—the bell tolling matins. Dawn approaches, and with it, my ordeal. I have not slept, but I am not tired. Instead, I feel a strange energy, like a soldier before battle, knowing that the waiting is almost over.

I kneel once more, not in desperation now but in determination. "Lord, I do not ask for victory, for I know their verdict is already decided. I do not ask for mercy from men who have forgotten its meaning. I ask only for the strength to speak truth, the courage to stand firm, the grace to remember that You are my ultimate judge. Let my words tomorrow ring with Your authority. Let my presence shame their corruption. Let my testimony stand as witness not just to my marriage but to the sanctity of all marriage, the authority of Your Church, the truth that no earthly power can overthrow."

The first pale light of dawn filters through the chapel's narrow window. It illuminates the crucifix above the altar, Christ in His agony, betrayed by those He loved, tried by those He came to save, condemned by those who feared the truth He spoke. If the Son of God could endure such injustice, surely I can endure this smaller calvary.

I rise, my decision made. Tomorrow—today now—I will go to their court, but I will not play their game. I will not be their defendant, their victim, their problem to be solved. I will be Katherine of Aragon, Queen of England, wife of Henry VIII, mother of Mary Tudor. I will speak truth to power even if power refuses to hear it.

My ladies are waiting outside the chapel, their faces drawn with worry and lack of sleep. They have kept vigil in their own way, these faithful souls who risk everything by standing with me.

"Your Majesty," María de Salinas says softly, "the dawn has come."

"Yes," I reply, "and with it, clarity. Help me dress. Not in mourning black, but in royal purple. I go to court today not as a widow or a defendant, but as a queen."

They understand immediately. This is not surrender but war, fought with dignity instead of swords, truth instead of armies. As they help me prepare, I think of all the queens who have faced unjust trials—Marie Antoinette before the Revolution, Anne Boleyn whom Henry will one day destroy as he now destroys me, even Christ's own mother watching her son tried and condemned.

We are a sisterhood of sorrow, we queens and mothers who must watch the men we love become the men who destroy us. But we are also a sisterhood of strength, enduring what would break lesser souls, standing firm when the world would have us kneel.

The sun rises fully now, flooding my chamber with light. In a few hours, I will enter Blackfriars monastery. I will face their court, their questions, their predetermined condemnation. But I will not face them as they expect.

I think of the words I will speak, not the careful Latin of legal argument but the plain truth of a woman's heart. I will remind Henry of our love, our children, our vows. I will challenge him before all the world to say truly whether I came to him virgin or not. I will make him look at me, really look at me, not as the problem he needs to solve but as the woman he once loved.

And then, when I have said what needs saying, I will leave. Not flee, not retreat, but leave with dignity intact, denying their right to judge what God has sanctioned. Let them continue their farce without me. Let them pretend to deliberate what they have already decided. I will not give them the satisfaction of my participation in this travesty.

"Your Majesty," María says, "it is time."

I nod, taking one last look around the chapel that has been my refuge. After today, everything will change. I may never be allowed to return here. This may be my last morning as Queen in fact as well as name. But that matters less than what I must do in the next few hours.

"Then let us go," I say, my voice steady. "Let us show them what a true queen looks like when she stands for truth."

We leave the chapel, my small procession of loyal ladies surrounding me like guards. Outside, I can hear the palace stirring to life, unaware that this day will mark a turning point not just in my life but in England's history. For if Henry can break a marriage sanctioned by the Pope, if he can cast aside a queen for convenience, if he can rewrite divine law to suit his desires, then nothing is sacred, nothing is safe.

The trial at Blackfriars will be remembered not for its verdict—that is foregone—but for what happens when power meets principle, when lies meet truth, when a king's will meets a queen's conscience.

I am ready. Twenty years of marriage, seven years of struggle, a lifetime of faith have prepared me for this moment. I go not to defeat but to testimony. Not to judgment but to witness.

The eve of judgment has passed. The day of truth has come.

Let it begin.

CHAPTER 23

THE COURT AT BLACKFRIARS

The great hall at Blackfriars Monastery has been transformed into a courtroom, though 'transformed' gives too much credit to what is clearly a hasty arrangement. The monastery's religious purpose shows through the secular staging like bones through thin flesh. Gothic arches soar overhead, designed to lift souls to heaven, now witness to an attempt to dissolve a sacrament. The irony is not lost on me—this sacred space perverted to serve profane purposes.

The June heat is already oppressive though it is still morning, making the crowded hall feel like one of Dante's circles of hell. Bodies press against bodies, all of London's nobility and gentry who could claim or buy a place cramming in to witness the spectacle of their Queen on trial. The air is thick with competing perfumes that fail to mask the underlying scent of sweat and excitement—that peculiar eager energy that attends public humiliation.

I enter through the main doors, my train carried by the two ladies still permitted to attend me in public—María de Salinas and Lady Willoughby. I have chosen my clothing with infinite care: a gown of deep purple silk, the color of royalty and martyrdom both. My hair is dressed in the Spanish fashion, severe and elegant, covered with a black veil that frames my face. Around my neck hangs my mother's cross, prominent against the dark fabric. Let them see that I come not as defendant but as Christian queen.

The noise that greets my entrance is like a physical force—gasps, whispers, the rustle of a thousand fabrics as everyone turns to stare. I keep my eyes forward, my pace measured and deliberate. Each step is a statement: I am here by command, not by choice. I acknowledge no authority but God's over my marriage.

The arrangement of the hall tells its own story of prejudice. Banners bearing the royal arms hang limp in the still air, their golden lions and lilies looking tarnished in the thick atmosphere. Two elaborate thrones have been erected on a raised platform for the papal legates—Cardinal Wolsey sweating profusely in his scarlet robes despite the early hour, and Cardinal Campeggio, the Italian whose gout clearly pains him, making his face even more sour than his disposition. Their thrones are placed to emphasize their authority as judges, representatives of papal power.

Another throne, even more elevated, has been set for the King. It sits empty for now, but its placement above even the cardinals' seats makes clear the true authority in this room. Henry will arrive later, timing his entrance for maximum effect, but his absence now allows me to survey the battlefield without the distraction of his presence.

And for me? A single chair, placed low, positioned so that I must look up at my judges like a common criminal in the dock. The insult is deliberate and crude. They seek to diminish me before we even begin, to establish visually what they hope to establish legally

—that I am nothing, nobody, a problem to be solved rather than a queen to be honored.

I take my seat with deliberate grace, arranging my skirts, folding my hands in my lap. My spine remains perfectly straight despite the chair's uncomfortable angle. I will give them nothing—no sign of distress, no acknowledgment of their petty humiliations.

The Boleyn faction clusters together like crows on the left side of the hall. Anne herself is not present—that would be too bold even for her—but her father Thomas Boleyn is here, his merchant's face alight with anticipation. Her brother George stands beside him, that beautiful, corrupt young man who sells his sister as eagerly as their father does. The Duke of Norfolk, Anne's uncle, has positioned himself prominently, already counting the rewards that will flow from his niece's elevation.

On the right, scattered and few, are those who still support me or at least support the law. Bishop Fisher stands near the front, his aged face grave but determined. Thomas More is further back, trying to be inconspicuous—he must walk a careful line between conscience and survival. Lady Margaret Pole catches my eye and nods slightly, a gesture of support that could cost her dearly if noted by the wrong observer.

The common people have been excluded, of course. This trial is meant to seem public while being entirely controlled. But I know they gather outside, hundreds, perhaps thousands of them. I could hear their shouts as my litter arrived: "God save the true Queen!"

"No Nan Bullen!" Their voices give me strength, knowing that whatever happens in this corrupt court, the people know the truth. The proceedings begin with all the pomposity that Wolsey can muster. He does so love his ceremonies, this butcher's son playing at being a prince of the church. A clerk rises and begins reading in Latin—the establishment of the court's authority, the papal commission that grants them jurisdiction, the grave matter that brings us here. The words drone on, impressive sounding and ultimately meaningless. No earthly court has jurisdiction over a sacrament. They might as well claim authority over the tide.

Then comes the reading of the King's petition, and here I must force myself to remain still, to show nothing as they publicly proclaim the lies Henry has convinced himself are truth. The clerk reads that the King's conscience is troubled, that he fears he has lived in sin these twenty years, that scriptural authority in Leviticus clearly forbids a man to marry his brother's wife.

They do not read—of course they do not—the verses from Deuteronomy that command such marriages when the brother dies childless. They do not mention the papal dispensation that explicitly addressed and resolved these very concerns before our marriage. They present only half-truths twisted into whole lies.

Next come the witnesses, and this is where the spectacle becomes truly grotesque. Men are brought forward who claim to have knowledge of my marriage to Arthur, though most were children when it occurred or not present at all.

Sir Anthony Willoughby testifies that he heard Prince Arthur boast the morning after our wedding night that he had "been in Spain" and found it "hot work." The words are clearly rehearsed, and I notice he does not meet my eyes as he speaks them. This man, whose wife serves me still, betrays truth for favor.

The Earl of Shrewsbury, ancient and trembling, is practically carried to the witness stand. He claims to remember bloodied sheets displayed after the wedding night, proof of consummation. But when questioned about details, he becomes confused, mixing up dates and places. It is painful to watch this old man forced to perjure himself in his final years.

One after another they come, these men who were not there, who saw nothing, who know nothing, but who speak with such conviction about the most intimate details of my life. They paint a picture of a marriage that never existed, of a young girl who was wife in full to Arthur, not the virgin I remained throughout those five months in Wales.

I do not respond to any of it. I sit in perfect stillness, my face a mask of royal composure. Inside, I burn with rage at the injustice, the crudity, the sheer blasphemy of it all. But I show nothing. They want me to react, to protest, to give them something they can use against me. I give them only silence and dignity.

Cardinal Wolsey presides over this travesty with obvious relish. He has waited years for this moment, to see me brought low, to remove the obstacle I represent to his ambitions. He believes, poor fool, that with me gone he will have complete control over Henry.

He does not yet understand that Anne Boleyn will destroy him the moment she no longer needs him.

Cardinal Campeggio seems more uncomfortable, shifting in his throne, his face pinched with pain from his gout but also, I think, from distaste at these proceedings. He knows this is wrong. He has secret instructions from the Pope to delay, to prevent any final judgment. But he is trapped between Roman authority and English pressure, and so he sits and watches this parody of justice unfold.

The afternoon drags on with more witnesses, more lies, more details that would make me blush if I were capable of feeling shame for things I did not do. They speak of my supposed pregnancy after Arthur's death, which proved false—as if the stress and illness of that time were not explanation enough for disrupted courses. They speak of my years of barrenness with Henry, as if this were proof of God's displeasure rather than simply God's will.

Through it all, the crowd watches with avid attention. I can feel their eyes upon me, some sympathetic, most simply curious to see how a queen conducts herself when her most private life is made public sport. This is what Henry has reduced us to—entertainment for the mob, our sacred marriage dissected for the amusement of courtiers.

As the shadows grow longer and the heat becomes even more oppressive, Henry finally makes his entrance. The doors are thrown open with theatrical force, and he strides in surrounded by his gentlemen, every inch the magnificent king. He wears cloth of gold that catches the late afternoon light streaming through the high windows, making him seem to glow with divine authority.

The entire court rises—except me. I remain seated until he has taken his throne, then rise slowly, offering the precise curtsey due from a queen to a king, no more, no less. Our eyes meet across the space, and for a moment, time stops.

He is still handsome, my husband, though the years have thickened his frame and hardened his features. But the eyes that once looked at me with love now hold only impatience and irritation. He wants this done. He wants me gone. He wants to be free to marry his concubine and get the sons she promises.

The crier steps forward, his voice booming through the hall: "Katherine, Queen of England, come into the court!"

The words echo in the sudden silence. They have called me, formally, officially. I am commanded to answer their charges, to participate in this theatrical destruction of my life.

I do not move.

I do not speak.

I keep my eyes fixed on the crucifix that hangs on the far wall, a reminder that there is a higher judge than these corrupt cardinals, a higher law than Henry's will. Let them call me. I will not answer to this false court.

The silence stretches, becoming uncomfortable. The crowd begins to murmur. This was not expected. I was supposed to come forward, to plead, to beg, to make some dramatic scene they could use against me.

"Katherine, Queen of England," the crier calls again, louder now, a note of desperation creeping into his voice, "come into the court!"

Again, I do not move. I sit in perfect stillness, my hands folded, my face serene. I am present in body as commanded, but I will not acknowledge their authority by answering their summons.

Wolsey's face is turning purple with rage. This defiance was not in his script. Campeggio looks almost relieved—any delay serves his purposes. Henry's expression is unreadable, but I see his hands clench on the arms of his throne.

The crowd's murmur grows louder. They understand what I am doing even if they did not expect it. The Queen refuses to recognize the court. The Queen denies their right to judge her. The Queen stands—or sits—on higher authority than theirs.

Someone in the back shouts, "God save the true Queen!" before being quickly hushed. But the damage is done. Others take up the cry, softly but audibly. The guards move restlessly, unsure whether to arrest half the audience.

This is my first victory—small but significant. I have disrupted their carefully choreographed performance. I have shown that I will not play the role they have assigned me. Tomorrow, perhaps, I will speak. But it will be on my terms, in my way, to make my own statement rather than answer their false charges.

The court officials huddle, conferring desperately. They cannot proceed without my participation, but they cannot compel me to speak. To drag me forward would destroy any pretense of legitimacy. To continue without me would be to admit the trial is a sham.

Finally, Wolsey, his composure cracking, announces that the court will adjourn until tomorrow. "Perhaps Her Majesty," he says with venomous emphasis, "will be better prepared to participate in the morning."

I rise then, smoothly, gracefully, and curtsey to the empty space where justice should reside. Then I turn and walk from the hall, my ladies falling in behind me. I do not look at Henry. I do not acknowledge the cardinals. I leave as I entered—a queen whose authority comes from God, not from courts or kings or cardinals.

Outside, the common people are waiting. When they see me, a great roar goes up. They press forward, reaching out to touch my gown, calling out blessings and encouragement. These people, who have no power, no influence, nothing but their voices and their faith, understand what those great ones inside do not—that truth cannot be judged false simply because power wishes it so.

Tomorrow, I will return. Tomorrow, I will speak. But not to answer their charges—to make my own. Not to plead for mercy—to demand justice. Not to accept their authority—to assert my own.

The first day of the trial has ended with nothing resolved except this: I will not go quietly. I will not make this easy for them. Every day of this trial will be a testament to their corruption and my constancy.

Let them call me again tomorrow. They will receive an answer they do not expect.

CHAPTER 24

THE QUEEN'S APPEAL

The second day of the trial dawns grey and oppressive, as if the heavens themselves recoil from what is happening below. I have not slept, but I am not tired. Instead, I feel a strange clarity, as if God has stripped away everything unnecessary, leaving only the essential truth that I must speak.

The great hall at Blackfriars is even more crowded than yesterday, word of my defiance having spread through London like wildfire. They expect drama today, these courtiers and nobles who have come to watch their queen humbled. They will receive drama, but not the kind they anticipate.

I enter as before, in royal purple, my mother's cross prominent against the dark fabric. But today there is something different in my bearing, a purpose that makes even my enemies step back as I pass. I have made my decision. I will speak, but not to the court. I will speak to the only earthly judge who truly matters in this case —my husband.

The cardinals are already seated, Wolsey's face set in lines of grim determination. He will not be caught off-guard today. Campeggio still looks uncomfortable, his gout clearly paining him, but there is also a wariness in his eyes. He senses that something is about to happen that will derail their carefully planned proceedings.

Henry enters with even more pageantry than yesterday, if such a thing is possible. He wears crimson today, the colour of blood, of passion, of sin. Anne Boleyn's jewel—one of my jewels that he gave her—glints on his chest. The insult is deliberate, crude, typical of the man he has become.

The crier steps forward again, his voice slightly tremulous. He remembers yesterday's defiance.

"Katherine, Queen of England, come into the court!"

This time, I move.

But not as they expect.

Slowly, deliberately, I rise from my seat. The entire court holds its breath, waiting to see if I will finally submit to their authority, answer their charges, play the defendant they need me to be.

Instead, I turn away from the cardinals entirely.

I gather my heavy skirts, feeling the weight of the fabric, the weight of twenty years of marriage, the weight of this moment that will define not just my fate but England's future. And I begin to walk across the floor of the court.

Not toward the witness stand where they expect me.

Toward Henry.

A collective gasp ripples through the hall. This is not done. This is not protocol. Defendants do not approach the King uninvited. Wives do not confront husbands in public. Queens do not break the elaborate choreography of royal justice.

But I am doing all of these things.

My steps are measured, deliberate. Each footfall on the stone floor rings out like a bell tolling, like a heart beating, like the drums of judgment day. I keep my eyes fixed on Henry's face, watching as his expression shifts from satisfaction to confusion to something that might be fear.

The guards move uncertainly, hands going to their weapons. One steps forward as if to block my path, but Henry raises his hand sharply, stopping him. He must allow this. To have me dragged away now would destroy any pretense that this is justice rather than persecution.

I reach the foot of his throne and sink to my knees on the cold stone floor. The position is one of submission—a wife before her husband, a subject before her king—but also of supplication, of appeal to whatever remains of his conscience, his memory, his heart.

The silence in the hall is absolute. Even breathing seems to have stopped. Every eye is upon us, this tableau of king and queen, husband and wife, betrayer and betrayed.

I look up at him, and for the first time in two years, I force him to truly see me. Not as the problem to be solved, not as the obstacle to be removed, not as the barren wife to be discarded, but as Katherine. The woman he married with such joy. The woman he crowned with such pride. The woman who bore his children and buried them with him. The woman who loved him completely, absolutely, until he made it impossible to continue.

His face is a study in discomfort. He wants to look away, to dismiss me, to return to the script where I am the defendant and he is the righteous king. But he cannot. My eyes hold his, and in them he must see the ghost of every promise he made, every vow he swore, every moment of happiness we shared before it all turned to ash.

"Sir," I begin, and my voice carries clearly through the silent hall, though I speak softly, intimately, as if we were alone. "I beseech you for all the loves that hath been between us, and for the love of God, let me have justice and right."

The words pour from me now, not the careful Latin of legal argument but plain English, the language of the heart. These are not prepared words but truth spoken directly from my soul to his, if he still has one to hear it.

"Take of me some pity and compassion, for I am a poor woman and a stranger born out of your dominion. I have here no assured friend, and much less indifferent counsel: I flee to you as to the head of justice within this realm."

I see something flicker in his eyes—memory perhaps, or shame. For a moment, just a moment, the mask of the righteous king slips, and I glimpse the man I married, confused and guilty and wishing this could all be different.

"Alas, Sir," I continue, my voice growing stronger, "wherein have I offended you? Or what occasion of displeasure have I given you, intending thus to put me from you? I take God and all the world to witness that I have been to you a true, humble and obedient wife, ever conformable to your will and pleasure."

I speak of the years we shared, the joy and the sorrow, the passion and the companionship. I remind him—and all who listen—that I never crossed him, never denied him, never gave him cause for complaint except in the one thing beyond my control: the bearing of living sons.

"I loved all those whom ye loved only for your sake, whether I had cause or no; and whether they were my friends or my enemies."

Let the court understand what this means. I accepted his mistresses, welcomed them to my household, smiled at them across my own table. I endured Elizabeth Blount, who bore him the son I could not. I endured Mary Boleyn, who warmed his bed while mine grew cold. All for his sake, all to keep peace, all because I understood that kings have appetites and queens must be patient.

"This twenty years and more I have been your true wife, and by me ye have had divers children, although it hath pleased God to call them out of this world, which hath been no default in me."

The pain of speaking about our lost children threatens to break my composure, but I hold firm. Those small coffins, those brief lives, those hopes destroyed—they were not my fault, not God's punishment for sin, but simply sorrow that we should have borne together.

Now comes the crucial moment, the heart of their case against me.

"And when ye had me at the first," I say, looking directly into his eyes, making him remember that night twenty years ago, "I take God to be my judge, I was a true maid without touch of man."

I pause, letting the words hang in the air, then deliver the killing blow: "And whether it be true or no, I put it to your conscience."

There it is. The challenge direct. He knows the truth. He found me virgin on our wedding night, despite my marriage to Arthur. He knows our marriage is valid. He knows this trial is built on lies. And now everyone in this court knows that I have called him to account before God and man.

His face flushes red, whether from anger or shame I cannot tell. His hands grip the arms of his throne so tightly his knuckles turn white. He wants to speak, to deny, to argue, but he cannot. To debate with me here would be to descend from his throne to my level, to admit that this is personal rather than legal.

I continue, my voice now ringing with absolute conviction. I speak of our fathers—his and mine—wise kings both who saw our marriage as good and lawful, who had it examined by the finest theologians and lawyers of Christendom. I speak of the Pope's dispensation, granted after careful consideration of all impediments.

"Therefore is it a wonder to me," I say, allowing a note of contempt to enter my voice, "what new inventions are now invented against me, that never intended but honesty."

I rise then, my appeal complete. I have knelt long enough. I stand before him now as his equal, his queen, his wife before God whatever he may claim before men.

"And I call God to witness," I say, my voice carrying to every corner of the hall, "that I have been to you a true and faithful wife, and that I have never in word or deed offended your person or your honor."

For a long moment, we stare at each other—king and queen, husband and wife, two people who once loved each other now separated by an unbridgeable chasm of ambition, lust, and betrayal.

Then I curtsey—not to him but to the space where justice should reside—and turn my back on the King of England.

The gesture is shocking, unprecedented. One does not turn their back on the king. But I am beyond caring for protocol. I have said what I came to say. I have spoken truth to power. Now let power do what it will.

Behind me, I hear Wolsey's voice, sharp with anger: "Madam, ye be called again!"

I do not acknowledge him. Wolsey is nothing—a butcher's son dressed in cardinal's robes, corrupted by ambition, who will soon enough be destroyed by the very forces he now serves. His words are wind.

My gentleman usher, Master Griffith, appears at my elbow, offering his arm. Dear, loyal Griffith, who risks the king's wrath by this simple gesture of support.

"On, on," I say, loud enough for all to hear. "It maketh no matter, for it is no indifferent court for me, therefore I will not tarry. Go on your ways."

And I walk out.

My ladies fall in behind me—María de Salinas, Lady Willoughby, the few who remain loyal despite the danger. We process through the great hall, past the stunned faces of England's nobility. Some look shocked at my boldness. Some show admiration they dare not voice. Some calculate what this means for their own positions.

The Boleyn faction looks triumphant, thinking my departure means surrender. They do not understand that I have just won the only victory that matters. I have spoken truth. I have challenged Henry before all these witnesses to deny what he knows to be true. I have transformed myself from defendant to accuser, from victim to victor.

As we near the great doors, I hear a voice from the crowd—Lady Margaret Pole, brave beyond measure: "God save Your Majesty!"

Others take up the cry, softly at first, then louder: "God save the Queen! The true Queen!"

The guards look to their captains, uncertain whether to arrest half the nobility of England. But they too know the truth, these simple men. Their wives, their mothers, their daughters all know that what is happening here is wrong, that a good woman is being destroyed for a bad woman's ambition.

The doors open before me, and I step from the dimness of the corrupt court into blazing sunshine. It seems like a sign, God's own light blessing my defiance.

But the true vindication comes from the square outside, where the common people of London have gathered in their thousands. When they see me, a roar goes up that shakes the very stones of Blackfriars.

"God save Queen Katherine!" "No Nan Bullen!" "The King's true wife!"

They surge forward, held back only by a thin line of guards who look distinctly uncomfortable with their task. Hands reach out to touch my gown, to receive my blessing. Women hold up their children. Men kneel in the mud.

These people, who have no power, no influence, no voice in the proceedings inside, have the only thing that matters: clarity of vision. They see this trial for what it is—a mockery of justice, a perversion of law, an attempt to legitimize adultery and call it marriage.

I raise my hand in blessing, making the sign of the cross over the crowd. Tears stream down my face—not tears of sorrow but of gratitude, of love for these people who risk punishment to show their support.

"God bless you all," I call out. "God save England!"

The cheers follow me as my small procession makes its way to the river, where a barge waits to carry us back to Greenwich. At every window, on every corner, people have gathered. The whole of London, it seems, has come out to show that whatever the corrupt court decides, the people know their true queen.

As the barge pulls away from the dock, I look back at Blackfriars, where even now they are probably scrambling to continue their farce of a trial without me. Let them. They can pronounce whatever judgment they wish. They have already lost in the only court that truly matters—the court of conscience, of truth, of God's own justice.

Wolsey will rage. Henry will fume. The Boleyn woman will scheme. But I have done what I came to do. I have spoken truth that will echo through history. I have shown that a queen's dignity cannot be stripped away by corrupt cardinals or faithless kings.

The Thames carries us eastward, toward Greenwich, toward an uncertain future. I do not know what comes next—imprisonment perhaps, exile certainly, possibly even death if Henry's rage grows hot enough. But I am at peace.

I have kept faith with my vows, my conscience, my God. I have shown my daughter what courage looks like. I have given the people of England a moment when truth stood up to power and did not blink.

Whatever comes next, I will face it with the same constancy that has carried me through twenty years of marriage, seven years of struggle, a lifetime of faith. I am Katherine of Aragon, daughter of Isabella, Queen of England in the sight of God if no longer in the sight of men.

And that, in the end, is enough.

CHAPTER 25

"I Call God to Witness"

Having knelt before Henry and seen the discomfort in his eyes, I know the moment has come to speak the full truth. Not the careful, measured words of diplomacy I have used these many years, but the raw, unvarnished truth of a wife to her husband, of a queen to her people, of a soul before its God.

I remain on my knees for a moment longer, gathering every ounce of strength my mother's blood provides. The hall is so silent I can hear the labored breathing of Cardinal Campeggio, the nervous rustling of silk as courtiers lean forward to hear better, the rapid beating of my own heart.

When I speak again, my voice is stronger, carrying to every corner of this vast hall. These words are not just for Henry but for history, for my daughter Mary who may one day read the record of this trial, for the generations who will wonder how England broke from Rome.

"I have been to you a true, humble and obedient wife," I continue, each word clear as struck crystal, "ever conformable to your will and pleasure. I never grudged a word or countenance, or showed a spark of discontent. I have loved all those whom ye loved only for your sake, whether I had cause or no, and whether they were my friends or my enemies."

Let them hear this, these courtiers who whisper that I was cold, difficult, too Spanish, too proud. Let them know that I smiled at

Elizabeth Blount even as she carried the son I could not give him. That I welcomed Mary Boleyn to my household even as she warmed the bed that had grown cold to me. That I endured every humiliation with grace because I understood that queens must be patient and kings must be forgiven their appetites.

"This twenty years and more I have been your true wife," I press on, "and by me you have had divers children, although it hath pleased God to call them out of this world, which hath been no default in me."

Here my voice catches slightly, the pain of those losses still fresh as new wounds. Our son, Prince Henry, those perfect fifty-two days before God called him home. The others who never drew breath, who I carried with such hope only to birth in blood and sorrow. I see Henry flinch at the memory, and good—let him remember that we suffered those losses together, that I broke my body again and again trying to give him what he needed.

But now comes the heart of it, the great lie upon which this entire proceeding rests.

"And when ye had me at the first," I say, raising my voice so none can claim they did not hear, "I take God to be my judge, I was a true maid without touch of man."

The words ring out like a clarion call. There it is—the truth that everyone knows but no one speaks. I came to Henry virgin and untouched despite my marriage to Arthur. He knows it. God knows it. And now all of England knows I have proclaimed it before the highest court in the land.

I pause, letting the weight of this declaration settle upon the court like judgment itself. Then I deliver the blow that will echo through history:

"And whether it be true or no, I put it to your conscience."

I watch Henry's face as these words strike home. His conscience—that convenient tool he has used to justify everything, to dress his lust in the robes of piety. Now I throw it back at him. If his conscience is so tender, so concerned with truth, let him declare before all these witnesses that I was not virgin on our wedding night. Let him perjure himself before God and man.

He cannot. His face is red as his robes, his jaw clenched so tight I can see the muscles jump. But he cannot speak the lie that would free him, not here, not with my eyes upon him and God watching from above.

I rise to my feet, no longer the supplicant wife but the queen I have always been. My voice grows stronger still, filling with the authority of righteousness.

"I have been your wife these twenty years and more, and you have had by me many children. When you had me first, I was a virgin, and I put it to your conscience whether I was or not. If there be any just cause by the law that you can allege against me, either of dishonesty or any other impediment, to put me from you, I am well content to depart, to my great shame and dishonor. But if there be none, then I beseech you, let me have justice at your hands."

The challenge is direct and unavoidable. If he has legitimate grounds, let him state them. But we both know he has none. The Leviticus argument is tissue-thin theology that any competent scholar could demolish. The claim of non-consummation with Arthur is a lie and he knows it. This entire trial is built on quicksand, and I have just pointed it out to everyone watching.

I continue, my words flowing now like a river that has broken through a dam:

"The King your father was accounted in his day as wise a prince as any in England had been for many years before. My father Ferdinand was esteemed one of the wisest princes in Spain. Both our fathers had gathered the finest minds in Christendom to examine our marriage. It was declared by the court of Rome, by the Pope himself, to be good and lawful."

I turn slightly, addressing not just Henry but the assembled court, making them all witnesses to this history:

"These learned men determined that our marriage was valid, that the impediment of my brief union with Prince Arthur was fully dispensed by papal authority. They were not fools or knaves but men of God, scholars of the highest reputation. Are we to believe that all of them were wrong? That they all failed to see what now seems so clear to those who have been paid to find it so?"

A murmur runs through the crowd at this—I have just accused the theological witnesses of being bought, which of course they have been. Wolsey's face is purple with rage, but he cannot interrupt without seeming to confirm my accusation.

"Therefore is it a wonder to me," I continue, allowing contempt to color my voice, "what new inventions are now invented against me, that never intended but honesty. And now to cause me to stand to the order and judgment of this court, which seems to me very prejudicial and partial."

There—I have said it plainly. This court is corrupt, bought, predetermined in its verdict. Everyone knows it, but I am the only one with the courage to speak it aloud.

"For you all know that Cardinal Wolsey is not my friend but my enemy, though he sits as my judge. And Cardinal Campeggio comes from Rome with, I doubt not, instructions to delay and obfuscate rather than deliver true justice. What justice can I expect from such a court?"

Wolsey starts to rise, his face apoplectic, but I am not finished. I turn back to Henry, and my voice softens, becomes almost tender:

"I have lived with you as your true wife for all these years. I have borne your children, kept your secrets, honored your name. When you were ill, I nursed you. When you went to war, I governed your kingdom and defeated your enemies. I have been more than wife to you—I have been partner, counselor, friend."

I see something flicker in his eyes—memory perhaps, or the ghost of the love we once shared. For a moment, he is not the tyrant king but the golden prince who rescued me from poverty, who crowned me with such joy.

"And now, in my age, when I should be enjoying the fruits of our long union, you seek to cast me aside for a younger woman, and you dress this cruelty in the garments of conscience and divine law."

The words hang in the air like an accusation. Several courtiers gasp at my boldness in mentioning Anne Boleyn, even obliquely. But why should I not speak of her? She sits at the heart of this matter like a spider in her web, though she dare not show her face in this court.

"But I call God to witness," I say, my voice rising to fill the entire hall, "that I have been to you a true and faithful wife, and that I have never in word or deed offended your person or your honor. I have done all that a wife should do, borne all that a wife should bear, forgiven all that a wife should forgive."

I pause, looking directly at Henry, making sure he understands what comes next:

"And if you cast me aside now, it is not for any fault in me, but for your own desires. History will record this truth, even if this court will not. Our daughter Mary will know this truth, even if you try to bastardize her. God knows this truth, even if you convince yourself otherwise."

The mention of Mary strikes home. I see Henry's face contort with something that might be pain. Good. Let him think about what he is doing to our daughter, the only living fruit of our union, the innocent child he would make illegitimate for his lust.

"I have been your true wife before God and man," I conclude, my voice ringing with absolute conviction. "No court can unmake what God has made. No king can dissolve what Heaven has joined. You may take my crown, my title, my freedom, even my life. But you cannot take the truth. I am your wife. I will die your wife. And when we stand before God's throne at the final judgment, He will know whose conscience was truly clear."

The silence that follows is deafening. Every soul in the hall seems to hold their breath. Henry's face is a battlefield of emotions—rage, shame, frustration, and something that might be grief for what we once were to each other.

Cardinal Wolsey finally finds his voice: "Madam, you must answer to this court—"

"I must answer to God," I interrupt, not even looking at him. "And I have given my answer. I am the King's true wife. Our marriage is valid. This court has no authority to judge otherwise."

I curtsey then—not to the corrupt cardinals, not even to Henry, but to the crucifix on the wall, to the God who sees all and judges truly. Then I turn my back on them all.

The gesture is shocking in its boldness. One does not turn their back on the King. But I am beyond caring for such protocols. I have spoken my truth. I have challenged their lies. I have called God Himself as my witness.

As I walk toward the doors, I hear voices calling after me, ordering me to return, to answer to the court. I do not acknowledge them. Their words are wind, their authority is nothing. I answer to a higher power than corrupt cardinals and a king enslaved by lust.

My ladies fall in behind me, their faces pale but proud. We process through the hall like queens in exile, dignity intact despite all attempts to strip it from us. As we pass, I see faces in the crowd—some shocked, some admiring, some calculating what this means for their own positions.

Lady Margaret Pole catches my eye and nods deeply, a gesture of profound respect. Bishop Fisher's eyes are bright with what might be tears. Even Thomas More, careful Thomas More, allows himself a small smile of approval.

These few, these faithful few, understand what I have done. I have not just defended my marriage—I have defended the very concept of marriage as sacrament. I have not just asserted my rights—I have asserted the rights of every wife whose husband might seek to discard her for convenience. I have not just called God to witness—I have reminded everyone in this hall that there is a judgment beyond the judgments of men.

As the great doors open before me and I step into the sunlight, I hear the crowd outside erupt in cheers. They have been listening, these common people of London, pressing their ears to doors and windows, catching fragments of what transpired within.

"The Queen spoke truth!" "God witness her words!" "Shame on the King!"

That last is dangerous—criticism of Henry could mean death. But they shout it anyway, these brave souls who have nothing but their voices and their faith.

I raise my hand in blessing, tears streaming down my face. Not tears of sorrow but of vindication. I have spoken the truth that everyone knows but few dare voice. I have stood before the combined power of England and not yielded.

Tomorrow, they will continue their sham trial without me. They will produce more false witnesses, more twisted theology, more legal sophistry. They will eventually declare my marriage invalid, as everyone knows they will.

But it will not matter. Because today, in this moment, truth has been spoken that can never be unspoken. Today, I have called God to witness, and that witness stands forever, beyond the reach of corrupt courts and faithless kings.

I am Katherine of Aragon, true wife of Henry VIII, Queen of England in the sight of God.

And that truth will outlive us all.

CHAPTER 26

THE DEFIANT EXIT

Having spoken my truth, having called God to witness, I turn my back on the entire assembly—on the corrupt cardinals, on the bought witnesses, on the husband who has betrayed every vow he made. The gesture is revolutionary. Queens do not turn their backs on kings. Wives do not walk away from husbands. Defendants do not abandon courts. But I am doing all of these things, because I am more than they have tried to make me.

The sound of my footsteps on the stone floor echoes through the suddenly silent hall. Each step is deliberate, measured, a drumbeat of defiance that seems to grow louder as I move toward the great doors. Behind me, I hear the explosion of voices I expected.

"Madam!" Wolsey's voice cracks like a whip. "Madam, ye be called again!"

I do not pause, do not acknowledge him. Thomas Wolsey is nothing to me now—a butcher's son dressed in stolen scarlet, a priest who has forgotten his God, a fool who believes Anne Boleyn will let him live once she has what she wants. His words have no more authority over me than the barking of a dog.

A court officer, young and clearly terrified of being caught between the cardinals' authority and a queen's dignity, hurries to intercept me. "Your Majesty," he says, and I note that he still uses my proper title despite the pressure to deny it. "You must return. The court commands—"

"The court commands nothing," I say, not breaking stride. "I do not recognize its authority. I answer to a higher judge than Cardinal Wolsey."

My gentleman usher, Master Griffith, appears at my elbow. Dear, loyal Griffith, who has served me for fifteen years, who could easily abandon me now for safer service but chooses to risk everything for principle. He offers me his arm with the same courtesy he would show if we were entering a state banquet rather than fleeing a corrupt trial.

"Your Majesty," he says quietly, "shall we proceed?"

"On, on," I say, loud enough for the entire court to hear. "It maketh no matter, for it is no indifferent court for me, therefore I will not tarry. Go on your ways."

The words carry to every corner of the hall, making my position crystal clear. This is not a legitimate court. These are not legitimate judges. This is a performance, a mummery, a lie dressed in legal robes, and I will not dignify it with my participation.

Behind me, chaos erupts. I hear Wolsey shouting orders, demanding I be brought back. I hear Henry's voice, lower but more dangerous, saying something I cannot make out. I hear the buzz of a hundred conversations as courtiers try to process what they have just witnessed.

But louder than all of that, I hear other voices:

"God save the true Queen!"

The cry comes from somewhere in the crowd, brave and clear. Lady Margaret Pole, I think, that indomitable woman who has survived so much and still dares to speak truth.

Others take up the cry: "The true Queen!" "God save Queen Katherine!"

There is a scuffle—guards moving to arrest those who dare support me—but there are too many voices, coming from too many directions. The hall is turning against the trial, the very witnesses to this travesty becoming my defenders.

My ladies fall in behind me—María de Salinas, who has been with me since Spain; Lady Willoughby, whose husband will certainly punish her for this loyalty; and a handful of others who value truth over safety. We process through the hall not as refugees fleeing injustice but as a queen and her court maintaining dignity in the face of corruption.

As we move through the crowd, hands reach out—not to stop us but to touch my gown, to receive a blessing, to show support that dare not speak itself more plainly. I see faces I know: Bishop Fisher, his aged face wet with tears; Thomas More, who nods almost imperceptibly; merchants' wives who have no business being here but have somehow gained entry to witness this historic moment.

"Shame!" someone shouts. "Shame on this false court!"

More scuffles, more guards pushing through the crowd, but they cannot arrest everyone. The sentiment is spreading like fire through thatch. These people—nobles and commons alike—have just witnessed something unprecedented. A queen has stood up to a king. A wife has spoken truth to a husband's lies. A woman has defied the combined power of church and state and walked away unbowed.

As we near the great doors, I see something that stops my heart for a moment. A group of young women, maids in the households of various nobles, have formed a line across our path. For a terrible instant, I think they mean to block us, to force me back to the trial. But then, as one, they sink into deep curtseys, creating a corridor of honor for us to pass through.

"Your Majesty," one whispers as I pass, barely audible but fervent. "We know the truth."

The great doors stand open, whether by design or accident I neither know nor care. Beyond them, sunlight streams in, so bright after the dimness of the hall that it seems like stepping from purgatory into paradise. The crowd outside is vast—thousands of London's citizens packed into every available space, on rooftops, hanging from windows, children perched on their fathers' shoulders.

When they see me, the roar that goes up shakes the very stones of Blackfriars monastery. It is not the polite applause of courtiers or the ceremonial cheers of state occasions. This is raw, emotional, overwhelming—the voice of England itself crying out against injustice.

"God save Queen Katherine!" "The King's true wife!" "No Nan Bullen!" "Shame on the false court!"

The guards who should control the crowd stand uncertain, overwhelmed. To suppress this demonstration would require violence on a scale that would turn all of London against the King. So they stand aside, these simple men who know where their wives' and mothers' sympathies lie.

The people surge forward, but not threateningly. They reach out to touch my gown, to kiss my hands, to receive my blessing. Women hold up their babies for me to touch. Men kneel in the mud, their caps in their hands, tears on their weathered faces.

"Your Majesty," an old woman cries out, pushing forward with surprising strength. "My husband left me for a younger woman after thirty years. If the King can put aside a queen, what hope for the rest of us?"

Her words strike to the heart of it. This is not just about royal marriage but about marriage itself. If the King can dissolve a union blessed by the Pope, witnessed by all of Christendom, what marriage is safe? Every woman in England sees herself in me—the aging wife discarded for someone younger, prettier, more fertile.

"Have faith," I tell her, taking her gnarled hands in mine. "God sees all. Truth endures. What He has joined, no man can separate, whatever earthly courts may say."

I move through the crowd slowly, blessing, touching, acknowledging these people who risk so much to support me. The contrast with the cold reception inside Blackfriars could not be starker. In there, power aligned against me. Out here, righteousness stands with me.

"Make way for the Queen!" someone shouts, and the crowd parts, creating a path to the river where my barge waits. But it is not the harsh command of guards that moves them—it is their own recognition of majesty that no court can strip away.

As I walk this human corridor, I hear fragments of conversation, opinions voiced openly that would be treason if spoken at court: "The Boleyn witch has bewitched him..." "It's about the monasteries' gold, mark my words..." "Breaking with Rome will damn us all..." "The Queen spoke God's own truth in there..."

My small procession reaches the Thames, where my barge waits, flying the royal standard that I still have the right to display, whatever the King wishes. The bargemen, simple rivermen who care nothing for politics, sweep off their caps and bow deeply.

"Your Majesty," the head bargeman says, "it's an honor."

As I board, I turn back to look at the crowd one last time. They fill every space, a sea of faces turned toward me—my true judges, my ultimate vindication. I raise my hand in blessing, making the sign of the cross over them all.

"God bless you, good people!" I call out, my voice carrying across the water. "God save England!"

The response is deafening. As the barge pulls away from the dock, the cheers follow us down the river. At every wharf, on every bridge, people have gathered. The word has spread through London faster than fire: the Queen has defied the false court. The Queen has spoken truth. The Queen remains the Queen.

I see them on London Bridge—hundreds of people waving, cheering, some holding up crude drawings of pomegranates, my symbol. Church bells begin to ring, not the solemn toll of judgment but the joyous peal of celebration. The churches are declaring their own verdict, whatever their bishops might be forced to say.

María sits beside me in the barge, tears streaming down her face. "Your Majesty," she says, "you were magnificent."

"I was necessary," I reply, though I too am crying now, overwhelmed by the love of these people I have served as Queen for twenty years. "Someone had to speak truth. Someone had to show that power is not the same as right."

"What will happen now?" Lady Willoughby asks.

I look back at Blackfriars, growing smaller as we move downstream. "They will continue their trial without me. They will find me guilty of whatever they need to find me guilty of. They will declare my marriage invalid and crown the Boleyn woman in my place."

"Then all is lost?"

"No," I say firmly. "Today proved that truth spoken bravely can never be fully silenced. Every person who witnessed what happened in that hall, every soul in these crowds, every child who will hear the story from their parents—they all know the truth. Henry can change the law, he can break with Rome, he can call Anne Boleyn queen. But he cannot change what is. I am his wife.

Mary is his legitimate daughter. Our marriage is valid. These are facts that no amount of legal sophistry can alter."

As we continue down the Thames toward Greenwich, where I will be allowed to stay for now—though for how much longer, God knows—I think about what I have done today. I have defied not just a king but the entire apparatus of power. I have shown that there is authority beyond earthly authority, law beyond human law, truth beyond convenient truth.

The sun is setting now, painting the Thames gold and red, like blood and glory mixed. Appropriate colors for this day when I have both triumphed and been defeated, when I have lost my worldly position but kept my immortal soul.

Behind us, at Blackfriars, they are probably scrambling to salvage their trial. Wolsey will rage. Henry will fume. They will eventually pronounce their judgment without me, declaring before the world that I was never truly married, never truly queen.

But ahead of us, all along the river, the people of England are lighting torches, creating a river of fire to guide their true Queen home. They know what the powerful refuse to acknowledge: that some truths are too fundamental to be overturned by courts, that some bonds are too sacred to be broken by kings, that some courage is too pure to be forgotten.

I have walked out on their false court. I have turned my back on their corrupted authority. I have chosen God's judgment over man's.

And in doing so, I have won the only victory that matters: I have kept faith with myself, with my vows, with the truth that makes us human rather than beasts.

Tomorrow, the legal persecution will continue. I will be stripped of my title, my homes, my freedom. But tonight, sailing down a river lit by the torches of the faithful, surrounded by the love of the common people who see clearly what the great ones willfully blind themselves to, I am still Katherine of Aragon, still Queen of England, still Henry's true wife in the sight of God.

And that, no earthly court can change.

Chapter 27
The Last Glimpse

The court has returned to Windsor Castle for the summer of 1531. Two years have passed since my defiant exit from Blackfriars, two years in which the legal machinery has ground on without me, eventually declaring what everyone knew it would declare—that my marriage was invalid, that I was never truly Queen, that Anne Boleyn could take my place. But declaring a lie does not make it truth, and I remain at court, a living reproach to Henry's conscience, though we live now as strangers in the same palace.

It is a grey, overcast morning in July when everything changes forever. I stand at my window overlooking the great courtyard, watching the organized chaos of departure. The entire household is preparing for the summer progress—wagons loaded with furniture and plate, horses stamping impatiently, dogs barking with excitement at the prospect of hunting. Henry is taking the court on a grand tour through the southern counties, a celebration of his freedom from Rome, from me, from any authority but his own will.

I watch him in the courtyard below, still magnificent despite the weight he has gained, still playing the role of the golden king though the gilt has long since worn thin. He laughs with Charles Brandon, Duke of Suffolk, the same false laugh he uses at council, all performance and no genuine mirth. Even from here, I can see the tension in his shoulders, the way he keeps glancing around as if looking for threats or perhaps for witnesses to his happiness.

And there she is, the cause of all this destruction—Anne Boleyn, dressed in green velvet despite the morning chill, mounted on a white mare that probably cost more than my entire household's expenses for a year. She rides astride like a man, her long neck extended, her dark eyes scanning the courtyard with proprietary satisfaction. She wears my jewels—I recognize the ruby pendant that was part of my wedding gift from Henry, now nestling against her throat like drops of blood.

This morning, Henry came to my chambers for what he claimed would be a brief farewell. It was the first time he had entered my rooms in months, and his discomfort was palpable. He stood just inside the door, as if afraid to come too close, as if my failure to accept his new reality might be contagious.

"I trust Your Majesty will be comfortable here during our absence," he said, the formality of his words a wall between us.

"As comfortable as a wife can be without her husband," I replied, watching him flinch at the word 'wife.'

"Madam, we have discussed—"

"We have discussed nothing," I interrupted. "You have dictated. You have threatened. You have acted. But we have not discussed, because discussion requires two people who respect each other, and you no longer respect me enough to even look me in the eye."

It was true. Throughout our brief conversation, his gaze had wandered—to the window, to the floor, to the tapestry behind my head depicting the judgment of Solomon. Anywhere but at me, his wife of twenty-four years, the woman who had shared his bed, borne his children, governed his kingdom.

"I will return in a few weeks," he said stiffly. "The household has instructions for your care."

My care. As if I were an elderly relative to be managed, a problem to be contained rather than a queen to be honored. But I saw the lie in his shifting eyes, in the way his hand moved unconsciously to the door handle as if already fleeing. He would not return in a few weeks. He would not return at all. This was goodbye, the real farewell that he lacked the courage to acknowledge.

"Henry," I said, using his name for perhaps the last time, making him stop at the door. "When you stand before God—and you will stand before God—He will ask you about the vows you made. What will you answer?"

For a moment, his mask slipped. I saw fear flicker across his face, the terror of a man who has convinced himself that his desires are God's will but knows, deep down, that he has built his house on sand. Then the mask returned, harder than before.

"God understands the needs of kings," he said coldly.

"God understands the nature of sin," I countered. "And He forgives those who repent. It is not too late, Henry. Even now, you could turn back from this path."

"The path is chosen," he said flatly. "And it leads forward, not back."

He left then, without a kiss, without a blessing, without even the courtesy of a proper farewell. The last time my husband touched me was to hand me the summons to Blackfriars. The last time he kissed me... I can no longer remember. The memory has been worn away by too much examining, like a coin rubbed smooth by desperate fingers.

Now I watch from my window as he mounts his horse, still graceful despite his increased weight, still every inch the king in his cloth of gold. He glances up at my window, and for a fleeting second, our eyes meet across the courtyard. I search his face for something—regret, sorrow, even acknowledgment of what this moment means. But I see only impatience. He wants to be gone. He wants to be free of the weight of my presence, the constant reminder of vows broken and sacraments defiled.

The procession begins to move, a river of color and noise flowing toward the gates. Henry rides at the front, the Boleyn woman beside him in the place where I should be. She turns in her saddle to look back at my window, and the triumph in her dark eyes is naked and ugly. She has won, that look says. The king is hers, the crown will be hers, the future is hers.

I do not give her the satisfaction of stepping back from the window. I stand there, visible, immovable, a monument to constancy in a world of change. Let her see that she has not defeated me, only displaced me. Let her know that winning Henry's body is not the same as winning God's approval.

The last of the procession disappears through the gates, the sound of horses' hooves fading into the distance. I remain at the window as the sun climbs higher, burning off the morning mist, revealing a world that looks exactly as it did yesterday but is fundamentally changed. Twenty-four years of marriage have ended not with death or grand ceremony, but with a lie about returning in a few weeks.

María de Salinas finds me still standing there as the bells ring for midday prayer.

"Your Majesty," she says softly, "you should rest."

"I am watching my life leave," I reply. "Twenty-four years, María. We have been together longer than we lived before we met. How does one separate threads so tightly woven?"

"One doesn't," she says firmly. "Whatever he says, whatever papers he signs, you remain his wife. God knows it. History will know it."

"History is written by the victors," I observe. "And today, I am not victorious."

But even as I say it, I wonder if it's true. Yes, Henry has left, choosing his concubine over his wife. Yes, I will be moved from Windsor to increasingly remote and mean accommodations. Yes, my title will be stripped away, my household reduced, my freedom curtailed. But I have kept my conscience clean. I have maintained my truth. I have shown my daughter what constancy means.

That evening, I walk through Windsor Castle like a ghost haunting my own life. These halls where I was crowned, where I gave birth, where I ruled as regent—they echo now with absence. The courtiers have fled with the king, rats following the piper. Only servants remain, and they scurry away when they see me coming, afraid that proximity to the abandoned queen might be contagious.

I find myself in the chapel where Henry and I heard Mass together countless times, where we prayed for sons, where we thanked God for victories. The altar is bare now, the candles unlit. I kneel where I have knelt so many times before, but tonight my prayers are different.

"Lord," I whisper to the darkness, "I do not understand Your plan. I have been faithful. I have been constant. I have defended Your sacrament against all attacks. Yet You allow me to be cast aside, humiliated, forgotten. What lesson is this meant to teach? What purpose does my suffering serve?"

There is no answer, only the sound of wind through ancient stones. But perhaps that is answer enough. Christ too was abandoned, betrayed by those He loved, left to face His trial alone. If the Son of God could endure such injustice, surely I can endure this smaller calvary.

The next morning, the orders come, as I knew they would. I am to remove from Windsor immediately. My new residence is to be The More in Hertfordshire, a property that has been little used since Wolsey's fall. The message is clear: I am to be buried in the countryside, far from court, far from influence, far from Henry's guilty conscience.

As my few remaining servants pack what little I am allowed to take, I take one last walk through the state apartments. In the great hall, my coat of arms has already been removed from above the throne, leaving a pale shadow on the stone where it hung for twenty years. In the queen's chambers—Anne Boleyn's chambers now—workers are already removing my things, my personal items being catalogued and locked away or redistributed to the new regime.

I stop at the nursery, that room of so much hope and heartbreak. It has been sealed since our son died, Henry unable to bear the reminder. I convince a servant to unlock it for me one last time. Everything is as it was—the tiny shirts laid out for dressing, the silver apostle spoons waiting for a hand that will never grasp them, the cradle that rocked so briefly.

I pick up the small rattle Henry gave our son, feeling its weight, hearing its gentle chime. Such a small sound in such a large silence.

"Your Majesty," María says gently from the doorway, "the carriage is ready."

I set the rattle down carefully, exactly where it was. Let it remain here, a ghost of what might have been, a reminder that Henry VIII once had a son with his true wife, even if only for fifty-two days.

As my carriage pulls away from Windsor, I look back one last time at the great castle rising from its hill, flags flying, magnificent and indifferent. Somewhere in England, Henry rides with his mistress, playing at being young and free. Somewhere, my daughter Mary wonders why her mother has disappeared from court, why her father looks through her as if she were a stranger.

And here I am, suspended between what was and what will be, no longer queen in practice but always queen in truth, beginning the long, slow journey toward whatever end God has planned for me.

The last glimpse of Windsor disappears as we round a bend in the road. I do not cry. I have no tears left for what is already dead. Instead, I begin to plan how to live with dignity in exile, how to remain constant when all around me changes, how to be Katherine of Aragon when the world insists I am nothing at all.

The summer sun beats down on the carriage roof, but inside I am cold, as cold as that first day in Plymouth when I arrived in this grey kingdom. Then, I was beginning. Now, I am ending. But between beginning and ending lies a life lived, a duty fulfilled, a vow kept.

That must be enough. It is all I have.

CHAPTER 28

My Shabby Palaces

The journey from Windsor is a descent into a grey, waterlogged hell. Henry's final departure was not an act of clean separation, but a slow, cruel erasure. He left on his summer progress with his concubine at his side, leaving me behind with a false promise to return in a few weeks. I knew, standing at my window watching his vibrant cavalcade disappear, that I would never see him again as my husband. The last glimpse I had of him was of a man glancing up at my window, his face not filled with sorrow or regret, but with a chilling impatience. He was eager to be gone, to leave behind the living monument to his broken vows. Two days later, the formal order came: I was to be removed from Windsor. My destination was The More, a property in Hertfordshire. The name itself felt like a cruel jest. More damp, more isolation, more misery.

The More rises from the Hertfordshire countryside like a great wounded beast, its brick walls stained with green and black damp, its many windows as dark and vacant as the eyes of a skull. This was once Cardinal Wolsey's pride, one of the many palaces he built to rival the king's own, a testament to his ambition and his exquisite, if worldly, taste. After his fall, it reverted to the crown. Now it serves as my first official prison, though they do not call it that. They call it my residence, my new establishment, as if I had chosen this exile, this slow, deliberate burial away from the world's sight.

My carriage lurches to a stop in the courtyard, the wheels sinking into mud that has the consistency of thick porridge. I see the full extent of my new reality. The famous gardens that Wolsey designed to mimic the great gardens of Italy are now a wilderness. Weeds taller than a man choke what were once intricate knot gardens. Brambles with thorns like claws catch at my skirts as I step down from the carriage. The great topiary beasts that once delighted visitors—lions and dragons and griffins—have grown wild, their shapes becoming grotesque and menacing in the dying afternoon light. The fountains, once fed by ingenious mechanics, are dry, their marble basins cracked and filled with a slurry of dead leaves and stagnant rainwater. It is a garden of decay, a perfect mirror for my life.

"Your Majesty," María de Salinas says, her voice tight with a mixture of pity and rage, "perhaps we should wait until the servants have prepared a path. This is not fit for you to walk upon."

"No," I interrupt, my voice steadier than I feel. "Let me see it all now, in its full honesty. Tomorrow I will have to pretend this is acceptable. Tonight, let me acknowledge what it truly is: a grave."

We enter through the great door, which groans on rusted hinges that scream in protest. Inside, the smell hits me with physical force—a complex perfume of damp, decay, and the droppings of the birds that now nest in the high rafters of the great hall. It is the scent of abandonment, of a place that has lost its purpose and is surrendering to the slow, inexorable siege of time. The great hall, which once hosted Wolsey's lavish entertainments for ambassadors and kings, is now a cavern of shadows. The painted ceiling, depicting the Cardinal's ambitious coat of arms repeated in an endless, arrogant pattern, is water-stained and peeling. In great patches, the plaster has fallen away entirely, revealing the bare, skeletal laths of the building beneath. A thick layer of dust covers everything, softening the edges of the room's former glory, dressing it in a shroud.

My apartments, such as they are, consist of three rooms in the south wing, a place known to be the dampest in the entire house. The furniture is minimal and mean—a heavy oak bed that looks more suited to a prosperous farmer than a queen, a single high-backed chair by the empty fireplace, a table that wobbles on uneven legs. The tapestries on the walls are so faded by damp and bleached by the sun that I cannot make out what scenes they once depicted. They are just ghosts of color, reminders that this room once held life and warmth. Everything speaks of deliberate insult, calculated humiliation. This is not simple neglect; this is a carefully staged production of my fall from grace.

My ladies, the few who have been permitted to remain with me, weep openly at the sight of it. Lady Willoughby, ever practical, begins issuing orders to the few, sullen servants who have been assigned to us, trying to bring some order to the chaos, demanding fires be lit, beds be aired. But María de Salinas simply stands in the center of the damp, cold room, her face a mask of Spanish pride struggling against a tide of despair.

"This is not fit for a queen," she says, her voice trembling with a fury I know she feels on my behalf. "It is not fit for a gentlewoman. It is an insult to you, to Spain, to God Himself."

"It is meant to be an insult, María," I reply, walking to the window and looking out at the ruined garden. The glass is so grimy I can barely see through it. "It is meant to break us. It is meant to make us forget who we are, to reduce us to the level of our surroundings. They hope the damp will seep into our souls."

I see the despair in their eyes, the slow draining of hope that is more dangerous than any physical hardship. They have followed me into this exile, these brave women, and their reward is this cold, damp tomb. They look at the peeling walls, the mean furniture, the encroaching wilderness outside, and they see an ending. If I allow this despair to take root, we are truly lost. I must be the rock. I must be the general. I must be my mother's daughter.

That evening, the first of our exile, is the lowest point. A fire is finally coaxed to life in the grate, but it gives off more smoke than warmth. We huddle around it, a small, miserable flock of displaced birds. The meal is an insult: a thin, greasy pottage with scraps of unidentifiable meat, served with bread so hard it could break a tooth. We eat in silence, broken only by the wind and the dripping of a leak. This, then, is my life now. This is what twenty-four years of faithful marriage have earned me.

After the meal, I watch my ladies: young Inés de Venegas weeping silently; the usually stoic Lady Willoughby staring vacantly into the fire; my oldest friend, María, her back rigid with a pride close to shattering. I know I must act before despair takes root.

I call them together. My voice, when I speak, is not the weary, defeated tone they expect. It is sharp, clear, and commanding.

"My ladies," I begin, and something in my tone makes them look up, their weary faces turning to me in the flickering, smoky firelight. "Look around you. This is what the King and his concubine believe will defeat us. Damp. Poverty. Isolation. They think that by taking away our palaces, they can take away our status. They believe that if they dress us in rags and feed us scraps, we will forget we are noblewomen. They think that if they bury us here in this ruin, we will accept that we are dead."

I let the silence hang for a moment, letting the full weight of our miserable situation settle. Then I stand, a slow, deliberate movement that draws every eye. I force myself to project an authority my aching body and breaking heart do not feel. "They are wrong."

I walk to the center of the small room, my worn black gown, now my only uniform, sweeping across the dusty floor. "From this moment forward, this is not a prison. This is the court of England. Because I am here. And as long as the true, anointed Queen of England resides within these walls, this is where the true court resides."

They stare at me, their faces a mixture of confusion and a dawning, fragile hope.

"We will maintain full court protocol," I declare, my voice ringing with a conviction I am willing into existence. "Our day will not be governed by misery, but by the proper order of a royal household. We will rise at the appointed hour. We will dress with care. We will attend Mass together, here in this chamber if we must, with a crucifix upon a table for an altar. We will dine at the proper time, and you will attend me as you would at Windsor or Greenwich. Every bow, every curtsy, every form of address will be as it should be. We will not descend into the chaos and despair they desire for us."

They have taken my palaces, but they cannot take my royalty. That is a state of being, an anointing from God, that no king can give or take away. This damp, stinking room is the court of England, because its true Queen resides here. Every reverent curtsy performed before me is an act of defiance against the whore who sits on my throne. Every meal, however meager, served according to the strict rules of court, is a public denial of their lie. They have stripped me of the trapping of queenship, so I must make queenship an act of will, a spiritual discipline. We will not be victims cowering in the dark. We will be a court in exile, a beacon, maintaining the sacred flame of legitimacy until the darkness passes or God calls us home.

"But Your Majesty," Lady Willoughby ventures, her practical English mind grappling with the reality of our situation. "We have so few servants. We have no proper plate. We have nothing."

"We have ourselves," I say firmly. "We have our dignity. We have the truth. These are weapons they cannot take from us. If we have no pages to serve us, we will serve each other with the same grace and ceremony. If we have no fine food, we will serve our bread and water on the pewter plates they have left us as if it were a ten-course feast. We will transform our poverty into a statement. This is not about pride, my ladies. It is a political act. It is a spiritual war. As long as we maintain the etiquette of a court, we deny their pretense that I am no longer the Queen. We deny their claim that Anne Boleyn is anything more than a whore in a stolen crown. We bear witness to the truth."

I look from face to face. I see a flicker of understanding in Inés's tear-filled eyes. I see a dawning resolve on Lady Willoughby's sensible face. I see María's back straighten even further, her pride no longer brittle but transformed into a weapon. I have given them not a command, but a purpose. A way to fight back not with swords and armies, but with spoons and curtsies and an unyielding adherence to the truth of who we are.

"Tomorrow," I say, my voice now calm and full of a power that comes not from my earthly position but from my soul, "we will begin. We will show them that a queen is not defined by her surroundings, but by her spirit. A court is not made of stone and gilt, but of loyalty and order. And the spirit of this court, the true court of England, is not broken. It is merely under siege. And we will not surrender."

That night, for the first time since leaving Windsor, I do not weep. I lie awake in the damp, musty bed and I plan. We will turn this shabby palace not into a home—it can never be that—but into a theater of resistance, where every small, mundane act of daily life becomes a performance of unwavering legitimacy. They meant this place to be my tomb. By the grace of God and the strength of my will, I will make it my fortress. And from within its decaying walls, we will wage a war of dignity that they, in all their finery and power, can never hope to win.

CHAPTER 29

The Break with Rome

A violent storm lashes Buckden Palace on a November night in 1534, a physical manifestation of the tempest that has engulfed my life and is now poised to swallow all of England. The rain does not fall; it drives against the leaded glass of my chamber windows like a volley of small, hard stones, demanding entry. The wind howls through the ancient stones of the palace, a mournful, keening sound that seems to echo the grief of the saints themselves. I huddle closer to the meager fire, pulling my worn fur-lined robe tighter around my shoulders, trying to ward off a chill that seems to emanate from the very marrow of my bones. But the storm outside is a pale imitation of the one raging within my soul, a maelstrom of fear, anger, and a sorrow so profound it threatens to extinguish the small flame of hope I have so carefully guarded.

My life here at Buckden has settled into a monastic rhythm of prayer, reading, and quiet endurance. We are forgotten, a small island of women marooned in a sea of hostility. News of the outside world arrives in whispers, carried by a sympathetic stable boy or a laundress who travels between the great houses. Each fragment is more bitter than the last: the rise of the Boleyn faction, the silencing of my supporters, the slow, methodical dismantling of the Church as I have always known it. But tonight, the whispers have ceased. Tonight, a shout has arrived.

It came in the form of a small, mud-stained packet, delivered not by any official channels but by a man whose face I did not see, who pressed it into the hand of my groom William at the postern gate and disappeared back into the storm. It is from Chapuys, my nephew's ambassador, my only remaining lifeline to a world that still acknowledges me as Queen. I know from the urgency of its delivery that it contains news of great import. I thank William, whose loyalty in these small acts of treason is a constant source of strength, and retire to the privacy of my chamber. María follows, her face a mask of anxious curiosity.

I break the seal with fingers that tremble, the wax crumbling like dried blood under my nail. The candlelight, our only luxury, flickers wildly in the drafts that snake through the room, making the words on the page dance and swim. I read, and the world, which had already tilted on its axis, shatters into a thousand irreparable pieces.

"Your Majesty must know," Chapuys's precise, coded script reads, "that the King has done what we feared but never truly believed possible. Parliament, a body now composed entirely of his creatures and those too terrified to speak against him, has passed the Act of Supremacy. His Majesty the King, his heirs and successors, are to be taken, accepted, and reputed the only Supreme Head on earth of the Church of England. The authority of the Bishop of Rome is utterly abolished. The break is complete and absolute."

The parchment falls from my nerveless fingers, floating to the floor like a dead leaf. For a moment, I cannot breathe. The air in the room feels thick, heavy, unbreathable. The roaring in my ears is not just the storm outside, but the sound of a world ending. María, who has been watching me with anxious eyes, retrieves the letter. She reads it herself, her face draining of all color. A small, strangled gasp escapes her lips, a sound of pure horror.

"This cannot be," she whispers, her voice a thread of sound against the roar of the wind. "He cannot... he cannot simply declare himself Pope of England."

But he has. The words echo in the cavern of my mind with the force of a physical blow, a sacrilege so profound that I feel the very air in the room grow thin and cold. *He has done it. He has committed the ultimate act of pride. He has become Lucifer, crying 'I will not serve' to God Himself.* The initial shock is a wave of pure, visceral horror, not for myself, but for his immortal soul. My own suffering, my own humiliation, pales into insignificance beside this cosmic act of rebellion. He has damned himself. He has taken the path from which there is no return. In this moment, I feel not anger, not the fury of a wronged wife, but a deep, aching pity for the man I once loved, the golden prince who was once so devout, so dedicated to the Faith that the Pope himself named him *Defensor Fidei*. What a bitter, terrible irony. The Defender of the Faith has become its destroyer.

I sink to my knees on the cold stone floor, the crucifix I always wear pressing into my chest. But this is not an act of collapse. It is an act of war. As the first wave of a wife's horror for her husband's soul recedes, my mind, trained for decades in theology by the finest scholars of Spain, trained in statecraft at my mother's knee, begins to dissect the act. I am not just a woman watching her husband fall into sin. I am a Queen, trained to see the political and spiritual consequences of such an act. The shock transmutes into a cold, clear energy. I rise from my knees and begin to pace the small chamber, my shadow looming and shrinking on the tapestried walls like a restless spirit. This is not just a sin. This is a strategy. And it is a deeply, catastrophically flawed one.

He has made himself Pope. The thought is absurd, a blasphemous comedy fit for a court jester's stage. But my mind, drilled in the intricacies of canon law, sees beyond the absurdity to the fatal theological error. *A Pope without apostolic succession,* I think, the words forming in my mind with the cold precision of a legal argument, *without the laying on of hands that stretches in an unbroken chain from his office back to Saint Peter himself, is nothing. He is just a king with a paper mitre. A temporal ruler dressing himself in spiritual authority he has no right to claim.* This is not just schism, a political tearing of the cloth of Christendom. Schisms can be mended. Wounds can heal. Popes and anti-popes have vied for power before, but always within the framework of the Church. This is something new. This is heresy. This is a poison injected into the very heart of the English church, a declaration that the Church in England is no longer part of the universal body of Christ. A schism is a quarrel within the family of God; heresy is a declaration that one is no longer part of the family at all. He has taken an axe to the True Vine, and a branch severed from the vine cannot live. It withers and dies.

The storm outside seems to intensify, the wind screaming around the turrets as if the very angels are weeping for this fallen kingdom. *Now,* I think, my mind racing with the terrible implications, *every man, woman, and child in England will be forced to choose. This is no longer the 'King's Great Matter,' a complex legal and theological debate for cardinals and universities, something that the common man could safely ignore. This is a simple, brutal choice for every soul in this kingdom: will you serve your King, or your God?* He thinks this act strengthens his position, solidifies his power, makes him absolute master in his own realm. He is a fool, blinded by lust and pride. He has just declared war on the conscience of every true Christian in his kingdom. He has turned a political problem into a spiritual crisis. He has sown the seeds of rebellion, civil war, and martyrdom in the fertile soil of English faith.

And then, a new thought, sharp and clear as a lightning flash illuminating the dark landscape, strikes me with its full, world-altering force. It is a thought so powerful, so transformative, that it stops my pacing. I stand still in the center of the room, the storm outside and the storm within for a moment perfectly matched.

My nephew. The Emperor. Charles.

Until now, my cause has been a matter of family honor for Charles. A difficult, embarrassing affair concerning his aunt's marriage, a diplomatic inconvenience that complicates his relationship with his English ally. He has offered support, applied pressure through his ambassadors, spoken sternly to the Pope on my behalf, but always within the cautious, calculated bounds of dynastic politics. He could pity me, he could honor my constancy, but he could not go to war over his aunt's marital dispute.

But this... this changes everything. The board has been overturned. The very nature of the game has been altered.

Charles is not just my nephew, my mind argues with a lawyer's precision. *He is the Holy Roman Emperor. His titles are not mere vanities. He is Defensor Fidei, the sworn protector of the Catholic Faith throughout Christendom. Henry is no longer just a problematic brother-in-law pursuing a distasteful annulment; he is a heretic king, a public schismatic who has torn an entire realm from the body of the Church. This is no longer a personal insult to the House of Habsburg. It is a direct challenge to the unity of Christendom, a mortal threat to the spiritual order of Europe, and an attack on the very foundations of Charles's own imperial and spiritual authority.* He cannot ignore this. He *must* act, not for my sake, but for the sake of the faith he is sworn to defend. To fail to act would be to show all of Europe that the title of Emperor is meaningless, that the Catholic princes cannot look to him for leadership against the tide of heresy.

"María," I say, turning to my friend, my voice no longer trembling but filled with a grim, terrible certainty. "He has made a mistake. A catastrophic mistake."

She looks at me, her eyes wide with confusion and fear. "Majesty, he has made himself a heretic and all of England with him. It is a disaster beyond imagining."

"It is," I agree, my hand closing into a fist at my side, my nails digging into my palm. "But even in the greatest catastrophe, there can be opportunity. Even in the deepest darkness, God can provide a sword. Henry, in his arrogance and his madness, has given me a weapon more powerful than any army, more persuasive than any diplomat. He has given me the cause of the true Faith. He has transformed me from a wronged and aging wife, a figure of pity to be argued over by canon lawyers, into the living symbol of Catholic resistance in this kingdom. He thinks he has won, that he is now absolute master in his own house. He does not see that he has just handed his enemies—myself, the Emperor, the Pope, every true Catholic in this land—their greatest rallying cry. He has made my personal battle the battle for the soul of England."

My weariness is gone, burned away by this new, cold fire. The years of passive endurance, of waiting for a verdict from Rome, of hoping for a change in Henry's heart—they are over. The nature of the war has changed, and so have I. I am no longer merely defending my own honor and my daughter's legitimacy. I am defending the honor of God Himself.

I go to my small, rickety writing desk. "Bring me the cipher," I say to María. "The one Chapuys left for matters of the gravest importance. We must write to the Emperor at once. He must be made to see this not as a family matter, but as a crusade. He must understand that this is not just about his aunt, but about the future of the Church and the stability of his own empire."

As María retrieves the coded book from its hiding place beneath a loose floorboard, I sit and stare into the fire. The flames leap and dance, consuming the dry wood, turning it to ash. Henry believes he can do the same to the Church in England, that he can consume its ancient traditions, its loyalty to Rome, its thousand years of faith, and forge something new in the fire of his own will. He has forgotten that the Church is not built on the wood of earthly kings, but on the rock of Saint Peter. And against that rock, the gates of Hell—and the ambitions of heretic kings—shall not prevail. The storm outside may be ending, its fury spent. But the real storm, the one for the soul of this kingdom, has just begun. And I, Katherine of Aragon, forgotten and exiled in this shabby palace, have just found myself at its very center, no longer a victim, but a standard-bearer.

CHAPTER 30

"PRINCESS DOWAGER"

The snows of December 1533 fall thick and fast upon Buckden, a silent, smothering blanket that promises to entomb us completely. The world outside my grimy window has been reduced to a monochrome of grey sky and white earth, the fenlands disappearing into a frozen, featureless void. It is a landscape of endings, a fitting backdrop for the arrival of the men who have come to pronounce the final death of my identity.

I know they are coming before I hear the horses. There is a shift in the air, a tension in the silence of the palace that speaks of an impending violation. My ladies, the few who remain, sense it too. They move about my small chamber with a nervous energy, their eyes constantly flicking towards the door. They have heard the rumors as I have, carried on the winter wind: the Boleyn has been crowned Queen in a ceremony of obscene magnificence, using my own crown, St. Edward's Crown, which no queen consort has ever worn. And she has given birth. Not to the son she promised Henry, the son for whom he has damned his soul, but to a daughter. A red-haired, squalling girl they have named Elizabeth. I allow myself a moment of grim, bitter satisfaction. He has broken the world in two for this, and God has given him another daughter. The irony is so profound, so terrible, it is almost beautiful. But the satisfaction is fleeting, because I know what must follow. With a new 'queen' and a new 'heir,' the old one must be definitively erased.

They come as the winter light begins to fail, their approach announced by the clatter of hooves and the jingle of harness in the courtyard below. It is not a small party. I see from my window a troop of armed men, their liveries stark against the snow, their breath pluming in the frigid air. They have come in force, as if they expect to lay siege to a fortress, not to confront one aging, ailing woman and her handful of ladies. The show of force is an insult in itself, designed to intimidate, to remind me that I am utterly at their mercy.

At their head ride two figures I know well. Thomas Howard, Duke of Norfolk, his thin, cruel face pinched by the cold and by a lifetime of ambition. He is the Boleyn's uncle, the chief architect of her rise and my fall, a man who would sell his own soul, and England's with it, for a moment more of the King's favor. Beside him rides Charles Brandon, Duke of Suffolk, my husband's oldest friend, the companion of his golden youth. He was once my friend, too. He danced at my wedding, laughed at my table, named a daughter for me. Now he comes as Norfolk's second, his face buried in the fur collar of his cloak, a man hollowed out by his own cowardice.

I take my time preparing to receive them. Let them wait in the cold. I dress with deliberate care, choosing my best remaining gown, a deep purple velvet that has faded with time but still speaks of majesty. I have María braid my hair, still more auburn than grey, in the severe Spanish style. I place my mother's simple gold cross around my neck. I will not meet them as a victim, but as a Queen.

I receive them in my presence chamber, such as it is—a cold, drafty room with a fireplace that gives off more smoke than heat. The tapestries are faded, the furniture sparse and mean. But I sit in my high-backed chair beneath my cloth of estate, which my ladies have carefully mended and hung. It still bears the royal arms of England and Spain, intertwined. Let them look at it. Let it remind them of the sacred alliance they have helped to shatter.

Norfolk enters first, stamping the snow from his boots with an arrogant swagger. His bow is a mere dip of the head, an insult he delivers with relish. Suffolk follows, his bow deeper, his eyes fixed on the floor. He, at least, has the grace to be ashamed.

"Madam," Norfolk begins, and the deliberate omission of my title is the first shot fired in this final battle. It is a word designed to strip me of everything, to reduce me to a nameless woman.

"Your Grace," I respond, my voice as cool and clear as the winter air. "You have traveled far in this weather. To what do I owe this armed visitation? Have I become so dangerous in my solitude that England's two greatest dukes require a small army to deliver a message?"

Suffolk flinches, but Norfolk's face hardens. "We come with news and instructions from His Majesty the King."

"My husband has instructions for me? How novel. I had thought he preferred to communicate his intentions through public proclamations and the pronouncements of his pet bishops."

Norfolk's face flushes, a blotchy red against the cold-whipped pallor of his skin. He thrives on this cruelty. "The King, madam, has taken a new wife, as all the world knows. By the judgment of a lawful ecclesiastical court held at Dunstable, your marriage to the King has been declared null and void from the very beginning."

He unrolls a document with a flourish, the parchment crackling in the quiet room. "The Lady Anne has been crowned Queen of England, and has, by the grace of God, borne the King a healthy and legitimate heir, the Princess Elizabeth."

They think the repetition of these lies will make them true. They think that if they say 'lawful court' and 'legitimate heir' enough times, the world will forget the truth. But truth is not a matter of decree. It is a matter of fact.

"The King has taken a concubine," I correct calmly, my voice unwavering. "And she has borne him a bastard. These facts are not altered by a sham ceremony performed by a heretic archbishop, nor by a piece of parchment filled with legal falsehoods."

"You speak treason!" Norfolk spits, his hand moving instinctively to the hilt of his sword.

"I speak truth. If truth has become treason in England, then England's soul is in greater peril than I had feared."

He continues, his voice tight with rage, ignoring my words. "The judgment of the court stands. You are therefore no longer to be

273

styled Queen. You are to be known, henceforth and by all persons, only as the Princess Dowager of Wales, in recognition of your brief and legal marriage to the late Prince Arthur."

There it is. The word, the title, the poison they have brewed for me. 'Princess Dowager'. An erase. A negation of twenty-four years of my life. A public declaration that my marriage to Henry never existed, that my children were born in sin, that my daughter, Mary, is a bastard. They offer it to me as if it is a recognition of some status, a piece of residual dignity. They think me a fool. They think me a weak, sentimental woman who will cling to any title, however demeaning.

They offer this title to me like an bone thrown to a dog, a scrap to quiet my barking. 'Princess Dowager'. Do they truly think me so simple that I do not see the legal serpent coiled within that seemingly innocuous phrase? The trap is ingenious in its cruelty, for it is a snare that I would set for myself.

My mind, sharp and cold, dissects it in an instant. *To accept that name is to accept everything. It is to agree, with my own mouth, that my marriage to Arthur was not only legal but consummated. It is to admit that the papal dispensation, the foundation of my life in England, was granted in error, based on a falsehood. It is to declare that my twenty-four-year marriage to Henry was therefore an incestuous abomination, a living sin. And if my marriage to Henry never existed, then my daughter, my Mary, the only living fruit of my womb, the true heir of England, is a bastard. It all hinges on this. This single title. This is not about my pride. God is my witness, my pride was burned to ash years ago in the damp rooms of Durham House. This is about the law. Divine and canonical. It is about my daughter's soul, her birthright, her very identity. I am not Katherine, the proud Spanish princess. I am Katherine, the Queen of England and the mother of its legitimate heir. And I am her last line of defense. To refuse this title is not an act of petulant defiance. It is my only remaining legal strategy. It is my sacred duty.*

When I finally speak, my voice is devoid of the passion they expect. It is cold, precise, the voice of a lawyer, a theologian, a queen. "I am the King's true wife. I was crowned and anointed by the authority of the Holy See. My title is Queen. I will be called by that name, and by no other."

Suffolk steps forward, his face a mask of pained sincerity. He, at least, has the decency to appear troubled. "Madam... Your Majesty... please, be reasonable. The King's mind is set. Parliament has confirmed it. The entire realm accepts the new order. Your resistance only makes things harder for yourself... and for the Lady Mary."

The mention of Mary is a deliberate, cruel twist of the knife. He knows she is my only weakness. "Do not speak to me of what is harder for my daughter," I say, my voice trembling for the first time, not with weakness, but with a mother's rage. "You keep her from me. You have stripped her of her household. You force her to serve the bastard child of the King's whore. You call her illegitimate when she is the only legitimate child Henry possesses. Her life is hard because her father has abandoned his duty to God and to his true family, not because her mother refuses to surrender to lies."

"Regardless," Norfolk says, his patience clearly at an end, "you *will* accept the title of Princess Dowager. Your household will address you as such. All correspondence will be directed to the Princess Dowager. We are here to enforce the King's will."

"The King may insist upon many things," I reply, my voice returning to its icy calm. "He may insist the sun rises in the west. He may insist that his adultery is a valid marriage. He may insist that a lie, repeated often enough, becomes the truth. But insisting, Your Grace, does not make it so. It only reveals the desperation of the liar."

Norfolk's face is now a mottled purple. He is not used to being defied, let alone analyzed with such contempt. "Madam, if you do not comply, measures will be taken. Your household will be dismissed entirely. Your allowance, already meager, will be stopped. You will be moved to less… comfortable accommodation."

I laugh. The sound is dry, brittle, utterly devoid of humour, and it clearly unnerves them. "Less comfortable than this? Your Grace, I invite you to look around you. I live in a damp ruin that you would not stable your horses in. I eat food that your dogs would refuse. I wear gowns that are more patches than original fabric. My ladies and I huddle by a smoking fire for warmth. What more can you possibly take from me that has not already been taken?"

"Your life," Norfolk says, his voice a low, venomous hiss. And the threat, naked and brutal, hangs in the cold air between us.

The chamber falls silent. My ladies gasp. Even Suffolk looks shocked that Norfolk would speak the unspeakable. But I am not shocked. I have known for months that this was the final currency they had to bargain with.

"If my husband wishes to add murder to his list of sins," I say, meeting Norfolk's gaze without flinching, "that is a matter for his conscience and his confessor. But I will not commit spiritual suicide to save him the trouble of committing a physical crime. I am more use to my daughter, and to God, alive and constant than I would be dead and compromised."

I return to my chair, sitting with a deliberate, unhurried grace, an assertion of queenship in this shabby room. "You have your answer, my lords. You may report to the King that you have delivered his message, and that I have delivered mine. I am the Queen. Now, you may show yourselves out."

They stand there for a moment, baffled. They came expecting tears, hysteria, a woman's weakness they could exploit. They found instead Spanish steel, tempered by years of suffering into an unbreakable blade. They have no more arguments, no more threats that I have not already faced and dismissed in my own heart.

"You will regret this, madam," Norfolk snarls as they turn to leave, his parting shot a confession of his own impotence.

"I regret many things, Your Grace," I reply to his retreating back. "I regret the loss of my sons. I regret the loss of my husband's love. I regret the peril this kingdom is now in. But standing for the truth of God and the rights of my child will never be among them."

They leave, their footsteps heavy with failure. The great door closes, and the silence they leave behind is profound. For a moment, I allow myself to tremble. The strength that sustained me through the confrontation drains away, leaving me weak and cold. My ladies rush to my side, María chafing my icy hands.

"Your Majesty was magnificent," she whispers, her voice thick with tears of pride and fear. "You were our Isabella."

"I was a mother defending her child," I correct, my voice weary. "It is the most basic instinct God gives us." The victory feels hollow, for I know what comes next. Retaliation. Swift and brutal.

Within the hour, it begins. The captain of Norfolk's guard returns. His face is impassive as he reads his orders. My entire household is dismissed. All who served me, who showed me loyalty, are to be cast out into the winter snow. The only ones permitted to remain are two servants deemed too old and insignificant to matter. They will be replaced by strangers, spies loyal to Norfolk and the Boleyn. My last friends, my last comfort, are to be torn from me.

I gather my ladies, my chaplain, my few loyal men-at-arms, in the cold presence chamber one last time. Their faces are pale with shock and fear for their futures. I have brought them to this. My constancy is their ruin. The guilt is a physical pain in my chest.

"I release you all from my service," I say, my voice breaking for the first time. "Go. Swear the oaths. Serve the new Queen. Survive. I do not wish you to suffer for my sake."

It is my chaplain, Father Abel, who answers. He is a simple man, not a great theologian, but his faith is pure. "We do not suffer for your sake, Your Majesty," he says, his voice clear and strong. "We suffer for Christ's sake. To deny you is to deny the sanctity of the marriage He blessed. We will not do it."

One by one, they refuse my offer of release. María, weeping, embraces me. "We are Spanish, Majesty. We do not abandon our Queen." Lady Willoughby, English to the core, kneels and kisses my hand. "I serve the true Queen of England, now and always."

The soldiers are not gentle. They tear María from my arms. They drag Father Abel away. I watch as my last friends, my family of exiles, are forced out into the snow, with no money, no prospects, nowhere to go. The door closes on their beloved faces, and I am utterly, finally, alone.

That night, alone in the vast, silent, freezing palace, I do not collapse into despair. The grief is a cold, hard stone in my heart, but something else is there too: a cold, hard resolve. They have taken everything. They have left me nothing. And in doing so, they have made me invincible. A person with nothing left to lose is a person who cannot be threatened.

I find a quill and a scrap of parchment that has been overlooked. By the light of a single, guttering candle, I begin to dictate a letter in my mind, a secret dispatch to be smuggled to Chapuys at the first opportunity. The words are not for him, but for my nephew, the Emperor. For Rome. For history.

"Make it known," I whisper to the shadows, my voice the only sound in the dead palace. "Make it known that they came with threats and false titles. Make it known that the title of 'Princess Dowager' is a legal trap, designed to bastardize the Princess Mary by my own admission. To accept it is to concede the entire case. This is the lynchpin. This is the heart of their legal strategy. My refusal is not pride. It is the only defense left to my daughter. They have stripped me of my household, my friends, my freedom. They think this will break my will. Inform His Imperial Majesty that they have instead forged it into something unbreakable. I am alone. But I am not defeated. The war continues."

The candle flickers and dies, plunging me into absolute darkness. But in my mind, a cold, clear light burns. I know my path. It is a path of suffering, of isolation, of slow death. But it is the path of truth. And I will walk it to its end, not as Princess Dowager, but as Katherine, Queen of England.

Chapter 31
The Cruelest Cut

Spring comes late to the fenlands in 1534, a reluctant greening of a landscape that has been grey for what feels like an eternity. The air loses its biting edge, but the chill within my heart remains, a permanent winter. The isolation at Buckden is now absolute. Since the violent dismissal of my household, I am attended only by strangers, their faces blank masks of obedience, their eyes watchful. They are my jailers, not my servants, and I know that every word I speak, every sigh I utter, is reported back to Cromwell. My only companions are the ghosts of my past and the ever-present ache for my daughter.

Mary. My jewel. *Mi perla.* The separation from her is a physical wound that does not heal, a constant, throbbing pain that is worse than any arthritis in my joints or dampness in my bones. I have not seen her face in almost three years. I have not heard her voice, have not held her hand. They keep her from me as a matter of policy, a tool of torture. They know she is the only weapon that can truly wound me. They use that knowledge with a surgeon's precision and a butcher's cruelty.

The news, when it comes, is delivered with the same calculated brutality as all their other pronouncements. I am in my chamber, trying to read a passage from St. Augustine, but the words blur on the page. My thoughts are with Mary. Where is she now? Hatfield? Hunsdon? They move her constantly, another turn of the screw. Is she well? Does she have enough to eat? Is she warm? Does she still remember her mother's face?

I hear the sound of horses in the courtyard, a sound that always brings a knot of dread to my stomach. It is never good news. I watch from my window as a small party dismounts. I recognize the livery of Sir William Fitzwilliam, the treasurer of the King's household, a man whose loyalty is as flexible as his ambition is vast. With him is Lord Mountjoy, a man of learning who once served in my own household in happier times, a man who should know better but has chosen survival over principle. The sight of them fills me with a cold premonition. This is not a casual visit. They have come to deliver a blow.

I receive them standing, though the effort makes my legs tremble and my back scream in protest. I will not show weakness to Henry's messengers. I am still the Queen, though my kingdom has shrunk to these three damp rooms. They enter without the proper courtesies, their bows shallow, their faces grim as executioners.

"Madam," Fitzwilliam begins, dispensing with even the pretense of respect.

"There is no madam here," I interrupt, my voice weak but steady. "If you seek Queen Katherine, I am she. Otherwise, you have wasted your journey on these muddy roads."

He ignores my correction, a small but significant act of power. He unrolls a parchment heavy with seals. The crackle of the stiff paper is the only sound in the room. "By order of His Majesty the

King, and for the better ordering of the royal succession, the household of the Lady Mary is to be dissolved."

My heart stops. I grip the back of a nearby chair, my knuckles white, the carved wood digging into my palm. *Mary.* They are going to harm Mary. I can feel it.

"She is to be stripped of the title of Princess," Fitzwilliam continues, his voice flat and emotionless, as if he were reading a list of household expenses. "And will henceforth be known, and addressed by all, only as the Lady Mary, the King's illegitimate daughter."

Illegitimate. The word strikes me with the physical force of a blow. I stagger, a wave of nausea and dizziness washing over me. They have called her this in whispers, in documents, but to declare it so, to strip her of her very name, her identity... It is a spiritual assassination.

But they are not finished. Mountjoy, the scholar, the man who once discussed Plato with me, now takes up the litany of cruelty, seeming to take a perverse pleasure in each syllable.

"Furthermore," he says, a slight smirk playing on his lips, "in order that she may learn her proper place, she is to be sent to live in the household of the Princess Elizabeth at Hatfield House. There, she will serve as a lady-in-waiting to her younger half-sister, attending her person and according her the respect due to the King's true and lawful heir."

The full, diabolical monstrosity of it breaks over me like a black, suffocating wave. My daughter. My Mary, the true Princess of

England, the legitimate heir to the throne, my serious, proud, devout child... reduced to serving the bastard of the Boleyn whore. Made to wait upon an infant. Forced to kneel before her, to address her as 'Princess,' to acknowledge with every breath, every curtsy, every moment of her waking life her own shame, her own illegitimacy, her own displacement. It is a form of psychological torture so refined, so exquisitely cruel, that only a mind like Cromwell's, or a heart as vengeful as Anne Boleyn's, could have conceived it.

"No." The word is not a protest. It is a tearing sound, ripped from my throat, a sound of pure, primal maternal anguish. "No, you cannot. He cannot. *Deus meus*, not Mary... not my child..."

"It is done, madam," Fitzwilliam says coldly, unmoved. "The Lady Mary has already been moved to Hatfield. She is there now, under the governance of the Lady Shelton."

Lady Shelton. Anne Boleyn's own aunt. A woman known for her harsh temper and her slavish devotion to her niece's cause. They have not just imprisoned Mary; they have given her to the wolves. The room begins to spin, the faded tapestries swirling into a vortex of meaningless color. This is worse than any blow they have struck against me. Take my crown. Take my freedom. Take my wealth, my health, my life. But leave my child her dignity. Leave her her identity. Leave her her birthright. To attack me is one thing. To attack my innocent daughter, to use her as a weapon to break my will, is an act of evil so profound it defies comprehension.

"She will never agree to it," I manage to say, my voice a ragged whisper. "Mary knows who she is. She has her mother's pride and her father's stubbornness. She is the legitimate daughter of a true marriage. No force on earth can make her acknowledge otherwise."

"Then force will be applied," Fitzwilliam says with a brutal shrug. "Lady Shelton has been given strict instructions. If the Lady Mary proves recalcitrant and refuses to acknowledge her new and proper status, she is to be... persuaded."

Persuaded. I know what that word means in the language of Henry's new England. It means beatings. It means starvation. It means public humiliation and cold, lonely isolation. It means every torment they dare not apply to me directly, the aunt of the Emperor, they will visit upon my innocent, defenseless daughter. Something breaks in me then, some last reserve of queenly composure, some final dam holding back the flood of a mother's terror. I lunge forward, my hands clawing, trying to rip the hateful document from Fitzwilliam's grasp. All dignity is gone, all reason consumed by a savage, protective rage. "You will not touch her! She is a princess of England and Spain! She is my daughter! She is innocent of any crime! If Henry has grievances with me, let him punish me! Let him take a sword and strike off my head, but leave our daughter alone!"

Mountjoy, stronger than he looks, catches my arms, his grip surprisingly rough. "Control yourself, madam," he says, his voice sharp with distaste. "You forget your position."

"I forget nothing!" I scream, struggling against his hold, all my Spanish reserve, all my royal training, all my Christian fortitude shattered by this one unbearable cruelty. "I am her mother! I have rights! God gave me rights over my own child!"

"You have no rights," Fitzwilliam says, his voice like the flick of a whip. "You are nothing but the Dowager Princess of Wales, and the Lady Mary is the King's bastard daughter. These are the facts as the law of this realm now recognizes them."

They release me and I stumble, falling to my knees on the cold stone floor, not in submission but in utter collapse. My strength is gone. The fight has drained out of me, replaced by an image that will haunt my waking hours and my dreams: my precious Mary, my serious, devout daughter, seventeen years old but small for her age and fragile in health, being forced to kneel before a baby in a cradle and call her 'Your Highness.' Being struck by the brutish Lady Shelton if she refuses. Being called 'bastard' by servants who once bowed to her.

"Does she know?" I whisper from the floor, my voice broken. "Have you told her... that she cannot see me? That we are to be kept apart?"

"The Lady Mary has been informed that all communication with you is forbidden," Mountjoy says, his tone leaving no room for doubt. "Any attempt by either party to send or receive letters, messages, or tokens will be considered an act of treason."

Treason. The love of a mother for her child is now treason in Henry's England. The word is the final nail in the coffin of my hope.

They leave me there on the floor, a heap of purple velvet and broken dreams. They have done their work. They have found the one weapon against which I have no defense. My ladies—the two ancient servants who are all that remain of my household—shuffle in, their faces masks of horror and pity. They try to help me to my feet, but I cannot rise. The strength has gone from my limbs. I can only kneel there and howl, a raw, animal sound of pure agony, all my years of restraint, all my dignity, all my faith swept away by this flood of maternal grief.

"My baby," I sob in Spanish, the language of my heart, reverting to my mother tongue in this extremity of pain. *"Mi niña, mi tesoro, mi única alegría."* My girl, my treasure, my only joy. They are torturing my only joy.

For hours I remain there, lost in a storm of grief. My ladies bring me water, wine, but I wave them away. How can I eat or drink when my daughter may be starving? How can I rest when she is in the hands of her enemies? The full scope of their cruelty is a physical presence in the room, a suffocating darkness. They will use Mary to break me. They will send me reports of her ill-treatment. They will offer to lessen her suffering if only I will sign their papers, accept their titles, agree to their lies. They are putting my daughter on the rack to force my confession.

When I can finally think again, my grief begins to cool, to harden into something else. Rage. A cold, pure, and utterly focused rage. They think this will break me. They have misjudged the daughter of Isabella of Castile. This will not break me. It will forge me into a weapon. My passive resistance, my war of attrition, is over. Now, I must become an active combatant. I cannot fight them with armies, but I can fight them with every tool I still possess.

That night, my war begins. I cannot sleep. Sleep is a luxury I will not afford myself while my daughter suffers. Instead, I plan. First, I must try to reach her. I summon the younger of my two remaining ladies, a girl named Elizabeth who is a distant cousin of the Willoughbys and whose loyalty I have come to trust.

"Elizabeth," I say, my voice low and urgent. "You have a cousin who serves as a laundress at Hatfield, do you not?"

The girl pales, knowing what I am about to ask. "Yes, Your Majesty."

"I need to get a letter to the Princess. Not a written letter, that is too dangerous. A message. A token." I unfasten the small, simple gold cross from my own neck, the one I wear beneath my gown every day. It is not valuable, but Mary will know it. "Take this. Find a way to give it to your cousin. Tell her to give it to my daughter. And tell her this message, word for word: 'Your mother sends this. She wears its twin. She prays for you without ceasing. She says remember who you are. Be constant. Endure. Truth will prevail.'" I make her repeat the words until she has them by heart.

I press a few of the Emperor's gold coins into her hand. "Bribe whom you must. But do not be caught."

She leaves on her secret, perilous mission, a small soldier in my new army. It is a desperate gamble, but I must do *something*.

Next, I turn to my other battlefield: the pen. I sit at my desk, the fire now stoked high, my chamber lit by a dozen candles. Let them see the light from my window and wonder what the old Spanish woman is plotting. I will wage a war of letters, a campaign on three fronts.

My first letter is to Henry. It will not be a letter of anger or accusation. That would only feed his self-righteousness. It will be a letter from a mother to a father, an appeal to the man he once was. I dip my quill, and the words flow, each one chosen with a strategist's care.

"My most dear lord, King, and husband," I write, using the titles that are both truth and defiance. "I do not write to you of my own sorrows, for they are of no account. I write to you of our daughter. Our Mary. I beseech you, Henry, by all the love that was once between us, by the memory of our dead sons who lie in their tombs, do not visit this great cruelty upon our only living child. I remember the day she was born. I remember the joy in your face, how you called her your pearl, how you held her up to the court and boasted that she had your Tudor spirit. Does that father no longer live in you? Can you truly condemn the child of your own body to such shame and misery? She is your daughter, Henry. Your firstborn. She has your eyes, your intelligence, your stubborn will. Whatever you may think of me, she is innocent. To punish her is to punish a part of yourself. For the love of God, for the salvation of your own soul, be a father to her, if you will no longer be a husband to me."

I seal the letter, knowing it is a plea aimed at a heart that may have already turned entirely to stone. But I must try.

My second letter is to Cromwell. Here, the tone is entirely different. No emotion. No appeal to shared memories. Only cold, hard, political logic.

"Master Cromwell," I write, affording him his proper title, for he is a man who respects power and procedure. "You are the King's chief minister, a man known for his pragmatism and foresight. I write to you not as a wife but as a political observer. The current treatment of the Lady Mary, daughter to the King and myself, is not only cruel but politically unwise. She is the niece of the Holy Roman Emperor. To publicly degrade her, to strip her of her title and treat her as a servant, is a grave insult to the House of Habsburg and to the Emperor's personal honor. It jeopardizes the treaties of trade with Flanders, upon which so much of London's prosperity depends. It risks turning a neutral Emperor into an active enemy. Is the satisfaction of the Lady Anne's personal vengeance worth the price of a potential trade war, or even a real one? I urge you, as a wise counselor to the King, to advise a more moderate and politically astute course of action regarding the Lady Mary. Her harsh treatment serves no strategic purpose and creates significant political risk."

This letter is a piece of cold steel. I am speaking Cromwell's own language. I am showing him that I am not just a weeping woman, but a political player who still understands the game.

My third and final letter is to Bishop Fisher, now imprisoned in the Tower, but whose voice still carries moral weight. This letter will be smuggled by a different, more dangerous route, through the network of those loyal to the old faith.

"My good and constant friend," I write. "They have now turned their cruelty upon my daughter. They seek to break her spirit as they have tried to break mine. I ask you, from your blessed confinement, to speak out. Write to the Pope. Write to the Emperor. Urge your fellow bishops who still have a shred of conscience to protest this unnatural persecution of an innocent child. Frame this not as a political matter, but as what it is: a spiritual abomination. A father warring against his own child is a sin that cries out to Heaven for vengeance. Remind them that a kingdom that devours its own children cannot stand. Pray for her, my lord Bishop. And pray for me, that my heart does not break entirely."

The dawn is breaking by the time I have finished. The letters are sealed, ready to be passed to the secret messengers who are my only contact with the world. I am exhausted, my body screaming with pain, my eyes burning from lack of sleep. But my mind is clear. My grief has not been vanquished, but it has been harnessed. It is no longer a flood that threatens to drown me, but a river that I have channeled to turn the mills of war. I have transformed my maternal anguish into action. I am no longer a passive victim in their drama. I am a combatant, a strategist, a mother fighting for her child with the only weapons she has left: her words, her wit, and her indomitable will. The cruelest cut was meant to silence me forever. Instead, it has given me a voice of fire.

Chapter 32
The Love of the People

They are moving me again, this time from Buckden to Kimbolton Castle, an even more remote fortress in the fens. It is May of 1534, and the morning mist rises from the marshes like the breath of ghosts. I am bundled into a litter—I no longer have the strength to ride—with only my two remaining servants attending me. The guards who escort us are surly and rough, clearly resentful of this duty to transport a woman they have been told is nothing.

But as our small, sad procession moves through the first village, something unexpected happens. The people come out of their cottages, at first just a few, then more, then what seems like the entire population. They line the muddy road, these common folk of England who have no power, no influence, nothing but their voices and their conviction.

An old man steps forward, cap in hand, and drops to his knees in the mud as my litter passes. "God save Your Majesty," he says, his voice clear and strong. "God save our true Queen."

The captain of the guard wheels his horse around, hand on his sword. "You speak treason, old man. That is the Dowager Princess of Wales, nothing more."

The old man looks up, unafraid. "I see Queen Katherine, wife of King Henry these twenty-four years. My eyes may be old, but they see truly."

Before the captain can respond, a woman pushes forward—a young mother with a baby in her arms. "Your Majesty!" she cries. "Bless my child! Let him be touched by the true Queen of England!"

Then another woman: "The Queen! The rightful Queen!"

And another: "God curse the Boleyn whore!"

The cry is taken up by others, spreading through the crowd like fire: "The true Queen! God save Queen Katherine!"

The guards are overwhelmed. They cannot arrest an entire village. They cannot stop the tide of love and loyalty that flows toward my litter. The people press forward, reaching out to touch the curtains of my litter, to kiss my hands when I extend them in blessing, to show in every way they can that they know the truth.

I am overcome. Tears stream down my face as I look at these people—my people, my subjects, the true judges of my queenship. They have not forgotten. Despite all Henry's laws, all his threats, all his propaganda, they know their true Queen.

"God bless you," I call out, my voice breaking with emotion. "God bless you all, good people of England."

A young girl, perhaps ten years old, manages to push through to the litter. She holds up a small bouquet of wildflowers—daisies and buttercups, the flowers of the poor.

"For you, Your Majesty," she says shyly. "My mother says you are the bravest lady in England."

I take the flowers with hands that tremble, and they are more precious to me than all the jewels I once wore. "What is your name, child?"

"Katherine, Your Majesty. My mother named me for you."

My heart breaks with love for these people who honor me still, who name their daughters after a rejected queen, who risk punishment to show their loyalty.

The captain of the guard has given up trying to control the situation. We move slowly through the village, the crowd growing larger as word spreads. They throw flowers in our path—not the cultivated roses of court but the honest flowers of English fields. They sing hymns, old Latin hymns that Henry has forbidden but which rise now in defiance of his new order.

At the edge of the village stands the priest, Father Edmund, whom I remember from happier times when I traveled these roads as acknowledged Queen. He wears his simple cassock, not the grand vestments of high ceremony, but he stands tall and unafraid.

"Your Majesty," he says, bowing deeply. "I have been commanded to recognize no queen but Anne Boleyn. I have been threatened with the scaffold if I pray for any but her. But I tell you now, before all these witnesses, that every Mass I say includes a prayer for Katherine, the true Queen of England, and for the Princess Mary, the legitimate heir."

"Father, you risk too much—" I begin.

"I risk my body," he replies firmly. "You risk your soul by standing for truth. Which is the greater courage?"

The guards hurry us on, clearly eager to leave this village where their authority means nothing against the people's love. But the scene repeats in every hamlet we pass. Word travels faster than our procession. By the time we reach the next village, the people are already gathered, already waiting to show their Queen that she is not forgotten.

In one town, the women have organized themselves. They stand in two lines, creating a corridor of honor for my litter to pass through. Each holds a candle, though it is broad daylight. As I pass, they curtsey in perfect unison, a choreographed declaration of loyalty.

"Why the candles?" I ask one of them.

"You are the light of truth in dark times, Your Majesty," she replies. "We hold these flames to show that your light has not been extinguished."

At a crossroads, we encounter a group of merchants traveling to market. They immediately stop their carts, and the men sweep off their caps while the women curtsey.

"Your Majesty," their leader says, "we are simple traders, but we know right from wrong. We know a true marriage from false pretense. You are our Queen, whatever London says."

One of them presses something into my hand—a small leather purse. "For Your Majesty's needs," he says quietly. "We know they keep you in poverty. It isn't much, but it's given with loyal hearts."

I try to refuse, knowing these people have little to spare, but he insists. "Let us serve our Queen in the small ways we can."

As we continue through the countryside, I see that my journey has become a pilgrimage route. People walk for miles to stand by the roadside as I pass. Mothers hold up their children. Old veterans of the French wars stand at attention, saluting as they would for any royal progress. Young lovers ask for my blessing on their marriages, saying they want the blessing of someone who understands the sanctity of true vows.

But it is not just the common people. As we pass through a larger town, I see familiar faces among the crowd—minor nobility who have traveled from their estates, merchants' wives I once received at court, even some clergy who risk their positions to show support. They cannot speak as boldly as the common folk—they have more to lose—but their presence speaks volumes.

Lady Exeter is there, heavily veiled but recognizable. She says nothing, but she drops into a deep curtsey as I pass, holding it until my litter is gone. Sir William Kingston, the Constable of the Tower, is there in civilian clothes. He meets my eyes and nods—just once, but with unmistakable respect.

Near Cambridge, we encounter something that makes even the guards stop in amazement. The entire student body of one of the colleges has turned out, standing in their academic robes along the road. As my litter approaches, they begin to sing—not in English but in Latin, a hymn to the Virgin Mary that is also, unmistakably, a hymn to me.

"Ave Regina Caelorum," they sing. "Hail, Queen of Heaven." But they look at me as they sing, and everyone understands the double meaning.

Their masters try to stop them, threatening expulsion, but they continue singing. These young men, the future priests and scholars of England, are declaring where their loyalty lies.

One young student, bolder than the rest, steps forward. "Your Majesty, we study theology and law. We know what is true and what is false. You are our Queen, and we will teach that truth no matter what laws are passed against it."

The captain of the guard has had enough. "Move on!" he shouts. "All of you, disperse, or face arrest!"

But how can you arrest a thousand people? How can you imprison an entire countryside? The people do not disperse. They follow us, a growing crowd that becomes a multitude, singing, praying, calling out blessings.

As we finally approach Kimbolton Castle, my final prison, the crowd has swelled to thousands. They cannot all have come from nearby villages. People have traveled from across the region to show their support. The guards are terrified, outnumbered hundreds to one, but the crowd is not violent. They are simply present, bearing witness, making it impossible for Henry to pretend that England accepts his new order.

At the gates of Kimbolton, I am helped from my litter. I can barely stand, weakened by travel and emotion, but I force myself upright to face this sea of love one last time.

"Good people," I call out, my voice carrying across the crowd. "My beloved subjects, my true friends. You have shown me today that truth lives in the hearts of the people even when it dies in the halls of power. You have given me strength to face whatever comes. I go now into this castle, perhaps never to emerge. But I go knowing that I am loved, that I am remembered, that I am still your Queen in the only court that matters—the court of conscience."

A great cry goes up from the crowd: "Long live the Queen! Long live Queen Katherine!"

I raise my hand in blessing one last time, making the sign of the cross over them all. "God bless you, people of England. God save you all from the darkness that has fallen on this realm. Remember the true faith. Remember the true Queen. Remember that right endures even when might seems to triumph."

The gates of Kimbolton close behind me with a sound like the ending of the world. But outside, I can still hear them singing, still hear them calling my name. They remain there for hours, until darkness forces them to return to their homes.

In my new prison, I am more isolated than ever. But I am also more certain than ever that I have been right to resist. The people know the truth. They see through Henry's lies, Anne Boleyn's pretensions, the whole elaborate falsehood that has been constructed to replace reality.

That night, as I kneel in the cold chapel of Kimbolton, I pray not for myself but for these brave souls who risked everything to honor their true Queen. Each face I saw today is etched in my memory —the old man in the mud, the young mother with her baby, the girl named Katherine, the defiant priest, the singing students.

"Lord," I whisper, "protect these Your servants who have chosen truth over safety. Let their loyalty be remembered when the history of these dark days is written. Let it be known that while kings and nobles bent to falsehood, the common people of England stood firm for truth."

I am in prison, but I am free. I am rejected by the court, but I am loved by the people. I am called Dowager Princess, but I remain Queen in every heart that values truth over power.

This is the verdict that matters. Not the corrupt judgment of Blackfriars, not the craven vote of Parliament, not the heretical pronouncement of the false Archbishop. The people of England have spoken, and they have called me Queen.

No castle walls can imprison that truth. No royal decree can silence it. It lives in every cottage and farm, every shop and mill, every honest English heart that knows right from wrong.

I am Katherine of Aragon, Queen of England in the eyes of God and the hearts of the people.

That is vindication enough for any woman, even one dying slowly in a forgotten castle.

CHAPTER 33

THE WALLS OF KIMBOLTON

Kimbolton. The name itself is a tolling bell. Of all the shabby palaces and decaying manors they have shuffled me between, this one feels the most final. It rises from the flat, weeping landscape of the Cambridgeshire fens, a squat, grim fortress of cold stone and colder history, surrounded by a moat of dark, still water that reflects nothing but the perpetually grey sky. The air itself is heavy, thick with the damp exhalations of the marshland, a place of agues and fevers. This is where they have sent me to die. It is not a residence; it is a tomb.

The journey here was another turn of the screw, another calculated degradation. I am weaker now, the constant pain in my joints making every movement a trial, the cough that has settled deep in my chest a constant, rattling companion. Yet I endure. As my small, sad procession made its way across the winter landscape, the people came. They lined the roads, these good, simple people of England, kneeling in the mud to receive a blessing from a queen their king had disowned. They offered me flowers, small loaves of bread, their prayers. Their love was a shield against the cold, a reminder that in the only court that matters—the court of the human heart—I am still their Queen. But the gates of Kimbolton have closed behind me, and their voices have faded, leaving only the sound of the wind sighing through the battlements.

My jailer here is a man named Sir Edmund Bedingfeld. He is a knight of some standing, a man who once served me with courtesy. Now he is charged with my keeping, and the task has soured him. He treats me with a brusque, formal coldness, addressing me only as 'madam' or 'Princess Dowager,' his face a mask of duty that cannot quite hide his resentment. He is a man caught between his orders and his conscience, and he has chosen to silence his conscience.

My world has shrunk to three rooms in the south range of the castle. A bedchamber, a small presence chamber, and a tiny oratory where a single crucifix hangs on the damp-stained wall. This is my kingdom now. The furniture is heavy and dark, smelling of age and neglect. The tapestries are faded beyond recognition. A perpetual chill seeps from the stone walls, a dampness that no fire can fully dispel. It is a cold that settles in the bones, a physical manifestation of the cold that has settled in my life.

I spend my days in a routine that is part prayer, part penance, part quiet defiance. I rise before dawn, my aching body a trial to be overcome. I dress not in the velvets of a queen but in the simple, rough habit of the Third Order of St. Francis, a vow I took in my youth that now seems prophetic. I wear it not as a sign of surrender, of retiring from the world, but as my new uniform, the armor of a spiritual warrior. Beneath it, against my skin, I wear a hair shirt. Its constant, scratching irritation is a reminder of my daughter's suffering, a small penance I offer up for her sake.

The days are marked by the canonical hours. Matins, Lauds, Prime, Terce, Sext, None, Vespers, Compline. The ancient rhythm of the Church becomes the rhythm of my life. My ladies are gone, my chaplain is gone, so I keep the hours alone, my voice a solitary whisper against the vast silence of the castle. Prayer is no longer a comfort; it is a battle. A battle against despair, against anger, against the terrible, seductive whisper of doubt that comes in the long, dark hours of the night.

The nights are the worst. The pain in my body intensifies in the darkness, a burning in my joints, a deep ache in my bones. But it is the pain in my soul that is the true torment. I lie awake on my hard bed, listening to the wind and the cry of the fen-birds, and I wrestle with God.

Why? The question hammers at my soul, a desperate, angry, ceaseless assault on the gates of Heaven. *Why, Lord? I have been constant. When all others fled from truth, I stood firm. I defended Your holy sacrament of marriage against a king's lust and a heretic's ambition. I sacrificed my comfort, my freedom, my daughter's happiness, everything, for the sake of Your law. I have kept the faith. And my reward is this? To die slowly in a swamp, forgotten by the world, separated from my only child, attended by my enemies? My obedience, my long years of suffering and prayer—has it all been in vain?*

I think of the promises of Scripture, the stories of the saints I have revered all my life. God protects the righteous. He confounds the wicked. He rewards the faithful. But where is my protection? Henry thrives, his whore sits on my throne, his new church tramples on a thousand years of sacred tradition. The wicked are not confounded; they are triumphant. My faithfulness has earned me nothing but pain and isolation. Where are you, God? Have you turned Your face from me? Have You abandoned England to its sins, and me to my enemies?

The anger is a poison, hot and bitter in my throat. I am angry at Henry, at the Boleyn, at Cromwell, at the cowards who betrayed me. But most of all, in these dark, honest nights, I am angry at God. I feel like Job on his dung heap, covered in sores, his life in ruins, crying out to a silent heaven. I have served You. I have loved You. I have sacrificed everything for You. And You have allowed this. You have permitted this evil to triumph. Why?

The struggle goes on for weeks, a secret, terrible war waged in the depths of my soul. I go through the motions of my day, my face a serene mask for my ladies—the two old women who are all that remain of my household, and who look to me for strength. I eat my meager meals, I read my devotional books, I even manage a weak smile for the guard who brings my firewood. But inside, I am a raging tempest of doubt and despair. My faith, the bedrock of my entire existence, is cracking.

The turning point comes not in a flash of divine revelation, but in a moment of quiet, human connection. A secret letter arrives from Mary. It has taken weeks to reach me, smuggled from hand to hand by a network of loyal servants who risk their lives for this small act of love. Her script is small and cramped, the parchment stained with what I know are tears.

"Dearest Mother and Queen," she writes. "They press me daily to abandon my title and my faith. Lady Shelton is cruel. My food is often scant, my chambers cold. But I do not yield. I cannot yield. For in my heart, I carry your example. I remember you standing before the court at Blackfriars, speaking truth when all others were silent. I remember your letters, telling me to be constant. Your suffering has become my strength. Your constancy is my shield. I pray for you without ceasing. Do not despair for me, for in obeying God and you, I have found a strange peace in the midst of this torment. I am your daughter. I will not fail you."

I read the letter again and again, the words blurring through my tears. But these are not tears of sorrow. They are tears of a profound, shattering realization. My suffering has not been in vain. It has had a purpose. It has been a lesson, a beacon, a source of strength for my daughter. My constancy was not a foolish, stubborn act that led to ruin; it was the seed from which her own strength has grown. I did not fail her. I armed her.

And if my suffering has served this purpose for Mary, perhaps it serves a greater purpose still. My mind, trained in theology, begins to see a new pattern in the chaos of my life. I have been thinking of my suffering as a punishment, a trial to be endured. But what if it is not? What if it is a vocation? A mission? My final and most important duty as Queen?

I rise from my bed and walk to my small oratory. The crucifix hangs on the wall, the body of Christ emaciated, broken, defeated in the eyes of the world. And in that image, I finally see my own. He was not defeated on the cross. He was triumphant. His greatest moment of worldly failure was his greatest moment of spiritual victory. His suffering was not a punishment; it was an act of redemptive love.

Enrico thinks he has buried me here. The thought comes with the force of revelation, a quiet explosion in my soul that rearranges everything. *Stolto.* Fool. He thinks this damp fortress is my prison, my tomb. He does not see. He has not imprisoned me; he has elevated me. He has stripped away everything worldly—my crown, my wealth, my freedom—and left me with only what is eternal: my faith, my conscience, my soul. He has inadvertently created the perfect cloister for me to wage my final battle.

My battlefield is no longer the court of England or the legatine court at Blackfriars. My battlefield is this bed of pain. My weapons are not legal arguments or diplomatic appeals. My weapons are my prayers, my patience, my unyielding constancy. Every painful breath I take is a prayer for the soul of England, a protest against the heresy that has poisoned it. Every day that I survive in this misery is a living, breathing accusation against his schism, a testament to the true marriage he has tried to erase. Every shiver of ague, every stab of pain in my joints, is a penance I offer up for the sins of my husband and my kingdom.

He wants me to disappear, to fade away into the grey mists of the fens. But in my very endurance, I become more visible. The story of the constant Queen, the good wife cast aside, suffering with dignity in her prison—this story is more powerful than any proclamation Henry can issue. It is a story that cannot be silenced. It whispers in the taverns, in the markets, in the confessionals. It becomes a legend, a symbol of the old faith, the true order of things.

My death will not be a defeat. It will be my final, undeniable victory. The world will not remember the verdict of a corrupt court. It will remember the death of a Queen, constant in her faith, faithful to her vows until the very end. That is a story that not even Cromwell, with all his spies and all his power, will be able to erase from the memory of the people. It will be a stone in the foundation of the true Church in England, a rock against which the waves of heresy will break.

This is my true legacy. This is my inheritance for Mary. Not a kingdom, not a crown that can be taken away by men. But an example. An example of a woman who knew what was right and stood for it, no matter the cost. An example is more powerful than a dynasty. An example is harder to destroy than a crown.

I kneel before the crucifix, but not in supplication. I kneel as a soldier before her captain, receiving her final orders. The anger is gone. The doubt is gone. In their place is a profound, unshakable peace. I understand my purpose now. It is not to win, but to witness.

The walls of Kimbolton are no longer my prison. They are the ramparts of my spiritual fortress. This sickbed is not my deathbed; it is my throne of suffering, from which I rule a kingdom of the spirit that Henry can never touch. Let him have his whore and his crown of lies. I have this. I have the truth. And I have a death to die that will speak more loudly than any words I ever uttered in life. The final act of the drama is mine to command. And I will play it with all the grace, all the courage, all the constancy of the Queen I was born to be.

Chapter 34
A Sickness of the Heart

A sharp pain in my abdomen takes my breath away, and I struggle to rise from my bed. It is November now, 1535, and the damp of Kimbolton has settled so deep in my bones that they feel made of ice rather than living matter. Each morning brings new agonies—joints that refuse to bend, a back that screams with every movement, hands so gnarled with arthritis that holding a spoon becomes an act of will.

But this pain is different. It burns like fire in my belly, radiating outward in waves that leave me gasping. When I press my hand to my stomach, I can feel the swelling there, hard and wrong beneath my fingers. My physician was dismissed long ago, so I must diagnose myself. A canker, perhaps. A growth. Or simply my body's final surrender after years of fighting battles it could never win.

They say I have a canker, a dropsy. The local physician Bedingfeld finally permitted to see me speaks in whispers to my servants, thinking I cannot hear. But I know what this sickness truly is. It is a sickness of the heart, a grief so profound it has become physical. Grief for my husband's lost soul, wandering further from God with each passing day. Grief for my daughter's suffering, which I am powerless to ease. Grief for England itself, torn from the body of Christ like a limb roughly amputated.

My body, worn out by years of childbearing and grief, is beginning to fail. The body that carried so many doomed children, that stood firm at Blackfriars, that endured seven years of poverty at Durham House, that survived the humiliations of The More and Buckden —this body has fought long enough. It wishes for rest.

The symptoms worsen with each passing week. I can no longer eat solid food without agony. Even thin broths cause my stomach to rebel. Water tastes of metal and ash. My skin has taken on a yellow tinge that no amount of washing can remove. Some days the pain is so intense I cannot leave my bed at all, can only lie there gripping my rosary, each bead a small anchor to consciousness.

Alice, my ancient chambermaid, tends to me with touching gentleness. She has nowhere else to go, this old Englishwoman who has chosen to share my exile, and so she stays, spooning water between my cracked lips, changing my soiled linens without complaint, sitting with me through the long nights when pain makes sleep impossible.

"Your Majesty should have proper physicians," she says one morning, tears running down her weathered face. "This isn't right, keeping you here like this, suffering without help."

"God is my physician now," I tell her, though speaking costs me breath I can barely spare. "He will heal me or call me home as He sees fit."

But I know which it will be. I am dying. I can feel it in the way my body grows lighter each day, as if my soul is already beginning to detach from its earthly vessel. I see it in the way even Bedingfeld looks at me now, with something approaching pity. He knows, they all know, that Katherine of Aragon's final battle is nearly over.

The nights are the worst. Pain keeps me wakeful, but it is not just physical pain. In the darkness, all my failures parade before me. The sons I could not give Henry. The marriage I could not save. The daughter I could not protect. The England I could not keep faithful to Rome. So many battles fought, so many lost.

Yet in my more lucid moments, I understand that perhaps losing was its own kind of victory. By refusing to yield, by maintaining my truth against all pressure, I have become something more than a rejected wife. I have become a symbol, a reminder that there are things more important than comfort, more vital than life itself. Truth. Faith. Constancy. These are the hills I chose to die on, and I regret nothing.

One December morning, I wake to find frost patterns on the inside of my window, delicate as Spanish lace. The sight triggers a memory so vivid I can almost smell it—the orange blossoms in the gardens of the Alhambra, my mother's hands braiding flowers into my hair before I left for England. How young I was, how certain that God had chosen me for greatness.

And perhaps He did, just not the greatness I expected. Not the greatness of a queen who bears kings and shapes nations, but the greatness of a woman who would not lie, even to save herself.

There is a kind of nobility in that, I think. A kind of holiness, even.

I call for paper and pen, though holding the quill is agony. There are letters I must write while I still can. To Mary first, always to Mary.

"My most beloved daughter," I write, each word a victory over my failing body. "By the time you read this, if you ever do, I may be with God. Know that every breath I have taken since we were parted has been a prayer for you. You are legitimate. You are royal. You are loved. Let no one tell you otherwise. When they hurt you—and they will continue to hurt you—remember that suffering for truth is noble. Your mother chose poverty, exile, and death rather than call you bastard. That is how much you are worth. That is how precious your legitimacy is. Stand firm, my jewel. Your time will come."

To Chapuys, the Emperor's ambassador, who has been my only friend in these dark years:

"Tell my nephew the Emperor that I die his loyal aunt and England's true Queen. Tell him that I forgive Henry and pray for his soul. Tell him that power without truth is nothing, and that I go to my judgment with a clean conscience. Thank him for his support, inadequate though it was. Blood is blood, even when diluted by distance and politics."

And finally, to Henry. This letter is the hardest, for what can I say to the man who was my husband, my love, my destroyer?

"My most dear lord, king and husband," I begin, the words coming slowly. "The hour of my death now drawing on, the tender love I owe you forceth me to commend myself to you, and to put you in remembrance of the health and welfare of your soul..."

I tell him I forgive him, though forgiveness still struggles with anger in my heart. I beg him to be a good father to Mary. I ask him to remember that he will face God's judgment one day, and earthly power will not help him then. And I end with truth that surprises even me: "Lastly, I make this vow, that mine eyes desire you above all things."

It is true, God help me. Despite everything—the betrayal, the humiliation, the long years of suffering—some part of me still loves the golden prince who rescued me from poverty, who crowned me with such joy, who wept with me over our dead children. That Henry is as dead as our son, but I love his memory. Perhaps that is enough. Perhaps love transcending betrayal is its own form of holiness.

The pain grows worse as December deepens into January. Eating becomes impossible. I survive on sips of water and the Host when Father Jorge can sneak in to give me communion. My world shrinks to this bed, these four walls, the crucifix on the wall that I stare at for hours, finding in Christ's suffering a companion to my own.

Strange visions come to me. Sometimes I see my mother, young and fierce in armor. Sometimes my lost children, the sons who never breathed, the daughters who never quickened, all grown and beautiful, waiting for me. Sometimes I see England itself, personified as a wounded woman, reaching out for healing I cannot give.

One night, I dream I am back in the Alhambra, standing in the Court of Lions. The fountain plays its eternal song, and the air is warm with the scent of jasmine. A figure approaches—Henry, but not as he is now. Henry as he was at seventeen, golden and laughing, full of love and promise.

"Katherine," he says, and his voice is young again, untouched by the harshness of kingship. "I'm sorry. I'm so sorry for everything."

"I know," I tell him in the dream. "I forgive you. But forgiveness does not change truth. I am your wife. I have always been your wife."

"Yes," he says, and tears run down his young face. "My only true wife. But I learned it too late."

I wake from this dream with my own tears wet on my cheeks. Is it prophecy or wishful thinking? Will Henry someday understand what he has done? Or will he go to his grave believing his lies, convinced that God smiles upon his serial adultery?

On January 6th, the Feast of the Epiphany, I feel a change. The pain, paradoxically, lessens. My mind becomes clearer than it has been in weeks. I know what this means—the final rally before the end. My body is gathering its last strength for the passage from this world to the next.

I ask Alice to help me sit up, to dress me in my best remaining gown—still black, but silk at least, with a touch of the dignity I once wore so easily. I want to die as a queen, not as a sick old woman forgotten in a cold castle.

"Summon Father Jorge," I tell her. "And whoever else will come. I would not die alone."

She goes, weeping, and I am left for a moment in solitude. I look around this chamber that has been my world for so long. The walls that imprisoned me have also sheltered me. The poverty that humiliated me has also purified me. The isolation that tortured me has also brought me closer to God.

"Thank You," I whisper to the crucifix. "Thank You for the suffering that taught me strength. Thank You for the losses that taught me what truly matters. Thank You for the long, hard road that led to this moment of clarity."

Outside my window, snow begins to fall, covering the ugly fenland in a blanket of pristine white. It seems appropriate—a cleansing, a purification, a preparation for what comes next.

My servants return with Father Jorge, and I see they have brought others—a few Spanish merchants who have somehow gained permission to come, old servants who served me in better days, even Bedingfeld himself, standing awkwardly in the doorway.

"Come in, Sir Edmund," I say. "Death makes equals of us all."

He enters, and I see his eyes are red. This man who has been my jailer, who has denied me every comfort, who has called me by false titles—even he is moved by the approaching end.

"Madam," he says, then stops, corrects himself. "Your Majesty. Is there anything...?"

"Yes," I say. "When I am dead, tell the King that I died blessing him. Tell him that I died as I lived—his true wife, England's true Queen. Tell him that truth survives even death."

The sickness in my belly is consuming me from within, but my spirit has never been clearer. Each breath is harder than the last, but each one is also a small victory—another moment of being Katherine, of maintaining my truth, of refusing to yield even to death itself until I am ready.

Father Jorge begins the prayers for the dying, his voice shaking with emotion. I join him when I can, the Latin coming easily to my lips even as English fails me. These are the words I learned as a child in Spain, the eternal words that connect me to my mother, to all the faithful who have gone before, to God Himself.

The pain is fading now, replaced by a strange lightness. The walls of the chamber seem to grow transparent. Beyond them, I can almost see it—the place where there are no lies, no betrayals, no false titles. Only truth, eternal and unchanging.

Not yet, though. Not quite yet. There are still words to speak, breaths to take, moments to live as Katherine of Aragon, Queen of England, wife of Henry VIII.

The sickness of my heart is killing my body, but it cannot touch my soul. That remains whole, constant, undefeated. And soon, very soon, it will be free.

Chapter 35

The Last Letter

I know the end is near. The pain that has been my constant companion these past months has strangely receded, leaving behind a peculiar lightness, as if my soul is already beginning to detach from its earthly vessel. It is January 7th, 1536, the day after Epiphany, and the weak winter sun filters through my chamber window at Kimbolton, illuminating dust motes that dance like tiny angels in the air.

My hands can barely hold a quill now, the joints so swollen with arthritis that each movement is agony. But I must write one last letter to Henry. Not for his sake—he lost any claim to my consideration years ago—but for mine. I need to speak my truth one final time, to set down in words that will outlive me the reality of what we were, what we became, what we might have been.

Alice props me up with pillows, her ancient face wet with tears she doesn't try to hide.

"Your Majesty shouldn't strain yourself," she says, though she knows I will not be dissuaded.

"Bring me the good paper," I tell her, "and the seal with the pomegranate and the rose. He should remember who writes to him."

She obeys, and I am left alone with the blank page that will carry my last words to the man who was my husband for twenty-four years, whether he acknowledges it or not. The quill trembles in my twisted fingers, but my mind is clear as spring water.

"My most dear lord, king and husband," I begin, each word carefully chosen, weighted with meaning.

The phrase itself is a declaration of war and peace simultaneously. I call him my husband, asserting the truth he has spent years denying. But I also call him dear, because despite everything, some part of my heart still holds the memory of the golden prince who rescued me from poverty, who crowned me with such joy, who held our dead son and wept.

"The hour of my death now drawing on, the tender love I owe you forceth me, my case being such, to commend myself to you, and to put you in remembrance with a few words of the health and safeguard of your soul, which you ought to prefer before all worldly matters, and before the care and pampering of your body, for the which you have cast me into many calamities and yourself into many troubles."

There—I have said it plainly. He has damned his soul for the sake of his body's desires. The calamities he has cast me into are nothing compared to the troubles he has brought upon himself. But I say it with love, the tender love I owe him still, God help me.

"For my part, I pardon you everything, and I wish and devoutly pray God that He will pardon you also."

The forgiveness comes harder than I expected. Part of me wants to rage, to curse him, to prophesy the doom that awaits those who break sacred vows. But what good would that do? Anger is a luxury the dying cannot afford. I need to travel light into the next world, unburdened by hatred.

"For the rest, I commend unto you our daughter Mary, beseeching you to be a good father unto her, as I have heretofore desired."

Here my pen falters. Mary, my jewel, my only living child, now forced to serve as a bastard in the household of Henry's subsequent children. What words can make him see her as I see her—legitimate, royal, precious beyond measure? But I must try.

"I entreat you also, on behalf of my maids, to give them marriage portions, which is not much, they being but three. For all my other servants I solicit the wages due them, and a year more, lest they be unprovided for."

Even now, facing death, I must be practical. These faithful souls who have shared my exile deserve better than to be cast into poverty when I am gone. It is a small thing to ask, considering all Henry has taken from me. Perhaps he will grant this if nothing else.

And now for the hardest truth, the one that surprises even me as I write it:

"Lastly, I make this vow, that mine eyes desire you above all things."

The words blur as tears fall onto the paper. It is true, incomprehensible as it seems. Despite the betrayal, the humiliation, the long years of suffering, despite his adultery and heresy and cruelty, my eyes still desire to see him above all earthly things. Not the Henry he has become—that bloated tyrant who kills wives and friends with equal indifference—but the Henry he was, the Henry he could have been, the Henry who perhaps still exists somewhere beneath the layers of sin and self-deception.

I sign the letter with a flourish that costs me the last of my strength: "Katherine, the Queen."

Not Dowager Princess. Not his discarded wife. The Queen, now and always, in this world and the next.

The letter is sealed with wax and my signet ring, the pomegranate of Granada intertwined with the Tudor rose. Let him see those symbols and remember the alliance we represented, the love we shared, the dynasty we began. Let him remember, if he is still capable of remembering anything beyond his own desires.

"Send it," I tell Alice when she returns. "Send it with all speed. I want him to receive it while my body is still warm."

She takes the letter reverently, understanding its importance. This is my last testament, my final word in the long argument that has been our marriage.

Later, Father Jorge comes to hear my final confession. I tell him of my sins, though they seem so small now—moments of anger, of doubt, of wishing harm on those who harmed me. He absolves me in Latin, the eternal words washing over me like warm water.

"Your Majesty has nothing to confess," he says when the ritual is complete. "Your life has been one long act of faith."

"I have been proud," I tell him. "Too proud to bend, even when bending might have saved others pain."

"Pride in truth is not a sin," he replies. "It is courage."

As the day wanes, more people gather in my chamber. Word has spread that the Queen—for they all call me Queen now, even Bedingfeld—is dying. Spanish merchants who have traveled from London, English servants who remember better days, even a few local people who have somehow gained entry. They kneel around my bed, a living rosary of grief and respect.

I think of other last letters I might have written. To my nephew the Emperor, chiding him for his inadequate support. To Thomas Cromwell, warning him that Henry will destroy him too, in time. To Jane Seymour, the new wife, telling her to guard her virtue and her head, for Henry's love is more dangerous than his hatred.

But there is only one letter that truly matters, and it is not written on paper. It is the letter of my life, written in suffering and resistance, in constancy and faith. That letter will outlive any words, any lies Henry tells about me. History will read that letter and know the truth.

Evening comes early in January, and with it a strange peace. The pain is entirely gone now, replaced by a floating sensation, as if I am already partially detached from my body. I can see everyone in the room, but they seem far away, separated from me by more than distance.

"Read to me," I ask, and someone—I can no longer distinguish faces—begins reading from my book of hours. The Latin washes over me, familiar as my own heartbeat. These are the words I learned as a child in Granada, the words that have sustained me through everything.

I close my eyes and see scenes from my life playing like a pageant. My arrival at Plymouth in the cold rain. My first sight of Arthur, so pale and weak. Henry at seventeen, golden and laughing. Our wedding night, full of genuine joy. Our son in my arms for those precious fifty-two days. Standing at Blackfriars, defying the court. The long years of exile. And through it all, like a thread of gold through dark fabric, my unwavering certainty that I am Henry's true wife, England's true Queen.

"Tell them," I say, though I'm not sure who I'm addressing. "Tell them I died as I lived. Constant. True. Undefeated."

Someone is crying. Several someones. But I am beyond tears now. I am approaching something greater than sorrow, greater than joy. I am approaching truth itself, naked and eternal, where all lies fall away and only reality remains.

The letter to Henry will reach him, I know. He will read it, perhaps with indifference, perhaps with the faintest stirring of conscience. He may destroy it, as he has destroyed so much else. But the words will remain, burned into his memory whether he wills it or not. In his last moments, whenever they come, he will remember that I forgave him, that I loved him still, that my eyes desired him above all things.

And perhaps—just perhaps—he will understand what he lost when he cast me aside. Not just a wife but a soul mate. Not just a queen but a conscience. Not just a woman but the one person who loved him enough to tell him the truth, even when truth meant exile and death.

The candle flickers, casting dancing shadows on the wall. Or perhaps it is my vision failing. Either way, the light is going, and I am ready to follow it.

My last letter is written. My last words are spoken. My last battle is fought.

Now, at last, I can rest.

CHAPTER 36

THE FINAL SACRAMENT

Father Jorge de Ateca arrives as the bells of Kimbolton strike two in the afternoon of January 7th. He has ridden hard from London, this Spanish priest who has risked everything to bring me the last rites. His cassock is mud-spattered, his face drawn with exhaustion and grief, but his hands are steady as he unpacks the sacred vessels from his leather satchel.

The local priest has been forbidden to attend me unless I acknowledge myself as Dowager Princess. Even now, at the very threshold of death, they try to force their lies upon me. But God has provided, as He always does. This good Spanish priest has come to ease my passage, to give me the final sacrament as Katherine, Queen of England.

My chamber has been transformed into a sacred space. The few servants and friends who have gathered kneel in a circle around my bed. Alice and William, my faithful English servants. Two Spanish women—María de Morales and Inés de Venegas—who appeared yesterday, having walked twenty miles through the winter cold to attend their Queen's final hours. Even Sir Edmund Bedingfeld is here, standing awkwardly in the doorway, unsure whether he is jailer or mourner.

"Come closer, Sir Edmund," I tell him, my voice barely above a whisper. "Death makes all earthly titles meaningless. You have been my keeper these years, but you are also a child of God. Join us."

He comes forward, this man who has denied me every comfort, and I see tears on his weathered face. Perhaps he finally understands what he has been part of—not the restraint of a difficult woman but the slow murder of a queen.

Father Jorge begins the ritual in Latin, the eternal words that have comforted the dying for fifteen hundred years. "Per istam sanctam unctionem et suam piissimam misericordiam..." Through this holy anointing and His most tender mercy...

The holy oil is cool on my forehead, my lips, my hands. Each anointing is a seal, a preparation for the journey ahead. I feel the weight of my sins—such as they are—lifting from me like a cloak removed. Pride, yes, I have been proud. Anger, certainly, for who could endure what I have endured without anger? But these are human failings, already forgiven by a God who understands human frailty.

"Do you forgive all who have wronged you?" Father Jorge asks in Spanish, knowing I will understand better in my mother tongue.

"I forgive them all," I reply, and I mean it. Henry, for his betrayal. Anne Boleyn, though she is already dead, executed by the man for whom she destroyed so much. Wolsey, Cranmer, Cromwell, all the architects of my suffering. I forgive them and pity them, for they have sold their souls for earthly power that will crumble to dust.

"Do you ask forgiveness from any you have wronged?"

I think of Mary, my daughter, suffering because of my refusal to yield. Would her life have been easier if I had accepted the annulment, taken the comfortable retirement they offered?

"I ask my daughter's forgiveness," I say, "for the suffering my constancy has caused her. But I could not purchase her comfort with lies about her legitimacy."

Father Jorge nods, understanding. Some prices are too high to pay, even for our children's ease.

Now comes the Viaticum, the final communion, food for the journey from this world to the next. Father Jorge elevates the Host, and even through my failing vision, it seems to glow with internal light.

"Corpus Domini nostri Iesu Christi custodiat animam tuam in vitam aeternam." May the Body of our Lord Jesus Christ preserve your soul for eternal life.

"Amen," I whisper, and receive the Host on my tongue.

The moment is transcendent. I have received communion thousands of times in my fifty years, but never like this. I can feel the Real Presence, not just as an article of faith but as a living reality. Christ is here, in this cold chamber, in this forgotten castle, in this broken body. He has come to walk with me through the valley of the shadow of death.

The wine follows, the Blood of Christ, sweet on my parched lips.

"Sanguis Domini nostri Iesu Christi custodiat animam tuam in vitam aeternam."

"Amen."

I am sealed now, prepared, ready. The sacrament is complete, but Father Jorge is not finished. He begins the Litany of the Saints, calling upon the whole company of heaven to receive me.

"Sancta Maria, ora pro nobis." "Sancte Michael, ora pro nobis." "Sancte Gabriel, ora pro nobis."

Holy Mary, pray for us. Saint Michael, pray for us. Saint Gabriel, pray for us. The names roll on, a roster of the blessed who have gone before. I close my eyes and can almost see them, rank upon rank of saints and angels, waiting to welcome another soul who chose truth over comfort, faith over convenience.

"Sancta Isabella, ora pro nobis," Father Jorge adds, though Isabella of Castile has not been canonized.

My mother, pray for me. Yes, she is there among the saints, whatever the Church has officially declared. I can feel her presence, strong and comforting, the warrior queen who taught me that some battles are worth losing if the cause is just.

"All holy men and women, pray for us."

The litany ends, and a profound silence falls. This is the moment between—no longer fully of this world, not yet of the next. I float in this space, aware of my body but not confined by it, conscious of the room but also of something vastly larger just beyond the veil of perception.

"Your Majesty," Father Jorge says softly, "is there anything else you wish to say?"

I open my eyes with effort and look at each face around my bed. These faithful few who have stayed with me to the end, who still call me Queen when the whole world insists otherwise.

"Tell them," I say, each word requiring immense effort. "Tell anyone who asks. I die as I lived. Katherine of Aragon. Queen of England. Wife of Henry VIII. I die in the faith of Holy Mother Church. I die forgiving all who wronged me. I die praying for England's return to the true faith."

A fit of coughing overtakes me, and when I pull my hand away from my mouth, it is spotted with blood. My body is failing rapidly now, systems shutting down one by one. But my mind remains clear, my soul at peace.

"The Psalms," I request. "Read me the Psalms."

Someone—I can no longer distinguish individual voices—begins reading Psalm 23. "Dominus regit me, et nihil mihi deerit..." The Lord is my shepherd, I shall not want...

The familiar words wash over me, but I am hearing them on multiple levels now. The Latin in my ears, the meaning in my heart, and something else—a music beyond words, the very harmony of creation itself.

"Though I walk through the valley of the shadow of death, I will fear no evil, for Thou art with me..."

No, I do not fear. I have walked through valleys darker than death these past years. I have been stripped of everything—husband, daughter, crown, freedom, health. But I have not been stripped of faith, and faith is all one needs for this final journey.

"Surely goodness and mercy shall follow me all the days of my life, and I will dwell in the house of the Lord forever."

Forever. Yes, forever. This suffering is temporary. This exile is ending. I am going home—not to Spain, not to any earthly palace, but to the eternal home where there are no false titles, no broken vows, no betrayals. Only truth, pure and eternal.

The afternoon light is fading, or perhaps it is my vision. The faces around my bed are becoming indistinct, but I can still feel their love, their grief, their prayers surrounding me like a warm cloak.

"Sing," I whisper. "Sing the Salve Regina."

They begin, these faithful souls, their voices blending in the ancient hymn to the Virgin. "Salve Regina, mater misericordiae..." Hail, Holy Queen, Mother of Mercy. The words carry me back to Spain, to the convent where I first learned this hymn as a child. I can smell the incense, feel the cool stone under my knees, see my mother's straight back as she knelt beside me. All the circles of my life are closing, completing.

"Ad te clamamus, exsules filii Hevae..." To thee do we cry, poor banished children of Eve...

Yes, we are all exiles, all banished from Paradise, all struggling to find our way home. But the exile is ending. The banishment is lifting. The gates are opening.

"Et Iesum, benedictum fructum ventris tui, nobis post hoc exsilium ostende." And after this our exile, show unto us the blessed fruit of thy womb, Jesus.

After this exile. After this long, painful, glorious exile. I will see Him face to face, the Christ I have served imperfectly but constantly. I will stand before the throne of judgment, and I will stand as Katherine of Aragon, Queen of England, knowing that I kept faith with the truth even when the whole world demanded I embrace lies.

The singing continues, but I am floating now, disconnected from my body though still tenuously attached. I see the room from above—my wasted body on the bed, the kneeling figures around it, the single candle fighting against the gathering dark.

But I also see beyond the room. I see Kimbolton Castle from above, a small fortress in the vast English countryside. I see England itself, torn and bleeding from Henry's schism. I see Europe, divided by wars of religion that will rage for centuries. And somehow, I see the future—my daughter Mary on the throne, trying to heal what her father broke; Elizabeth, Anne Boleyn's daughter, ruling with the strength that should have been Mary's; the long centuries when my story will be told and retold, twisted and straightened, forgotten and remembered.

Father Jorge is giving me the final blessing now, his hand making the sign of the cross over my failing body. "Go forth, Christian soul, from this world in the name of God the Father Almighty, who created you, in the name of Jesus Christ, Son of the living God, who suffered for you, in the name of the Holy Spirit, who was poured out upon you..."

Go forth. Yes, it is time to go. Time to leave this broken body, this cold castle, this England that no longer knows me. Time to go where I am known truly, loved completely, vindicated eternally.

"Go forth, faithful soul..."

Faithful. Yes, I have been faithful. To my vows, to my conscience, to my God. It is enough. It is more than enough.

The candle flickers one last time, and in that flicker, I see everything clearly—my whole life like a tapestry finally viewed from the proper distance, the pattern visible at last. Every thread had its purpose, even the dark ones. Especially the dark ones.

The last sacrament is complete. The final journey begins.

I am ready.

CHAPTER 37

THE UNCONQUERED QUEEN

The world fades. The pain is gone. The cold stone of Kimbolton dissolves. A single shaft of weak winter sunlight breaks through the clouds and illuminates the dust motes dancing in the air of the chamber. They are like tiny, golden angels, swirling in patterns that seem to spell out words in a language older than speech.

My thoughts are no longer coherent in the way of earthly thinking, but flow like a river approaching the sea, all boundaries dissolving. Images cascade through my consciousness, not in sequence but all at once, a lifetime compressed into a single eternal moment.

The sun of Granada, warm on my face as a child in the Alhambra gardens, my mother's hand in mine as she shows me the pomegranate trees that share my symbol. "Remember, *hija*," she says, "the pomegranate must break open to reveal its treasures. So too must we sometimes break to show our true worth."

My mother's proud smile when she told me I would marry the Prince of England, her hands steady as she placed her own crown on my head for practice. "You will be a queen, Catalina. Never forget that. No matter what they call you, you will be a queen."

Arthur's shy, pale face that first night at Dogmersfield, the tremor in his hand as he took mine. Poor, fragile boy, racing toward death from the moment of his birth. I was never meant to be his wife, only his companion for that brief journey from wedding to grave. I see that now, see how God used even that sorrow to prepare me for what was to come.

Henry, my golden prince, laughing on horseback the day he came to claim me after his father's death. So alive, so certain that God favored him above all men. That Henry is as real to me now as the tyrant he became. Both exist simultaneously in this moment outside time—the lover and the betrayer, the protector and the persecutor, the husband and the stranger.

My baby son, Henry Duke of Cornwall, safe now in the arms of the Virgin, those fifty-two days when I knew perfect happiness. He is here, in this space between worlds, grown to the man he never became on earth. "Mother," he says, though not in words, "your suffering was not punishment. It was preparation. You had to learn to lose everything to gain everything."

Hija mía, Mary, a queen in her own right now, though I shall not live to see it. I see her future, a premonition of trials and sorrow, a crown that will bring her more grief than glory as she struggles to heal the wounds of this kingdom. "Oh, my daughter," I whisper to her across time, "be wiser than that. Faith cannot be imposed by fire. I fought with constancy, not cruelty. Remember that."

The vow. Always the vow. I see it now not as chains but as wings. Every time I refused to break it, I flew higher, closer to truth, closer to God. The world called it stubbornness, but heaven calls it sanctity. To keep faith when all the world demands faithlessness—that is the greatest victory of all.

In manus tuas, Domine, commendo spiritum meum. Into your hands, O Lord, I commend my spirit.

The Latin comes not from my lips—I am beyond speech now—but from my soul itself. These are the words Christ spoke on the cross, the words of ultimate surrender and ultimate triumph. I speak them now as Katherine of Aragon, daughter of Isabella and Ferdinand, wife of Henry VIII, mother of Mary Tudor, Queen of England in the sight of God if no longer in the sight of men.

The room below me—for I am above it now, somehow, watching my own death—erupts in quiet weeping. Father Jorge is praying, the others are kneeling, even Bedingfeld has tears on his face. They see an ending. I experience a beginning.

Light. Not the weak winter sunshine but a brilliance that makes the sun seem like a candle. It doesn't hurt my eyes—I don't have eyes anymore, not really—but fills me with warmth that goes beyond any physical sensation. This is the light of truth itself, and in it, all lies are burned away.

I see Henry receiving my letter, hours or days from now. He reads it with a face that shows nothing, but I can see inside him now, see the small boy who still lives within the bloated king, frightened and alone. He will keep the letter. He will read it again on his own deathbed, eleven years hence. Too late, always too late, but he will know, finally, what he lost.

I see Thomas Cromwell, efficient and ruthless, ordering my burial in Peterborough Cathedral with the honors due to a Dowager Princess, not a Queen. But I also see the people who will come to that burial, calling me Queen still, leaving pomegranates on my tomb for centuries to come. The lies of power are temporary. The truth of love endures.

I see the long future stretching out—a vision of fire and blood, of crowns lost and won, of a kingdom struggling for centuries with the schism born of my husband's sin. My story will be told and retold, twisted and restored, forgotten and remembered. Some will call me a victim, others a hero. Some will pity me, others admire me. All will be right and wrong simultaneously, for no earthly story can capture the truth of a soul.

But now, in this moment of transition, I know the truth complete. I was not a victim but a victor. Every loss was a gain, every humiliation an elevation, every earthly defeat a heavenly triumph. I kept faith. I maintained truth. I refused to lie even to save myself. In the economy of heaven, these things matter more than crowns or kingdoms.

The light grows brighter, and in it I see figures approaching. My mother, young and fierce as she was at Granada, wearing armor that shines like stars. My lost children, all of them, the ones who never drew breath and the ones who lived their brief moments— they are here, whole and beautiful, welcoming me home.

And behind them, a figure in rough robes, with wounded hands and feet, whose face is both terrible and beautiful beyond description. Christ Himself, come to receive a soul who chose His truth over Henry's lies.

"Well done, good and faithful servant," He says, though not in words that any earthly ear could hear. "You have kept the faith. You have finished the course. Enter into the joy of your Lord."

The last thread holding me to my earthly body snaps. Katherine of Aragon, the body, lies still on the bed at Kimbolton, worn out at fifty years, defeated in all earthly terms. But Katherine of Aragon, the soul, soars free, victorious, eternal, unconquered.

Behind me, in that cold chamber, they are already arguing about how to announce my death, what title to use, where to bury me. Let them argue. Let them call me Dowager Princess on my tomb. Let them erase me from the records, rewrite history, pretend I was never Queen.

I know who I am. God knows who I am. Truth knows who I am.

I am Katherine of Aragon, Queen of England, wife of Henry VIII, mother of Mary Tudor. I lived in truth. I died in truth. I exist now in Truth itself, where all lies fall away and only reality remains.

The winter sunbeam that illuminated my last moments on earth continues to shine through the window at Kimbolton, catching the dust motes that still dance in the air above my still form. To earthly eyes, it is just light and dust. But from where I am now, I can see them for what they truly are—angels, countless angels, bearing witness that a queen has come home.

My story on earth is over, but my testimony is eternal. Let anyone who doubts the power of constancy look to my life. Let anyone who thinks truth can be defeated by lies remember my stand. Let anyone who believes might makes right consider my end.

I was cast aside, impoverished, imprisoned, and allowed to die in neglect. By every earthly measure, I lost everything.

And yet, I am unconquered. I kept my vows. I maintained my truth. I refused to yield to lies, even unto death.

Is this not victory? Is this not triumph? Is this not the greatest conquest of all—to lose everything temporal and gain everything eternal?

The last earthly sound I perceive is the bell of Kimbolton tolling the hour. Two o'clock in the afternoon, January 7, 1536. The exact moment matters to those who mark time. But I am beyond time now, in the place where all moments exist simultaneously, where beginning and ending are one, where every tear is wiped away and every truth is vindicated.

I am Katherine of Aragon. I was a queen on earth. I am a soul in heaven. I kept faith with my vows, my conscience, my God.

And that is enough. More than enough. That is everything.

The dust motes continue their dance in the winter sunlight, spelling out in their swirling patterns a message that only the faithful can read: Here died a queen who would not lie. Here ended a life that never yielded. Here began an eternity of vindication.

My earthly voice is silenced. But my testimony echoes through the centuries: Truth matters. Vows are sacred. Constancy is its own victory.

I am Katherine of Aragon, forever Queen, forever true, forever unconquered.

Finis.

Printed in Dunstable, United Kingdom